HINDSIGHT

A note from the publisher

Dear Reader,

At *Pantera Press* we're passionate about what we call *good books doing good things*™.

A big part is our joy in discovering and nurturing talented home-grown writers such as Melanie Casey.

We are also focused on promoting literacy, quality writing, the joys of reading and fostering debate.

CAN YOU READ THIS?

Sure you can, but 60% in our community can't. Shocking, isn't it? That's why *Pantera Press* is helping to close the literacy gap, by nurturing the next generation of readers as well as our writers. We're thrilled to support *Let's Read*. A wonderful program already helping over 100,000 pre-schoolers across Australia to develop the building blocks for literacy and learning, as well as a love for books.

We're excited that *Let's Read* operates right across Australia, in metropolitan, regional and also remote communities, including Indigenous communities in Far North Queensland, Cape York, and Torres Strait. *Let's Read* was developed by the *Centre for Community Child Health* and is being implemented in partnership with *The Smith Family*.

Simply by enjoying our books, you will be contributing to our unique approach and helping these kids. So thank you.

If you want to do more, please visit www.PanteraPress.com/Donate where you can personally donate to help *The Smith Family* expand *Let's Read*, and find out more about the great programs *Pantera Press* supports.

Please enjoy *Hindsight*.

For news about our other books, sample chapters, author interviews and much more, please visit our website: www.PanteraPress.com

Happy reading,

Alison Green

HINDSIGHT

MELANIE CASEY

PanteraPress
great storytelling

PanteraPress
great storytelling

First published in 2013 by Pantera Press Pty Limited
www.PanteraPress.com

This book is copyright, and all rights are reserved.
Text copyright © Melanie Casey, 2013
Melanie Casey has asserted her moral rights to be identified as the author of this work.
Design and typography copyright © Pantera Press Pty Limited, 2013
PanteraPress, the three-slashed colophon device, *great storytelling, good books doing good things, a great new home for Australia's next generation of best-loved authors,* WHY vs WHY, and *making sense of everything* are trademarks of Pantera Press Pty Limited.
We welcome your support of the author's rights, so please only buy authorised editions.

This is a work of fiction, though it may refer to some real events or people. Names, characters, organisations, dialogue and incidents are either products of the author's imagination or are used fictitiously, and any resemblance to actual people, living or dead, firms, events or locales is coincidental or used for fictional purposes.

Without the publisher's prior written permission, and without limiting the rights reserved under copyright, none of this book may be scanned, reproduced, stored in, uploaded to or introduced into a retrieval or distribution system, including the internet, or transmitted, copied, scanned or made available in any form or by any means (including digital, electronic, mechanical, photocopying, sound or audio recording, or text-to-voice). This book is sold subject to the condition that it shall not, by way of trade or otherwise, be lent, re-sold, hired out, or otherwise circulated in any form of binding or cover other than that in which it is published and without a similar condition being imposed on the subsequent recipient.

Please send all permission queries to:
Pantera Press, P.O. Box 1989 Neutral Bay, NSW 2089 Australia or info@PanteraPress.com

A Cataloguing-in-Publication entry for this book is available from the National Library of Australia.

ISBN 978-1-921997-20-4 (Paperback)
ISBN 978-1-921997-21-1 (Ebook)

Cover and Internal Design: Luke Causby, Blue Cork
Front cover image: © quavondo, © Rudolf Vlcek
Back cover image: © iStock
Editor: Kylie Mason
Proofreader: Desanka Vukelich
Author Photo: Andrew Dunbar
Typesetting: Kirby Jones
Printed in Australia: McPherson's Printing Group

Pantera Press policy is to use papers that are natural, renewable and recyclable products made from wood grown in sustainable forests. The logging and manufacturing processes are expected to conform to the environmental regulations of the country of origin.

For Mum

PART ONE

Chorus: *Come, poor thing, leave the empty chariot.*
Of your own free will try on the yoke of Fate.
Aeschylus, *Agamemnon*

CHAPTER 1

The man settled back into the shadows. He pulled his collar up to his chin and thrust his hands deep into his pockets. It was a bitter night and he'd been standing there for over an hour.

The doorway that concealed him was so dark he could hardly see his own feet. Sickly yellow light from the street lights died well before it reached him. This alleyway serviced the businesses that lined the two main streets of Jewel Bay and the council had decided that lighting was an unnecessary expense. He loved small-town thinking.

The wind picked up and he felt the chill start to sink into his bones. Still, he couldn't move. He had to remain invisible. His breathing was shallow and fast. His pulse was beating in time to the music in his head: Beethoven's Ninth, *Ode to Joy*.

A sound made him tense and sneak a quick look into the laneway. A figure was moving quickly in his direction, weaving between the scattered boxes and crates, stepping around a bin that was tipped over onto its side, spewing rotten food and crumpled packaging across the uneven bitumen.

The blood began to thunder in his ears and saliva flooded into his mouth. The person was close now, only a few metres away. It was her. He held his breath until she passed his doorway.

Stepping up behind her he threw one arm around her left shoulder, covering her mouth and nose with his hand. With the other hand he plunged a syringe into her neck. She started to thrash against him. He locked both arms around her. She kicked and struggled, grunting with fear and panic. He loved it when they fought; loved feeling all that desperation in his arms. She tried to scream, a muffled, gasping sound, before collapsing against him. Her arms and legs went slack and she made a strangled gurgling noise. Her bladder released and the smell of warm urine scalded his nostrils.

He held her until he was sure she was out. Then, leaning close to her ear, he whispered then laughed. Grasping her under the armpits he dragged her backwards into the deeper shadows. He turned her around to face him. Her eyes were closed — pity.

'Never mind,' he whispered, 'there will be plenty of time later.' He dragged her the remaining few metres back to the doorway. He checked his watch: three minutes, fifteen seconds. Not bad. Her head sagged forwards, her hair shrouding her face. Her mouth was slack and her tongue protruded. Saliva glistened in a long drool onto the front of her shirt.

He cocked his head, listening. A car drove down Main Street and receded into the distance. There were no other sounds of life, no voices, no footsteps; just the wind and the distant crashing of the sea.

He picked the woman up, one arm under her armpits, the other under her knees and hefted her into the crate, puffing with the weight of her. She felt heavier than her seventy or so kilos, but then again, she was almost a dead weight. He sniggered softly to himself as he lifted the lid into place.

The symphony in his head restarted as he stepped out of the doorway and walked down the lane back to his car on Main Street with a spring in his step. It was nice when things went to plan. He would come back in the morning, with the van.

As the sound of the man's footsteps faded, an untidy pile of packaging a few metres away from the doorway shuddered and started to move.

As the sheets of cardboard fell away, the pile took shape and unfolded into an old man. He stepped out of the shadows. Shooting a glance at Main Street, he took a few wobbly steps forward.

He'd woken just before the man leapt from the doorway and grabbed the girl. It'd happened so quickly. At first he'd thought he was dreaming; now he wished he had been. He'd huddled there listening to the shuffles and grunts punctuated by something that he couldn't quite grasp until it dawned on him that the man was laughing. He'd had to press his fist into his mouth to stop from gagging.

He leant out of the doorway and risked a quick glance down the laneway again just to make sure the man wasn't coming back. He looked at the crate in front of him. The lid didn't look like it was nailed down. With a bit of effort he managed to lift it. Holding his breath, he peered inside.

The young woman was folded into the foetal position, her hair covering her face. Tentatively, he touched her — she felt warm. He shook her. No response. Fumbling, he reached further into the crate, groping for her neck. He pushed her head to one side and felt for a pulse. Nothing. Bile flooded his mouth again. He gave way to the urge and retched onto the ground.

She was dead; there was nothing he could do. After a few moments he reached back into the crate and started to feel around her body. Puffing, he lifted her legs and was rewarded when his fingers brushed smooth leather. Tugging hard he pulled her handbag from under her. His nerves got the better of him and he turned and did a half shuffle, half run to the end of the lane then stepped cautiously around the corner looking for any sign of the man. No people, no cars. Just the empty street with a few shop windows dimly illuminated. Ducking back into the laneway, he rifled through the handbag, pulling out a wallet before throwing the bag into one of the bins lining the laneway.

HINDSIGHT

He shuffled off down Main Street to find another spot to settle for the night, keen to get as far away from the crate and its contents as he could. He passed a phone booth, its glass crazed and orange light flickering, and stopped. He walked back to it and paused with his hand on the door. Muttering to himself, he pushed it open and stepped inside. With a shaking hand he lifted the handset and dialled.

'Hello? Police … Hello? Yes I want to report a murder … Johns Lane, Jewel Bay … Yes … There's a body in a crate. No, he's gone now. No, no, I can't.' He slammed the receiver back in its cradle.

He left the booth and hurried down the street, throwing nervous glances over his shoulder until he was well away.

CHAPTER 2

I looked at the clock on the wall again, willing the seconds to tick by. I resisted the urge to drum my fingers on the timber of the kitchen table. The sounds of scoffing coming from the corner finally ceased and Shadow sauntered over to the table and jumped onto a spare chair. It was a remarkably elegant manoeuvre for the nine and a half kilo cat. In human terms it'd be equivalent to a hundred-kilo gymnast leaping onto a balance beam.

The minute hand finally shifted and with a sigh of relief I plunged and poured myself a large mug of coffee, then added milk and two spoons of sugar. The aroma, rich and dark with just a hint of vanilla and cinnamon, teased my nostrils as I took my first sip of the day. Closing my eyes, I let the hit take me. The blend was my own secret recipe and it was heaven in a cup. Opening my eyes, I saw Mum wrinkling her nose. Even after more than ten years of watching me drink coffee every morning she still can't get used to the idea. In her world there is no situation that can't be improved by a cup of tea.

As I sipped and slowly felt the tendrils of warmth and life seep into my limbs I listened to snippets of the conversation between the two people who were my entire world.

'I'm going into town later today,' Mum said. 'I thought I'd stop in and have a cup of tea with Mrs O'Grady. Last time she came to visit there was a shadow hanging over her. I'm sure her sister passed last night.'

Surprising as it might seem, this was normal conversational fare in our household. The women in our family are what most people describe as 'gifted'. In Salem we would have been burned at the stake but there you have it; we were blessed to be born in an era of relative tolerance.

Mum can touch someone and see glimpses of their future. She dresses it up a bit for the sake of the townsfolk and pretends to be reading their palms. Gran and I both know that palmistry has nothing to do with it. She's also selective in what she tells her clients. I always know when she's seen something that makes her grieve: I find her in the same place in the garden, sitting under the oak tree and looking out over the bay. She looks older and sadder, like there's a weight on her shoulders. It's part of the territory. The sight is a burden as much as it's a gift.

'Well, if you're going into town could you drop some chamomile and peppermint at the store? Mr Johnson rang me last night and

HINDSIGHT

he's sold out again,' Gran said. Gran has the most marvellous herb garden. If some people have green thumbs I think Gran must have green arms because there is nothing that won't grow for her. It's part of her own version of the family gift. She can help people to heal by channelling her energy into them. Plants and animals also respond well to her touch. I've often wondered if Shadow's panther-like proportions have as much to do with the affection she lavishes on him as his love affair with his food bowl.

She turned away from the stove and piled a mountain of pancakes in front of me. I've given up on protesting. There's no point; there's nothing that makes Gran happier than feeding her family. To be honest, it's pretty hard to resist her cooking anyway. I've resigned myself to having more curves than I probably need and to exercising for at least an hour a day to ensure they don't turn into bulges.

'I'll stop by on my way. I need to get some more candles anyway. Is there anything you need, Cass?' Mum said.

I forced down my mouthful of pancake and took a deep breath. 'I think I might come with you. I want to go to the library. Apparently they have some amazing new historical texts.'

Mum and Gran both fell silent. I could hear the birds singing out in the garden accompanied by the sounds of Shadow vigorously washing his ample pelt and the grandmother clock ticking away next to the pantry. I plastered on a smile that I hoped looked more real than it felt. 'I'll be fine.'

Mum was the first to recover. 'Good, well, perhaps I'll stop in at the library as well. I need a new book.'

If you knew my mother, you would know this was an outright lie. Her idea of a good novel is a soppy romance and she probably reads three of those a decade.

'No, really, Mum, I want to go by myself and stay for a few hours. You'd be bored stiff and you've got things to do anyway.'

I deliberately turned my attention back to my breakfast without looking at Gran. I knew the expression I would see on her face: it would be worry and sadness all rolled into one.

We finished breakfast in silence and I went upstairs to shower and get dressed. I knew that I was taking a risk but I'd made up my mind. I couldn't spend my entire life cooped up in the house, as much as I loved the place.

The cause of all the angst was my own special version of our family gift. The first seven years of my life were unremarkable; I was an ordinary child, leading a pretty average life, going to school and coming home. The only thing unusual about me was my eccentric family. Mum and Gran decided I had no special talents. For some reason I'd missed out. That was until Gran took me into the neighbouring town of Clifton one day when I was nearly eight.

I was crossing the road with her when I froze in the middle of the road. Gran tells me that my eyes glazed over and I just stood there until I let out a piercing scream that sliced down her spine like a knife. All I remember is being behind someone else's eyes. I turned as a car hurtled towards me and screamed as metal crunched into bone. Then, as soon as it had started, it was over. I was still standing in the middle of the road, cars were beeping their horns and Gran was trying to move me onto the footpath.

HINDSIGHT

The experience left me shuddering and crying on and off for days. For a few brief seconds I'd been someone else. I'd felt their fear and seen every detail of the car as it bore down on them. I'd seen and somehow recognised the face of the driver. Worst of all though, I felt the impact.

Mum made a few enquiries through her extensive network of clients and found out that back in the early fifties, a local girl had been run down by her boyfriend while she was crossing the road. He was in a jealous rage because she'd broken it off with him and he thought she had another lover.

That was the first time my gift manifested itself. Mum and Gran hoped that it was a one-off but I think deep down we all knew better. The really horrible part about it is that out of all of our talents, mine is the strongest.

As time went by we came to realise that all I have to do is pass over a place where someone has died suddenly, where their spirit was wrenched from their body, and it happens. The greater their fear and pain, the stronger the vision. As I got older and started going further afield it started happening more often. Each episode left me feeling like I'd been killed along with the victim.

Thankfully we lived in a place with a low crime rate but that didn't account for the people who had died in violent accidents or by their own hand, and my gift didn't seem to be limited by time. A death one hundred years ago felt the same to me as one yesterday. The earliest I'd experienced dated back almost one hundred and fifty years. It was a teenage boy killed by his father in an alcoholic rage.

Jewel Bay is a quiet town for most of the year. Settled in 1890 by a few farming families, today the stable population is about seven thousand, if you include all the outlying farms and properties. It's nestled along the rugged southern coastline of South Australia's Fleurieu Peninsula between Clifton and Fairfield. Fairfield is the largest town in the region and most of the infrastructure for Jewel Bay is run out of there. In summer, Jewel Bay explodes to about nine thousand as city folk descend on us. Over the years, the townspeople have developed split personalities, running small farms and properties for three-quarters of the year and then turning their hands to the tourist trade for the summer months. They run B&Bs, farm stays, cafés, tour groups, give riding lessons, surfing lessons, run fishing charters, bake cakes and biscuits; the list is almost endless and for nearly four months a year the town booms before settling back into the slow and steady rhythm of the quieter months.

For someone with a gift like mine it's a reasonably safe place to live. As I grew up I got to know the hotspots where deaths had occurred. Some I discovered by accident but most I researched in the local records. By the time I was a teenager I'd developed a very detailed map in my head of all the places I could and couldn't go. In some ways that gave me a false sense of security.

The crunch came when I was nineteen on a trip into town with Mum. She'd tried to talk me into staying at home, she said she had a bad feeling about it but I'd carried on like a pork chop until she finally gave in. At that age my mum's gift for seeing into the future tended to infuriate me. I thought it was a gross invasion of my privacy. Even though I had developed the knack of blocking her attempts to read me, when something affected all of us, as it often did, she could usually get a pretty good take on it.

Things were going fine until we walked into the new pharmacy. The store had only opened a few months before and we both assumed it would be a fairly safe bet, 'phantom free' as I liked to call it. Nothing in the local history told us any different. An abandoned building had stood on the site before it was redeveloped.

I took about three steps into the crowded store before a wave of searing pain and despair hit me. I was seeing through the eyes of a young woman — my mouth, hands and feet were taped and I could hardly breathe because my nose was swollen and blocked with blood.

A man came into view. He had grey eyes and hair so pale it was almost white. He stood in front of me and showed me a long thin blade. Slowly, savouring every moment, he started to make a series of cuts along my arms and chest. Each cut was like fire, the cold steel sent pain shooting along my nerves. I tried to scream but couldn't.

Finally, everything went black and I lost consciousness. I woke up in hospital. My head throbbed and swam as I looked around me. Gran and Mum were sitting by my bed. Gran had bags under her eyes and Mum had been crying.

What followed was a series of tests to see if I had epilepsy or any other abnormalities of the brain. Mum told me I'd collapsed in the pharmacy and had what they thought was some kind of fit. I'd banged my head as I'd fallen, too, and given myself concussion.

Gran and Mum understood what had really happened, of course, but knew better than to try to explain it to a group of doctors, who would more than likely want to book them in for tests if they started giving paranormal explanations.

After a few days I was sent home with a bunch of pills I knew I didn't need. I wallowed around feeling sorry for myself. I hardly left my room. I had nightmares all night and slept all day, exhausted and depressed. In my dreams the man with the white hair and grey eyes was always there, waiting, his knife glinting in the light.

Mum and Gran were at a loss and decided the best way to deal with things was to let me come to terms with it in my own way. They brought me trays of food and hot cups of tea. One day Gran came into my room and put some copies of old newspaper clippings in front of me. Twenty-three years earlier a girl had gone missing after a party. They found her body abandoned in a park near the site of the new pharmacy. Her hands, feet and mouth were tied and she'd died slowly, losing blood from a series of cuts her murderer had made over her arms and torso. He'd killed her slowly and painfully, torturing her.

'I'm so sorry, Cass. I knew about this one but it never occurred to me that the site of the pharmacy might be where she died.' Tears glistened in her eyes.

I reached out and gave her a hug. 'Don't be silly, Gran. I knew about this case too. There was no way you could've known she died there. Even the police assumed she died in the park.'

'Well, at least you know who she was now.'

HINDSIGHT

'Yes, and I can stop avoiding the park.' I gave her a watery smile. 'Did you know her?'

'Not really, she was a lot younger than me. Her family had only just moved to Jewel Bay. I met them a couple of times but they were a bit suspicious of your mother and me.'

'Ah — the two witches on the hill.'

Gran smiled. 'It's three witches now, dear, and yes, some people prefer to keep their distance.'

She was being polite. The townsfolk fell into three categories. Some people were happy to know us and make use of Mum's and Gran's special talents. Others didn't want to believe in anything except for what their five senses told them and preferred to keep away from us. They wouldn't cross the road to avoid us; they took a polite but distant approach.

The last category covered the people who would probably have fitted right into Salem in the witch-hunt days. They didn't bother to disguise their contempt or animosity. They thought we danced naked under the moonlight, sacrificing small children and worshipping Satan. Thankfully there weren't very many of them.

I looked down at the photocopies Gran had placed on top of my rumpled bedspread, then reached over and switched on the bedside light. The face of a pretty young woman looked back at me. She was probably in her mid-twenties. She looked like she had fair hair and light-coloured eyes. Her name was Kerry Sampson. She was laughing.

I scanned the text. The police had questioned some local men and rounded up the regular shady customers for questioning but none of their enquiries yielded any solid leads. In the end it was assumed the killer was from out of town. Kerry was just in the wrong place at the wrong time. It was a comforting spin from the local police. People could start getting on with their lives without looking askance at every person they met in the street.

I put the papers down and looked up at Gran, who must have been anticipating the question that was already forming on my lips.

'So what should I do, Gran? You know I saw him. I can't stop seeing him. I'll never forget what he looks like. The police were right you know, I've never seen him around here.'

'What do you want to do?'

I sighed. Gran never gave people straight answers. She should have been a psychiatrist, or a politician.

'I think I should let the police know what he looks like, but will they still be interested?'

'The police are always interested in closing unsolved murder cases. Plus, if her family is still alive I am sure they would want to see the murderer caught.'

'So they don't live around here any more?'

'No, they couldn't stand it here after Kerry died. Everyone's well-meaning sympathy was too much to take. They needed a fresh start. I think they moved back to the city.'

'So how do I do it? I can't just front up to the police station and ask to see the sketch artist.'

'I'm not sure. Come downstairs and we'll talk to Anita about it. She's made your favourite biscuits and we'll take tea in the garden and try to work out what to do.'

HINDSIGHT

'Mum's baking? Things must be bad. OK, I'll be down in five, I just want to wash my face and clean the week's worth of fur off my teeth.'

We spent the afternoon talking things through and in the end we decided an anonymous tip was the best solution — the local police weren't ready to deal with the reality of my gift just yet. Mum posted them a letter with a full description of the murderer. For weeks we scanned the local papers hoping to see an article about fresh leads in the Kerry Sampson case. Nothing ever appeared.

The episode left me feeling like I'd failed. I had a niggling doubt that I should have done more. Over time I thought less about it but I never forgot and I never really got over it. The one thing I knew for sure was that I never wanted to experience another death as brutal as Kerry Sampson's.

That was nine years ago. I'm twenty-eight now and I've been living like a recluse ever since.

CHAPTER 3

Ed Dyson felt like he'd been beaten about the head with a blunt object. His eyes were stuck together with sleep and his tongue had grown its own shag pile rug.

He'd spent the night before with a bottle of the best Irish his limited resources could afford and Jeff Buckley to keep him company. When the phone screamed into his consciousness it was like surfacing from a deep, black pool. He looked blearily at the clock for long enough to register that it had just gone 5 AM. He took the call with a deep sense of dread.

'Yeah.'

'Dyson, we got a DB. I'll pick you up in ten.' And with that his partner, Phil Steiner, rang off.

Ed hauled himself out of bed and shuffled into the bathroom. The harsh glare of the fluorescent light sent fresh needles of pain through his eyeballs into what was left of his grey matter. He sniffed under one arm and decided that he couldn't go without a shower. No way would Phil put up with him smelling that bad. He turned the shower on and grabbed for his toothbrush — might as well deal with the shag pile at the same time. Standing under the steady stream of hot water he battled the urge to retch and began brushing.

The drive over from Jewel Bay took Ed and Phil less than twenty minutes. When they arrived on the scene there was only one uniform there. He was from the small station in town and Ed hadn't come across him before. He was so new his uniform looked like it was just out of the packet.

'So what is the story here, Constable …?'

'Forsyth, sir.'

'Tell me what you found, Constable Forsyth.'

'I was on call last night when the emergency operator put one through. It was a man saying that there'd been a murder. He was really hard to understand and I wasn't sure if it was someone winding me up or not.'

He swallowed a couple of times, his Adam's apple bobbing up and down. Ed twitched impatiently.

'Anyway, he told me there was a body in a crate in Johns Lane. He said the killer wasn't there any more but he couldn't wait, he had to go. Then he hung up. I got here about twenty minutes later. I just had a quick look, found the crate with the body and called it through to you.'

Phil looked up from taking notes. 'Did he actually say the body was in Johns Lane?'

'Yes, sir, I mean ma'am.'

'Isn't this Stuart Lane?'

'Yes, ma'am, but the older locals still call it Johns Lane. John's was a pub that used to be on the corner over there.'

'So he must have been a local?' Ed asked.

'Yes, I suppose so, sir.'

Ed stood there for a few seconds digesting this. 'How long have you lived here?'

'I was born here.'

'Do you know many of the locals?'

'I know a lot, sir, but not everyone. We have over five thousand people if you include the outlying properties.'

'Yes, I know that. Do you have any idea who phoned it in?'

The young officer fidgeted and dropped his glance to the ground. 'I'm not sure but it might have been Old Mick.'

'Who's he?' Phil asked.

'A homeless man who wanders in and out of town.'

'A homeless man?' Ed rolled his eyes.

'Yes, sir.'

'Jesus Christ, I suppose he's a drunk as well?'

'Yes, you could say that, sir.'

'So our only witness is a homeless drunk?'

'Witness, sir?'

'Yes, witness, Constable Forsyth. He did tell you the killer was gone, didn't he?' Ed snapped.

'Well, yes, I suppose so.'

'Did he or did he not say that the killer was gone? What were his exact words?'

A deep flush started to creep up the young man's neck. Dark patches of sweat had appeared under his arms despite the chill of the morning. He sucked in a breath.

'He said the killer was gone now.'

'Which suggests he might have seen him and possibly even witnessed the murder?'

'Yes, sir.'

'Did you think to look for him once you'd secured the scene?'

'No, sir.'

Ed's eyes bored into the young man. 'Did you recognise the victim?'

'No, sir.'

'Did you touch anything?' Phil asked.

Forsyth looked put out. 'No, well that is, I touched the lid of the crate to open it and check for the body but then I secured the area and called for assistance.'

'Good lad. So the lid was closed?'

'Well no, not exactly.'

'What do you mean not exactly? It was either open or closed, which was it?' Ed barked, losing his patience.

The young officer's Adam's apple went into a frenzied dance. Phil shot Ed a look.

'You're doing great, Constable, just tell us exactly what you saw when you found the crate.' She flashed him a thousand-watt smile, patting his arm reassuringly.

'It was pretty dark so I was using my flashlight. I saw the crate and the lid was half on, half off. I moved it slightly so I could shine my torch inside and see what was in there. When I saw her, I reached in and checked for a pulse.'

'So you touched the lid and the body?' Ed asked.

'Yes, sir.'

'I'll finish up here with Constable Forsyth if you like?' Phil said, giving Ed a very pointed look.

Ed thought about arguing but decided Phil was probably right. He wasn't in the mood for dealing with a rookie. Phil's bedside manner was better suited for the conversation with the wet-behind-the-ears Constable Forsyth.

'Fine by me.'

'So back to what you did when you discovered the body …'

Ed wandered off and left them to it.

An hour and a half later he was by the side of the road freezing his balls off. The sun was struggling over the horizon and a wind straight from Antarctica was whistling around the collection of vehicles gathered to witness the unravelling of another tragedy. Police tape fluttered and cops in uniform stood around, shifting from foot to foot. They were waiting for the final scene; the crew who would take the corpse to the morgue.

Phil was standing next to him but they hadn't spoken much. They'd worked together for more than ten years. Phil was his closest friend and partner and there was no need for words. She'd sent Constable Forsyth off to write his official report instructing him to be back by 9 AM when the local businesses opened, to check whether any of them had CCTV cameras turned on the street outside their shops. It was unlikely in a sleepy town like this, but it was worth a shot.

Ed felt Phil's eyes boring into the side of his head for about the tenth time in as many minutes. She'd been shooting him concerned glances on and off all morning. He was doing his best to ignore it. He didn't have the energy to get into it.

When she'd picked him up her only comment was, 'You look like shit.' It was both a reprimand and a statement of fact. Phil knew about the drinking; she knew about the all-consuming depression that Ed had fallen into after his wife, Susan, disappeared two years ago. Susan had been four months pregnant and they were planning for their new baby, renovating their 100-year-old house and looking forward to a long, happy future together.

In an instant, that had all vanished. Susan went to work as usual one day and just never came home. Over and over again he'd replayed that final morning in his mind. He was tired and grumpy. A triple fatality on one of the most notorious stretches of the local roads had kept him up until the wee hours of the morning. He was angry at yet another senseless waste of life caused by testosterone mixed with alcohol.

HINDSIGHT

He and Susan had talked briefly about it. Then she mentioned going shopping for baby things and he upset her by saying he thought it was too soon. She accused him of always being pessimistic. It was true enough, but after two miscarriages he was afraid to get his hopes up. Then she'd disappeared and he'd felt his pessimism was somehow the cause of it.

In the first two weeks after she'd gone missing, he was frantic. He phoned hospitals, checked with every friend and distant relative he could think of and pestered colleagues from neighbouring towns and Adelaide every few days.

Once his initial panic abated it was replaced with a burning anger — anger at himself; anger that she was still missing; anger at the people he worked with. Then the whispers started, the sideways looks. Some people were saying she'd left him because of the job. Others were hinting that there was another man. The most malicious gossipers were convinced he was responsible.

The humiliation of having to be questioned about her disappearance was the final straw. It sent him into a rage so violent that the Chief had been forced to send him home for the day.

After that he'd walked around in a daze. He couldn't feel anything, couldn't cry, couldn't accept what had happened. He was on autopilot.

Eventually the storm broke. It happened suddenly, when he was at the supermarket. He caught a glimpse of a woman who looked so much like Susan from behind that he almost called out her name. She turned around, sensing his eyes drilling into her back and it was then that he saw she was holding a baby, not more than a few months old. She returned his intense gaze with a puzzled frown, wondering why this stranger was staring at her.

He'd dropped what he was holding and ran out of the shop. He ran until the pain in his lungs forced him to stop. He threw himself down on a bench in a park and cried, deep, gut-wrenching sobs. He didn't give a damn about who might see him. All he cared about was the agony that was ripping his insides apart. He'd cried until he was drained. After he'd sat there for hours, he called Phil.

She knew he'd gone to pieces as soon as the first word left Ed's lips. She dropped everything to come and get him and take him home. She put him to bed and he'd fallen instantly into an exhausted sleep.

After the breakdown, Ed sank into a pit of alcohol and depression. He couldn't get out of bed, couldn't eat, couldn't be bothered doing anything. The only thing that took away the pain was the booze, and that didn't last for long enough.

Three months passed in a drunken stupor until Phil finally reached the limit of her tolerance. She marched in one morning, dragged Ed out of bed and forced him into a freezing cold shower. She made him eat and drink what felt to him like a litre of black coffee and then she started talking.

She told him that she couldn't imagine what he was feeling but that Susan would be ashamed of him if she could see him. She told him how proud Susan had been when he'd solved the last case they'd worked before her disappearance. She told him it was time to fuckin' pull himself together.

After that day the blackness had started to lift. He made an effort to live and within a month he was back at work. The moods still hit him but less often.

The arrival of the meat wagon snapped Ed back to the present. The cold wind penetrated again and he stamped his feet and shoved his hands under his armpits to try to bring back the circulation. The empty street stretched in front of him. He and Phil headed over to talk to Sonya, the pathologist. She stood at the entryway to the lane. Weak sunlight had started to stretch its fingers into the shadows but it would be another hour before it was bright enough to see properly. Floodlights illuminated a doorway about a third of the way down. Sonya was hunched over a pile of rubbish next to a large wooden crate that took up most of the doorway.

She straightened up and turned to shoot them a smile. A pleasant-looking woman in her early forties, she had chestnut brown hair pulled back in a simple ponytail. Her face was bare of any make-up, not surprisingly considering the hour. When she smiled she showed a wide mouth full of straight white teeth. The effect was a bit startling and slightly horsy.

She swept a glance over Ed and laughed. 'Jesus, I've seen corpses that look more alive than you do this morning.'

'Thanks for that. I know where to come when I need my ego stroked. What have we got?'

'It's a nightmare of a crime scene for the forensic team, lots of traces of bodily fluids of one type or another, mainly urine. It's really too contaminated to be certain that anything they collect belonged to the killer. I might have more luck with the body when I get her back to the lab.

'I'm not sure what killed this one. No obvious wounds or injuries. No marks around her neck to indicate strangulation, although there is a small red mark over her carotid artery that could be a puncture wound. I'll have a closer look back in the lab.

'There are traces of fresh urine just outside the doorway over there. It could be hers. Looks like she soiled herself. There's also a pile of vomit next to the crate. It looks fresh and smells of alcohol. Doubt it was hers but it might belong to either the killer or the guy who called it in.'

'What about the crate?' Phil asked.

'I don't think there's anything special there but the team are checking. It looks like a standard shipping crate. It'll go back to the lab to be checked for prints. I don't like your chances though. This one looks planned.'

'Can we have a quick look before she's bagged?' Ed asked.

'Yep, I'm done here. Knock yourselves out.'

They edged closer and stared into the crate. Its sad contents were illuminated by the floodlights. The victim was curled into a ball. She was wearing a navy skirt, cream blouse, thick tights and sensible looking black court shoes with a medium heel. She had long blonde hair, like pale straw in the cold winter sun. It was tangled and partly covered her face. Her skin had taken on

HINDSIGHT

a blue tinge. Ed could imagine what she would have been like; conservative, neat, probably the quiet, serious type.

Phil and Ed looked at each other. Their faces wore identical expressions — the same mixture of sorrow and anger they felt at the start of every murder investigation.

CHAPTER 4

I'd be lying if I said that I felt relaxed about venturing into town. I could count the number of times I'd visited in the last nine years on one hand. If anyone asked, which didn't happen too often, Mum and Gran always explained my housebound state by saying I suffered from agoraphobia. It made me sound like a bit of a head case but it was better than telling them the truth.

Upstairs, as I got dressed and psyched myself into some semblance of calm, I could hear Mum and Gran talking in muffled tones down below — no doubt debating the wisdom of my latest bid for freedom. I love our house, I love living with Mum and Gran, but the problem is I'm on the wrong side of twenty-five and at some point I need to prove to myself that I can go it alone.

Long-lived as the women in my family might be, Mum and Gran won't be around to mollycoddle me forever. Also, at some point I just need to get a life. Despite our family history, I kind of like the idea of meeting someone and settling down to have a couple of kids. Don't get me wrong, Mum and Gran have had their loves — obviously, otherwise I wouldn't be here. The men just didn't stay around for very long. Grandad died of cancer at the age of forty-one. It was a terrible thing for Gran that she couldn't heal the one person who meant the most to her.

My own father just couldn't deal with my mum's gift. Before they got married he swore to her it wouldn't be a problem for him but as time wore on he became more and more resentful of people asking her to read for them. It got to the point where they argued about it on a daily basis. He couldn't understand why she couldn't just ignore her gift. The problem is, anyone who has a talent as strong as Mum's can't just put it in a box and pack it away in the closet like an unwanted wedding gift. It's an intrinsic part of who she is. To ignore it would be like cutting off her arm.

When I was two, Mum and Dad decided to have a trial separation. Mum moved in with Gran and Dad moved to Queensland. That's the way it's been ever since. I see Dad every so often. It was more regular when I was younger, before he remarried and started his second family; before I developed my version of the family gift. He sends me birthday and Christmas cards. I probably should feel more pissed off than I do by the fact that he so obviously doesn't need me in his life but I can't remember any different and I can't imagine it any other way.

HINDSIGHT

Still, my acceptance of my lot was one thing. Convincing a date that my family was just a different version of 'normal' was another.

Forget about Mr Right, the hard truth is that at twenty-eight I haven't even found Mr Close-Enough. I dated plenty of boys back in school but most of them just seemed too immature or too full of testosterone to even begin to deal with the complexities of a house full of women with paranormal tendencies. Those relationships ran a pretty predictable course: everything was pretty normal until they started to want to take me to places that I hadn't checked or they came to pick me up and met my mother and grandmother.

One poor sod, Michael James, got the double whammy. He wasn't meant to come inside but nerves got the better of him and he needed to use the bathroom and of course that meant I had to introduce him. Mum and Gran were in the kitchen sorting Gran's home-grown herbs for the local health food store complete with Shadow's predecessor (who was also black) purring around their ankles — it was like a scene from *Macbeth*.

It was all downhill from there. Michael compounded the issue by taking me to a lookout I hadn't been to before and where some unhappy soul had ended it all by jumping. Imagine it: he leans in for a snog, I freeze, my eyes glaze over and I let out a blood-curdling scream as I feel myself plummeting to the bottom of the cliff.

I had one serious relationship when I was in my early twenties. Poor Geoff; almost fifteen years older than me, kind and patient and willing to accept my talent and my reluctance to venture very far afield. He was a wonderful, caring man and I should have felt blessed to be loved by him. I just couldn't make myself feel that way. We parted ways; me feeling like an ungrateful cow, him gentlemanly as always.

I knew if I was ever going to meet someone I had to get out and about more. Working as an editor didn't exactly help. I mostly dealt with my clients by email and I tended to work all hours of the day and night. My social life was non-existent.

I'd been teetering on the brink of trying to take control of my life for a long time; I just hadn't been able to take the last step into the unknown. What'd pushed me over was a visit from an old school friend, Julie. We were close through our school years but then she moved away and gradually we stopped phoning each other, stopped sending cards until finally we drifted out of each other's lives.

Julie had always been a good friend. She understood that my family was a bit unusual but accepted them without hesitation. Years later, when she turned up on our front porch, I didn't recognise her. She was glowing and her eyes sparkled. In her arms was a little boy. She spent the afternoon with me and we caught up on all the missing years. She had married a man she met working in a large finance firm in Adelaide.

I was happy for her. She'd come into her own and motherhood obviously agreed with her. At the end of the afternoon she jumped in her car and drove off to meet Richard, who was at a business meeting in a nearby town. As I stood on the front porch and watched them leave a wave of self-pity swept over me.

HINDSIGHT

What followed was three days of black moods that had Mum and Gran ducking for cover. I'm normally a fairly easy-going person and I don't let too much worry me. Not this time.

I felt like there was a thundercloud perched permanently over my head, I couldn't shake it and I couldn't explain to Mum and Gran the muddle of thoughts going through my head. I'm sure they figured it out. Their few brave attempts to draw me out were met with snarls and hostility. They beat a strategic retreat and tiptoed around me until the mood passed.

Things gradually got back to normal. What was left was that annoying stream of consciousness that popped into my head more and more frequently. It was like an alter ego, pestering me to get off my butt and do something with my life. So here I was, about to take on the big bad world again. A chill slithered down my spine and I shivered involuntarily. Don't be an idiot, little Miss Alter Ego said.

Mum chattered ceaselessly on the drive into town. I just sat back and made appropriate noises, feeling like a prisoner who'd just been let out after a long period of incarceration. Everything looked newly painted. I could feel a thrill of energy and excitement building in the pit of my stomach. It seemed like I could take on the world and win and all of a sudden it wasn't just good to be alive, it was bloody fantastic. A manic grin spread over my face. Mum must have caught it out the corner of her eye because the tone of her voice suddenly changed and I was drawn back into her stream of chatter by her sudden probing.

'Well, that's the biggest smile I've seen on your face in ages. What brought out the sunshine?'

'Nothing in particular, Mum. Just feeling glad to be alive.'

'I wish you'd let me have a peek at your future, Cass, I'm sure it would be good for you to know.'

'No, what you mean is that it would be good for *you* to know.'

A scowl replaced my smile. Mum had been pestering me to read my future for years and it annoyed the crap out of me. I really didn't want to know and she just couldn't understand it. Being more psychically gifted than your average person, I'd learnt how to block her. She couldn't read me unless I let her and it drove her nuts. Sweeping aside my momentary irritation, I tried to recapture the sense of exhilaration. I looked over at her and decided to extend an olive branch.

'Mum, you know I love you, don't you?'

'Yes, Cass, I know,' she murmured.

'How about we just enjoy this outing and agree to disagree?'

She sighed. 'Yes, I suppose that's really all we can do, I just wish …'

'Mum, please don't spoil today. I don't want to fight with you.'

'Well, no, I don't want to fight either but …'

'I'll buy you a piece of mud cake from Mrs McCredie's.'

'Ah now, that's not playing fair. How can I refuse an offer like that?' She finally let the matter drop and the conversation returned to less controversial issues, such as how she could tell

HINDSIGHT

Mrs Henshaw that her husband was cheating and whether or not she should tell Mr Mooney that his sister who lived overseas was in for a period of long and serious illness.

With a sense of relief I went back to looking at the passing scenery. The sun was peeking out from behind the clouds and the fields were lush and green from the winter rain. In the distance cows dotted the hills like specks of lint on a bright green jumper. I rolled the window down and inhaled deeply, breathing in the cool sharp air that smelled of eucalyptus and the sea.

Gradually the landscape started to change and the occasional building popped up among the greenery. Eventually the buildings won the battle with nature and we entered the town centre. I studied everything intently, trying to see what was different from the last time I was there a couple of years earlier. Things looked much the same. There was a new coffee shop where the old haberdashery store used to be but other than that it looked like the army of progress had halted at Jewel Bay, taken a look and then passed it by.

The town was slowly grinding into second gear for the morning. People were walking at a brisk pace to get to their destinations and the traffic was starting to fill the streets. I felt a sense of wellbeing as the rhythms of the town hummed around me. I grew up in this place, went to school here. The familiarity settled around me like a comfortable blanket.

Mum pulled up in front of the library and I smiled at her with more confidence than I really felt.

'So I'll see you for lunch at Mrs McCredie's at twelve thirty?'

'Are you sure you don't want me to come with you, Cass?' I could see genuine worry in her eyes.

I glued a smile on my face. 'Mum, please. I really need to do this by myself. I remember the safe paths and nothing has happened on them since I was last in town. I checked.'

Safe paths were my key to survival when I was younger. I carefully plotted the roads I could take without having visions. I leant over and gave her a quick kiss on the cheek and before she could think of anything else to say I was out of the car.

The library always struck me as an amazing piece of architecture for a small town. It stood there like a grand old dame dressed in satin and jewels among Amish neighbours. Its Corinthian columns were oddly mixed with gothic-styled windows and detailing, right down to the token gargoyle on the roof. One of the town's founding fathers commissioned the building. Money was not an issue and I spared a moment of pity for the architect he'd hired to pull together all his favourite elements from a wide range of styles.

I walked up the steps to the imposing front doors and pushed them open. The familiar smell of books greeted my nose and the hush embraced me as I started to make my way to the reference section.

'Can I help you, dear?' It was the delightful Mrs Jones, senior librarian, professional busybody and advertisement against spinsterhood.

I switched on the smile again and slowly turned around, bracing myself for the barrage I knew was coming.

HINDSIGHT

'Mrs Jones, how nice to see you.' I silently congratulated myself on my A-class acting skills.

The woman turned and studied me over the top of her glasses.

I sighed. 'Cass, Cass Lehman. It's been a while …'

'Of course, Cass, my dear, why, how lovely to see you again after such a very long time. What brings you into town? Are you feeling better?' The wattles of skin on her neck quivered excitedly and her eyes gleamed behind the gold rims of her spectacles.

I could imagine her mouth watering at the thought of spreading this bit of news around her gaggle of cronies. Cass Lehman, back in town! More than two years since the last time, agoraphobia you know, very unfortunate, not surprising, though, when you consider how unusual her mother and grandmother are, didn't have a chance of being normal the poor child, needed a healthy environment to grow up in, not a house full of superstition and fancy. 'I am very well thanks, Mrs Jones. Just here to do some research in the special reference section. I'll see you later.'

I turned and hurried away before she could pump me for more information. I could feel her gaze scorching the fabric on my retreating back. With a sigh of relief I reached the small reference section and slipped between two rows of books.

I wanted to look up the history of the neighbouring town of Fairfield. I needed to look at its history from the time it was founded to the present and I was hoping that some of the local chronicles that were only available in hard copy would have the information I was looking for. Once I'd searched those, I planned to move on to the microfiche to look at the newspaper clippings from the local papers.

What I hadn't wanted to share with Mum and Gran was that I was making plans to venture further than Jewel Bay. I figured a good first step to finding my freedom might be to explore the bigger town and maybe eventually find a home of my own there. Before I could set foot in the place though, I needed to know where the psychic hotspots were.

For me, that meant doing painstaking research into every murder or tragic death since the town was established and plotting them onto a street map. Hopefully I could work out some safe paths and navigate my way around the town without having any unexpected episodes. The only danger was unknown or unrecorded deaths that I could inadvertently stumble over.

I was willing to take the risk. I'd come to realise that I desperately needed to get out and make my own life. I couldn't keep going the way I was — I would go crazy and end up as a mad old lady with a dozen cats. I'd die without anyone realising for weeks and end up as kitty chow.

I was soon immersed in my research and before I knew it, I had only an hour left before I was due to meet Mum. Gathering up my notes I decided to move to the newspaper archives and start some work there. Two hours of trawling through dusty tomes of local history written in quaint language describing the ebb and flow of rural life in a small town was enough for the moment. For a change of pace I decided to start in the present and work backwards. I sat down at one of the computers and

HINDSIGHT

pulled up the *Local Tribune* from the previous month and started browsing.

Forty-five minutes of mostly uneventful skimming passed until an article popped up that caught my attention: Local Girl Found Murdered.

I remembered the case well. Back in 2001, Louise Anderson, a pretty young girl who was born in Fairfield but was studying in Adelaide, went missing mid term. A campaign to find her followed and ended with the tragic discovery of her body somewhere in the city. I scanned the article. It was written before she was found and the police were appealing for information. There was some uncertainty about where she went missing from. The Fairfield police were working with the Major Crime Investigation Branch in Adelaide. The article included a picture of one of the local detectives investigating the case, Detective Ed Dyson.

The photograph showed a man weighed down by his job. He looked like he hadn't slept or eaten anything for weeks. The article quoted him calling for anyone who might have seen Louise on the day of her disappearance to come forward and assist police with their investigations. The request smacked of desperation.

I scanned further down the microfiche looking for related articles. I soon found what I was looking for. The front page article described how her mutilated body was found in the Adelaide Parklands. The autopsy results confirmed that she'd been tortured and dumped while she was still alive. No useful evidence was found on the body. From what I remembered they never caught the killer.

Without really knowing why, I printed out the articles. The case wasn't relevant to my research but for some reason it bothered me intensely. I picked up the pages from the printer and sat there looking at the picture of Ed Dyson. There was something about him that appealed to me. I wondered if he was still a cop. I sat back and stared into space. Maybe I was going about this the wrong way. Maybe I should be confronting my demons instead of running away from them.

A glimmer of an idea started to burn in the recesses of my brain. If Ed was still a detective maybe he could use some help. A nervous knot formed in the pit of my stomach. What if I offered to help him solve the case? I could visit the place where they found her. If I could pick up on her last moments I might be able to see her killer through her eyes. The thought made me shudder. The word 'tortured' leapt out of the page at me. If she died from the torture that meant I would feel what she felt.

I was still sitting there staring at the page when a hand descended on my shoulder.

'Jesus, Mum,' I gasped. 'You just scared ten years off my life.'

'Sorry, darling, I thought you must have heard me coming — I made quite a racket walking across the floorboards in my heels. What's that you're reading so intently?'

'Just an article I came across about the Louise Anderson murder while I was doing some research. It bothers me for some reason.'

'I remember that one. Turned out it was one of the security guards on her campus, which was why it took so long to figure it out. The guy gave the police false information about a possible suspect that turned out to be a complete fabrication.'

'Oh, I didn't realise they caught the guy.' I felt a weird mix of relief and disappointment as I said it.

'Yes, it took them a long time, if I remember. Anyway, are you ready for lunch? I've been waiting for you at Mrs McCredie's for the last twenty minutes.'

I glanced up at the clock and groaned. 'Shit! I'm sorry. I completely lost track of time. Yes, let's go. I need to settle up with Mrs Jones for my printing and photocopying and then we can eat. Looks like I'd better shout you lunch, not just cake, to make up for keeping you waiting.'

'Well, if you insist, Cass. It's not often I get taken out to lunch these days. By the way, you might as well hear it from me because the town's all abuzz with it — someone was killed last night. Her name was Janet something or other. I didn't know her. She'd only been in town for about eighteen months. Have you heard of her?'

'Me? Not likely. How did she die?'

'Well, it hasn't been confirmed officially, but Mrs O'Grady says she was murdered.'

'Oh no! Do you think she's right? You know she likes a good bit of gossip. She could be stretching the truth.' I could feel a sense of panic starting to rise in my stomach. 'Shit! Do you know where it happened?' Mrs Jones was shooting me daggers. My voice had risen well above the acceptable murmur that she expected from those entering her hallowed domain.

'It's OK, Cass, the police have had Stuart Lane taped off all morning. It happened there.'

I sighed with relief. That was a place I didn't need to visit any time soon.

'Tell me the rest over lunch, Mum, I'm starving and if we don't stop talking soon, Mrs Jones is going to burst a blood vessel.'

CHAPTER 5

By 10 AM the police knew who the victim was: Janet Hodgson, twenty-seven years old, a bookkeeper employed by a local farm machinery business that had a showroom and offices on Jewel Bay's Main Street.

They'd been hard at it, talking to her co-workers, the owners of the business and neighbouring businesses; pretty much anyone who could help them piece together a life that so far seemed unremarkable. They knew that she was last seen in her office at 9 PM the previous night when the cleaner left. They knew she had no family: her parents were both dead, and there were no siblings. There was no partner that anyone knew of. She was well liked but didn't seem to have any really close friends.

She was in the habit of working late at least once or twice a week to take advantage of the peace and quiet. She usually parked her car on the street running parallel to Main Street because it didn't have the same two-hour parking restrictions. The quickest way for her to get to her car was to cut down Stuart Lane. It probably hadn't even occurred to her that the shortcut might be dangerous.

Ed joined Phil, who'd just finished talking to a group of wide-eyed sales and office staff. 'Hey, how about we grab a bite? I could eat a damned horse.'

'Yep, sounds like an idea. We can compare notes at the same time.'

They headed for the only café that was open, ordered bacon and egg sandwiches to go, and retreated to the warmth of their car.

'So basically we don't know shit,' mumbled Phil through a mouthful. 'We don't know her habits, we don't know of anyone who was close to her who can tell us where she went, who she spent time with outside work — nothing.'

Ed sighed. He felt like he was standing at the bottom of a steep slope wondering if he had the energy to get to the top. All he wanted to do was find a comfortable spot, stretch out and let oblivion take over. He yawned.

'Come on, buck up, we'd better go check out her car and apartment before you nod off. Maybe by the time we get back to the station the lab work will be in — let's hope he's a sloppy prick.'

Janet's car was still parked on the street from the day before. It was a late-model red Ford hatchback. They peered through the windows. It was reasonably clean, no rubbish piled up in the footwells.

'Let's have a look shall we?' Phil said, snapping on some gloves. She jimmied open the door.

'Man, I hope you never decide to turn to a life of crime,' Ed said.

They rummaged through the glove box and carefully checked for any papers. There was a handful of receipts, a card for a local hairdresser and the service history for the car but nothing else. The only other paraphernalia was a hairbrush, a couple of pens, registration papers, some food wrappers and a street directory.

Phil looked at Ed and shrugged. 'Hopefully we find a diary or something useful in her apartment that will tell us more about this woman than her favourite hairdresser.'

'Hey, don't knock hairdressers, Phil. People have been known to bare their souls in the course of a good haircut.'

'Well, yours wouldn't know much about your soul. When was the last time you paid him a visit?'

'Yeah all right, I know.' Ed ran a hand over his head, making tufts of sandy hair stick out in all directions. 'I reckon it's worth getting the guys from the lab to check over the car. She might have known her killer. He could have sat in this very car.'

'Ah, the return of the optimist, that's what I like to see.' Phil shot him a half smile. 'Next stop, Janet Hodgson's apartment.'

They climbed back into Phil's bright yellow Mustang, her pride and joy. The only thing closer to her heart was her partner, Grace. Grace'd tell you that it was a pretty close thing sometimes;

if it came to a toss-up between her and the car she wouldn't like to put money on herself.

'There's something not right about this girl,' Phil said. 'Nobody knows her — not one person we spoke to today told us anything about who she really was and what she was like. Shit, Ed, how many women do you know who don't have any close friends that they talk all kinds of crap with?'

'Maybe we just haven't found them yet. Might be that she likes to keep her work life and personal life separate. Her apartment might give us some more to go on.'

They didn't have long to wait. Within a couple of minutes they pulled up outside the apartment. It was in a two-storey block; one of the newer high-density developments that had caused an uproar when it was built back in the nineties. A glass door gave way to a small entry foyer housing a wall of letterboxes and an intercom system so visitors could be buzzed in. There was a phone next to the intercom with an emergency number. After trying the phone and discovering it was out of order, Ed punched the number into his mobile and got the apartment manager. She only lived a couple of blocks away and she reluctantly agreed to come over to let them in.

She arrived bad tempered and flushed, greying hair hanging limply to her shoulders, a floral dress stretched tight over her ample waistline and breasts.

'So what's all this about?' she snapped. 'I can't have police coming in and out of here. I hope Miss Hodgson hasn't been causing trouble. I like to keep a certain tone of tenants. These apartments are in great demand, you know.'

Ed looked slowly around the cheap décor of the foyer, taking in the lifting vinyl and flaking paint, then switched on his iciest smile.

'Janet Hodgson was found murdered this morning, ma'am. We need to have a look through her apartment as part of the investigation.'

He watched as her mouth opened in an O of surprise. She said, 'Well I suppose you'd better come with me then.'

They trudged after her, watching the veins in her legs bulge and strain as she tackled each stair, finally arriving at apartment 17.

'This is it. Don't be making no mess or disturbing the other tenants,' she spat out as she turned to go.

'The key please, ma'am. We may need to come back with forensic teams and we would hate to have to disturb you,' Phil said in saccharine sweet tones.

The manager thrust the key at her and stomped off down the corridor.

'Thanks for your help,' Phil called out, before turning to Ed, who was surveying the inside of the apartment from the door.

There wasn't a lot to see: a couple of newish cream couches with scatter cushions in a range of yellows and blues, a patterned rug on the floor and a coffee table with a couple of magazines on it. A small television sat in one corner. A couple of pot plants here and there added a bit of greenery. A set of bookshelves lined one wall, full of novels and historical texts. They gloved up and slowly and methodically worked over the room.

Next they walked through to the kitchen and surveyed the immaculately clean benchtops and neatly arranged contents of the cupboards and drawers. The bathroom told the same story. A limited selection of cosmetics and toiletries were carefully stacked in the drawers and vanity cupboard. Lastly they turned to the bedroom.

A décor of pale blue and white greeted them. The bed was made, the dressing table neat and tidy. A novel and a radio alarm clock sat on the bedside table next to a reading lamp. They did a quick check of the drawers in the dressing and bedside tables. A few bills, an address book and a diary were the only items of interest.

'Shit, I've never met a woman with so little crap,' Phil said, snapping off her gloves.

'Yep, we haven't found a single photo or photo album either. It's like she's just been camping out here.'

Ed's phone interrupted their conversation. He took the call and then turned back to Phil.

'That was the Chief. She wants us back right now. Preliminary forensics are back and if I'm any judge something else has come up too — she sounded like someone put salt in her sugar bowl.'

Phil groaned. 'Oh great, that's just what we need, a round with the fire-breathing dragon.'

They were back at the station within half an hour. They'd taken less than ten steps down the corridor before Senior Constable Samuels popped his head out of an office and called out to them.

'Sorenson's waiting for you in her office. She's got a couple of trained monkeys with her too.'

HINDSIGHT

Samuels was the office busybody. He made everyone else's business his own; handy when you needed to know something but a pain in the arse when it was your life he was sticking his nose into.

'Thanks for the warning, buddy,' Ed called out as they made their way to the Chief's office. He glanced at Phil. He could tell she was thinking the same thing as him: 'trained monkeys' was slang for the Crime Service Detectives from Adelaide and that meant that they were about to lose control of the case.

They knocked on the door and received a curt 'Enter'. Walking in they saw DCI Sorenson and two detectives. They both knew the older of the two; they'd worked with him before. The younger man was unfamiliar.

DCI Sorenson was a red-head in her late forties. She was tall and lean and quite attractive when she stopped frowning, which wasn't very often. Today she looked weary, tiredness carved into the flesh around her eyes and mouth.

'Detectives Dyson and Steiner, thank you for joining us. Take a seat. I believe you know Detective Byrnes. This is Detective Rawlinson. They will be helping us with our investigation into the Hodgson murder.'

'Excuse me, Chief, but is Crime Service involvement necessary at this stage? Nothing we've come across has indicated that this is anything but a routine murder investigation.' Phil stared at the two detectives as she said it, the contempt in her voice coming across loud and clear.

About five years ago they were working on a double homicide with the Noarlunga police and Phil fell into the trap of taking it very personally. One of the victims was an eight-year-old girl, the other a ten-year-old boy. Their murder was brutal. The children were abducted, raped and tortured before they were left to die in an abandoned warehouse.

Phil and Ed worked day and night to try to break the case. The Crime Service detectives working with them believed the murders were part of a series of killings that had taken place throughout the country. They arrested and charged a man from Darwin while a suspect Ed and Phil had identified walked free. Two years later he was convicted of killing a five-year-old girl. Phil had never got over it.

'Detective Steiner, you know as well as I do that with no obvious suspect this becomes a Tier 2 murder, but there's some additional information that's relevant to the investigation so if you don't mind, I was just going to ask Detective Byrnes to explain.' Sorenson gave Phil the full blast of a Medusa-like glare.

'Thank you, DCI Sorenson.' Byrnes took his cue. 'As you said, on the surface this case appears to be a Tier 2 murder which automatically warrants our involvement —'

Phil snorted.

'— however, the victim, Janet Hodgson, was also in the witness protection program so we need to investigate her death to see if her murder was related to her previous life.'

There was silence as Ed and Phil processed the bombshell.

Ed recovered first. 'Well, that would explain why her apartment felt like she was only camping there and why she didn't have any close friends or family.'

Byrnes turned to him. 'She'd been in the program for about eighteen months. She moved here from Sydney. She was married to a schmuck who was into everything from cocaine to money laundering. She met him when she was only nineteen, he turned on the charm and they got married a year later. She didn't realise what the family business was until it was too late. She threatened to leave him. He threatened to kill her and her mother. A real class act, this guy.

'Her mother passed on about two years ago. Up until then she put up with his crap. He was a violent, abusive thug and she finally decided she'd had enough when he just about beat her to death. She was in hospital for two months. That was when she agreed to give evidence against him on the condition that we put her in the program.'

'So where is he now?' Phil asked.

'Serving life. He got done for killing another scumbag. The real issue is whether one of his cronies managed to somehow track Janet down. Her ex's not a very forgiving guy and I'm sure he won't be heartbroken when he hears she's dead.'

'Mmm, I don't normally believe in coincidences,' Ed commented, 'but this just doesn't feel like an organised hit. It's too personal. A hit is normally cold and clean.'

'Yep, but if that's true then this chick must have been one of the unluckiest women on earth,' Rawlinson drawled.

A knock on the door interrupted them.

'That'll be the preliminary results from the pathologist,' Sorenson said. 'Come in. Yes, Sonya, we're ready for you now.'

Sonya wore the professional mask she always wore. Ed and Phil had known her for years and respected her talent and dedication. They'd shared too many cases with her to remember them all and had drunk just as many beers to help them forget the rest.

'The lab results have come back negative for just about everything. No foreign blood, no semen, no skin cells and no clean fingerprints. The preliminary autopsy report indicates that the victim died from a heart attack induced by severe stress. She had a congenital heart defect that she probably wasn't even aware of, but the attack caused enough stress to trigger a massive heart attack. He literally scared her to death.

'What's interesting is the small puncture wound on her neck. She was injected with a combination of a sedative and a fast-acting muscle relaxant. It's a curious one. If she hadn't had a heart attack the small dose of muscle relaxant would have hit quickly, rendering her immobile and then the sedative would have knocked her out after about ten minutes and would have kept her out of it for about ten to twelve hours. The attacker didn't want her dead. My guess is he wanted her unconscious until he could come and collect her.'

She stopped talking and passed a hand wearily over her face to tuck a stray strand of hair behind one ear. The humming of the air conditioner and the murmur of voices from outside the office filled the silence. No one said anything until Sorenson finally broke the spell.

'So we don't actually know whether or not he was planning on killing her?'

HINDSIGHT

'She's dead. That makes him a killer,' Phil said.

'Phil's right. He's a killer whether or not he meant to be,' Ed said.

'The drugs in her system didn't kill her. If he planned on killing her it would've been by some other means. We'll probably never know what he had in mind,' Sonya said.

'I hope he never gets the chance to show us,' said Ed.

'Yes, we have a first-class nutter out there. I want you to work your butts off until we have him behind bars. This is not someone we want among the general public. We need to work as a team so I expect nothing but co-operation from everyone,' Sorenson said staring Phil down.

Phil glowered and was about to start bitching again when Sorenson's phone rang. She answered the call and gave them all a very obvious 'your presence is no longer required' look. Grumbling, they filed out.

'Hey, sorry to hear about your wife, mate,' Rawlinson said as they walked along the corridor into the squad room.

He was the younger detective, probably in his early thirties, dressed to kill in a suit that made Ed feel like he'd bought his own clothes from the welfare store and then slept in them for a few days. He was a strange mixture of arrogant and eager, vacillating between them.

'Thanks,' was Ed's curt reply.

Phil glared at Rawlinson, trying to decide whether the guy was being a prick or whether he was just stupid. She decided to give him the benefit of the doubt, turning instead to Byrnes.

'So Detective Byrnes, in your expert opinion, how would you like us to proceed?'

Byrnes's face hardened and a vein started to throb in his temple. 'How about you and Detective Dyson fill us in on where you're up to? Then we'll tell you what we know and we can work out a plan of attack from there.'

'OK, well, what we have is sweet FA. We searched the victim's car and apartment, interviewed her colleagues and spoke to her landlady. So far we know nothing about her. All we have is a few bills, her purse with a couple of ATM cards and a book with a half-dozen numbers in it. We were about to start interviewing her neighbours and checking out the contacts in her address book when we were interrupted.' Phil's summary came out like bullets from a machine gun.

'We know she worked late on a regular basis, kept pretty much to herself, didn't have any close friends at work and has the cleanest bloody apartment I've ever seen,' Ed added.

'Is that all?' Byrnes asked.

'Yes — that's all,' Phil snarled. 'Do you think we're keeping the juicy stuff to ourselves so we can claim all the glory? Sounds more like something I'd expect from you lot.'

Byrnes gave Phil a long hard look but either he couldn't think of anything to say, or he had plenty but thought better of it. He turned back to Ed.

'And what about the officers in Jewel Bay? What are their names?'

'Constable Forsyth and Sergeant Johnston. We saw Forsyth this morning, he was the first on the scene, but we haven't caught up with Reg yet. We'll head over to see them both this afternoon. Forsyth was checking for any CCTV footage of the street. So what do you have?'

Rawlinson looked at Byrnes and, getting a slight nod, started to fill them in. 'Her previous name was Alicia Mazzone. Her husband was Louis Mazzone, part of the mob from the eastern states and involved mainly in drugs and money laundering.

'He's a real bastard, likes to use his fists. When her mother died, Alicia finally saw her way out. She was a pretty smart woman. She'd been collecting information about Louis for a long time and gave us enough to put him away until he's a very old man. He's still got twenty years to go before he even gets to think about a parole hearing.'

Byrnes took up the thread. 'So that's why we think it's highly likely that someone, somewhere recognised her and fed the information back to Louis. He's got pretty long arms, even in gaol.'

'Yeah, it seems obvious but it just doesn't feel right,' Ed said. 'There's something about this one that sets off alarm bells.'

'Jesus, Ed, I hate it when you get those feelings.' Phil grimaced. She looked Byrnes straight in the eye. 'I've worked with Ed for longer than I like to remember and if he thinks we've got ourselves a fuckin' weirdo, I reckon we're in for fun times.'

'Yeah, well, as talented as Detective Dyson might be, Detective Steiner, we need a bit more to go on than a tingle in his big toe,' Byrnes said impatiently. 'We need to know more about her life, her movements yesterday, where she ate, anyone she called. I want to know everything, right down to how many times she went to the bathroom. I didn't think she was the type, but just maybe she called someone from her old life and they let the cat out of the bag.

'I suggest you continue to follow up her movements locally, the numbers in her phone book, her habits, all the usual stuff. See if anything stands out. In the meantime we'll go and put some pressure on some known associates of the Mazzone family. See if we can find out anything.'

'Sounds fine to me; less we have to work in the same space the better,' Phil muttered.

'Right, call me if anything comes up, otherwise we'll meet again tomorrow and compare notes.' Byrnes turned and strode out of the room with Rawlinson loping along behind him like an eager puppy.

'Fun coupla guys,' Ed said.

'Yeah, life of the party,' Phil snorted. 'Don't think I'll be adding them to my Christmas card list.'

'Yeah, well, let's get back out there, hey? I can feel the trail going cold every minute we hang around here.'

Phil grabbed her coat and keys. 'Jesus, Ed, you're all cheer today. Let's go see Reg and Constable Newbie and see what they've been up to.'

CHAPTER 6

Ed and Phil stopped at a café to grab a late lunch. When they walked in everyone looked at them. A couple of the patrons knew them, having assisted them with investigations, but nearly everyone recognised them as the detectives from Fairfield. Their pictures had appeared in the local rag on and off for the last fifteen years; that amounted to minor celebrity. They ordered and settled into a table and the conversation around them gradually resumed.

Word of the events in Stuart Lane had spread. Jewel Bay was a small town and people didn't like it when their idyllic life was shaken by any crime, least of all murder. Like most country towns, suicide and car accidents claimed far too many lives, but generally people lived content with the knowledge that the most serious crime was drunk and disorderly behaviour on Friday and Saturday nights.

The café owner soon bustled over with their lunches. She put their food down in front of them and stood there fidgeting.

'Sorry to bother you, but can you tell me anything about what's happened? Everyone wants to know.'

Ed fielded the question. Small towns were not places where they could move with anonymity and they had encountered this type of questioning in every case they worked.

'We can't tell you much yet. It's still too early. Reg, Sergeant Johnston, will fill you in when we know more.'

'But was she murdered?'

The word 'murder' stopped all conversation in the café as if by magic and an anticipatory hush descended as the customers waited to hear the detective's response.

'She was attacked and the attack caused her death. The final autopsy results will be available in the next few days. We can tell you more then.'

'Do you know who did it?'

'Unfortunately not.'

'So it could be anyone?' A note of hysteria crept into her voice.

'Let's not panic. In nearly every case the killer and victim know each other and there's a clear motive. Random attacks are extremely rare.'

She looked like she wanted to ask more but Ed cut her off. 'Is my banana smoothie on the way?'

She looked blankly at him for a few seconds. 'Yes, yes it is. I'll just get it now.'

Slowly people turned back to their meals and Ed and Phil got stuck into theirs.

'So what's with the health kick?' Phil said, eyeing Ed's meal. 'I can't ever remember you ordering a banana smoothie.'

'I read that vitamin B was good for hangovers.'

Phil's smile vanished. 'You gonna tell me about that?'

'It was our wedding anniversary.'

'Shit, I'd forgotten. I should've remembered.'

'Yeah, some best woman you are.'

'I would have kept you company. Why didn't you say something?'

'Look, I appreciate it, but you can't keep hovering over me every time a significant day comes up. Grace'd get fed up with that pretty quick.'

'Grace understands.'

'Grace has the patience of a saint, how else could she put up with you? But even she'll get sick of it one of these days. I don't want to be responsible for that. God knows we work long enough hours without you adding after-hours babysitting to it all.'

Grace was an amazing woman; an accomplished artist and businesswoman, she breezed her way through life seamlessly, organising herself and Phil without breaking a sweat.

'Yeah, I can't believe she hasn't got sick of me yet, but you know she loves you and if she thought you needed some company she would have been shoving me out the door herself.'

Ed glanced around the room. Most people's eyes slid away as his gaze swept over them, embarrassed to be caught listening and watching, but one pair of eyes met and locked with his, catching him by surprise. They belonged to a young woman at a window table.

She was in her late twenties and attractive in an old-fashioned kind of way. She had curly, honey blonde hair, carelessly pulled back in a clip. Her eyes were what transformed her face from plain to interesting: a warm hazel with flecks of gold. She smiled at him as she returned his stare. He blinked then looked away. The smile made him nervous for some reason he couldn't fathom. He turned back to Phil and started to tackle his meal.

'So where do you want to start this afternoon?' Phil asked. She had ordered her staple diet of hamburger with the lot. She took an enormous bite, dripping sauce down her chin.

Ed never ceased to be amazed at the food Phil put away. She was about five-eight and had a thin, wiry frame without a pick of fat on it. Her clear skin and shiny crop of short strawberry blonde hair completed the picture of glowing good health. Anyone who didn't know her would have been forgiven for thinking she led the lifestyle of a yogi.

'Jesus, Phil, you gotta stop eating that shit. Just watching you makes my stomach churn.'

'Hey, one salad wrap and a bloody smoothie doesn't give you the right to give me diet counselling. When you start looking after yourself properly I might start to listen.'

HINDSIGHT

'Fair enough. I just don't understand why you aren't the size of a small whale.'

'I keep telling you, it's all in the genes. I was just blessed with a fast metabolism.'

'Women everywhere would pay thousands for what you have if only you could bottle it and sell it.' He took another bite of wrap. 'After we're done here we might check out the crime scene again now that the techs have left. I want to get a feel for the place and see if I can get into the killer's head.'

'It's as good a place as any to start. We'd better head in to see Reg and his rookie too or he's likely to get his nose out of joint. You know what he's like. He hates to feel excluded.'

Reg had been a police officer since the dawn of time. He was part of the local landscape, a career uniform, steady and reliable. He wasn't a shining star but he was familiar, and his stern but fair approach made him a favourite with the locals. Ed and Phil had worked with him on every major crime in Jewel Bay.

'Yep, I thought we might ask him to organise all the local interviews. We can conduct them here and he and his offsider can either sit in or watch.'

'Sounds good. We might want to get his theory on who the killer could be too. I know the suits think it's mob related but I'm not so sure. The crate bothers me. If it was a professional hit why bother to knock her out and stuff her into a crate?'

'Yeah, too risky and messy for a pro.'

'You'd have to have a van with a hydraulic lifter to move it,' Ed commented.

'Yep, or more than one person.'

'Two of them? Nah, I doubt it. I reckon we start by looking at any van owners with priors.'

'Perfect job for the newbie if Reg agrees,' Phil said.

They left as soon as they finished their meals. Stuart Lane was a bit of a hike but they decided to leave their car and walk. The local cop shop was only a few hundred metres further than the lane.

The day was cool and crisp. The sun broke through the clouds every so often but its pale rays did nothing to banish the bite in the breeze coming directly off the sea. The trees along the street were bare and the overall impression was of a summer haven that had hunkered down for the winter months. There were plenty of people out and about but they had the purposeful stride of locals about their business, not the dawdle of holiday makers.

At the lane, the tape had already been taken down. They stood looking at the doorway where the body had been abandoned. As they were standing there a car squeezed its way down the lane, forcing them to step into the alcove while it passed. It stopped a bit further down and a bloke jumped out and started to unload cartons from the boot.

Ed stepped out of the doorway. Watching the man, a piece of the puzzle fell into place. 'The killer was coming back for her. I wonder what he was planning on doing?'

'I don't want to know.' Phil sighed.

'Hate to say it but I think this one has an agenda,' Ed said.

'Great, let's keep that idea to ourselves for a while shall we? We don't want to start a panic. I can just imagine what would

HINDSIGHT

happen if they thought there was a serial killer or rapist in their midst.'

'Yep, let's go see what Reg has for us. You never know, Constable whatever-his-name-is might have found some camera footage.'

'Yeah and I'm gonna win Lotto tonight.' Phil gave him a crooked smile.

They headed down the laneway, turning left at the end and covering the short distance to the police station. They passed the phone booth.

'I can't remember, did forensics say they found prints on the phone or not?'

'Yeah, lots of them, we'll check with Reg to see if Old Mick has a record. With a bit of luck we might at least be able to identify his prints and confirm that it was probably him who called it in.'

They spent the rest of the afternoon with Reg and his offsider, whose first name turned out to be Alex. Alex Forsyth was a good kid — enthusiastic and willing to do anything asked of him. He'd had no joy finding any camera footage. Jewel Bay just wasn't the sort of place where the local shopkeepers felt they needed CCTV. Most shops didn't even have cameras and the ones that did mostly didn't use them in the winter months.

Phil and Ed filled Reg and Alex in on the morning's proceedings over in Fairfield and ran them through their theory about the van and its driver. Reg couldn't hide his annoyance at the Crime Service.

'So they've breezed in now that she's dead and told you that she's been living here under the witness protection program for the last eighteen months?'

'Yes, that's pretty much it,' Phil muttered.

'I can't believe they didn't tell me when they moved her here.'

'Yeah, sometimes they don't. It just depends on how connected they think the people are who're after the witness.'

'They thought I might be dirty? You've gotta be kidding?'

'They don't know you like we do, Reg.' Ed tried to soothe the older man's obviously wounded pride.

'What, they thought I might let it drop after a few too many pints?'

'Something like that.'

'Well, it's a bit bloody rich.'

They got the feeling he would have liked to say a lot more but was holding back for the sake of Constable Forsyth's delicate young ears.

They spent the rest of the afternoon reviewing records that Alex pulled for them, looking at people who owned vans in Fairfield, Jewel Bay and Clifton. It was surprising how many there were. There were a total of 327 registered in the three towns. No one really leapt out as a likely suspect. Twenty-six owners had committed previous offences, mostly minor. A few had records for drink driving. A couple had records for assault or other misdemeanours but none of them stood out as potential murderers.

By the time six o'clock rolled round, Ed's head was ready to explode and his eyes were dry and gritty. Reg was clearly over it too. He wasn't used to working much past five o'clock. They decided to call it a day.

'Ed, come back to my place and have dinner with us,' Phil urged. 'Grace would be glad to see you.'

'I'd love to but, honestly, last night caught up with me again about three hours ago and I need to sleep. Tell Grace I promise I'll come and visit soon.'

'No worries. If you're sure you'll be OK?'

There was a question under the question and Ed knew it.

'I promise I'm just going home to sleep.'

'No booze?'

'No booze.'

'OK, let's go, I'll drop you home.'

Ed was as good as his word. He went home, took a handful of painkillers and crashed into bed at 7 PM. He didn't move a muscle until he was woken by the sound of the rubbish trucks doing their usual 6.30 AM rounds. His head felt clearer than it had in months. Something about this new case was hitting a nerve and he knew he needed to be at his best.

He couldn't put his finger on what was bugging him. He was at work by 7.30 AM and the first thing he did was revisit the list of van owners with priors or a history of violence. He found a couple who were probably worth speaking to but no one that gave him that glimmer of excitement he felt when they were on the trail of a suspect.

Phil sauntered in an hour later and stopped dead when she saw Ed at his desk, glued to the screen in front of him. 'Did you wet the bed?'

'Nah, but I slept like a baby.'

'Only people who have never had kids use that expression,' Phil quipped, then, realising what she'd said, the smile dropped from her face. 'Shit, sorry. I forgot to take my sensitivity pills this morning.'

Ed forced a smile. 'It's OK. I don't expect everyone to watch every word they say around me in case they happen to say something that's a bit close to home.'

'Yeah, I know. So, anything leapt out at you now that you've unpickled your brain cells?'

'No, there's not much. We're going to have to look at nearly all of them. Reg and Alex are going to be busy.'

'Bugger. Want a coffee?'

'Nah, I've already had three.'

'Is the boss in yet?'

'She got in half an hour ago. I filled her in on yesterday. No word from the suits.'

'Hopefully they've crawled back under their rock for a while.'

'Do you want to have a look at these again?' Ed nodded at the list on his desk.

'Yeah, you never know, for the first time in history you might have missed something.'

They spent the morning in relative silence, trawling through online records, breaking for a quick sandwich at lunchtime. They'd been back at it for a solid couple of hours when they were interrupted by Sorenson.

'That's what I like to see, my two best detectives hard at it.'

The honey in her tone instantly alerted them that something was up.

'Ed, can you step into my office for a few minutes. There's someone I'd like you to meet.'

Ed looked at Phil. Phil responded with a slight shrug. He followed Sorenson along the corridor to her office. She opened the door and waved him inside. Seated with her back to them was a young woman. She stood up and turned around as they entered. With a jolt, Ed recognised her as the young woman who'd been having lunch at the café in Jewel Bay the day before. Her intense eyes locked with his again.

'Detective Dyson, I'd like you to meet Cass Lehman. Miss Lehman is the daughter of one of my dearest friends. She lives in Jewel Bay and she thinks she might be able to assist you with your enquiries.'

There was an edge in Sorenson's voice that told Ed there was more to it. He switched on his most charming smile.

'Miss Lehman, pleased to meet you. We'd be very grateful for any assistance.' He shook her hand and glanced over at Sorenson.

'Perhaps you can take Miss Lehman into a private interview room and she can fill you in.'

'OK, I'll grab Phil.'

'No, I think only you for the minute.'

He paused, trying to work out what the hell was going on. 'OK, right this way, Miss Lehman.'

The woman, who'd said nothing but a murmured hello up until this point, followed him down the passageway to one of their two interview rooms. He opened the door for her and scanned her face as she passed him. She looked nervous. Ed pulled out a chair for her on one side of the melamine table and sat down opposite her.

'So, Miss Lehman, what do you know about Janet Hodgson?'

'Call me Cass. Janet Hodgson, was that her name? I don't know anything about her.'

'Right, so, did you see or hear something that might help us find who killed her?'

'Um, no, not yet.'

Ed leant back. 'Not yet? So how exactly do you think you can help us?'

Cass took a deep breath. 'I see things.' She winced.

'You see things?'

'I have a special ability. When I visit a place where someone died violently I experience their death.'

'Uh huh.' Ed was already imagining what Phil would say if she was in the room. He could understand why Sorenson had wanted him to handle this. It was only the knowledge that this was the daughter of one of Sorenson's 'dearest friends' that stopped him from dismissing her as a crank and marching her out of the station. 'And how will that help us exactly?'

'I see and feel what the person felt while they were dying. It's like an imprint of their death. For a few minutes it's like I'm the one who died.'

'So ...?' He let the question hang.

'I want to visit the place she died and see if she saw the man who attacked her. I might be able to give you a description.'

Ed sat there staring at her. Sorenson had to be kidding.

HINDSIGHT

'If you'll just excuse me for a minute I'll go and fill my partner in. Would you like a coffee while you wait?'

'No thanks, Mr Dyson.'

'Call me Ed. Mr Dyson was my father. It makes me feel ancient.'

He gave her a quick smile and ducked out of the room. It dropped from his face as soon as the door shut behind him. He strode back down the passageway to Sorenson's office. Giving only a cursory rap he barged in.

'Before you say anything, Detective Dyson, this is not open for debate. If Cass Lehman says she thinks she can help, she means it. I won't have you belittling her or refusing her assistance.'

'But —'

'No buts. You will take her to the crime scene and let her see what she can see. As a matter of fact I'll come with you.'

'But Phil —'

'You can tell Phil what's happening and tell her she's on strict orders to mind her manners.'

'She's not going to like it.'

'Exactly, which is why I want you to be the one to work with Cass. Besides, she asked for you.'

'Why? Do you really think she's legit? She saw us in the Jewel Bay Café yesterday, you know. She could be a voyeur.'

'Cass is no voyeur. She might be a bit strange, as are the rest of her family, but they're good people and they don't offer assistance lightly. Go and brief Phil. We leave in fifteen minutes.' She turned back to her computer, dismissing him.

And that was that.

As the four of them approached the squad car, Cass turned to him and asked, 'Has anyone died in this car?'

The question floored him. Phil snorted and answered her before Ed had a chance.

'We're not in the habit of bumping people off in the back of police cars.'

Cass flushed crimson. 'No, I just thought …'

Sorenson's eyes burned into Phil. 'It's all right, Cass, the car is less than a year old and no one has died in it.'

The trip took place in uncomfortable silence. Ed could feel Phil's barely contained annoyance. Cass and Sorenson were in the back and he regarded the young woman in his rear-view mirror every so often. She'd said very little since they'd left the station. She was clearly nervous and he wondered if she was having second thoughts.

Her long curly blonde hair was parted simply in the middle. She wore no make-up. Her face was a classic oval with a high brow. Her hazel eyes were definitely her best feature. She wasn't exactly plain but she had an aloof, distant kind of beauty.

Still, there was something about her. He'd barely looked at other women since Susan disappeared. He'd been too busy wallowing in misery and self-recrimination, until now.

They pulled up at Stuart Lane and Cass got out of the car. Ed walked up beside her.

'How do you want to do this?'

'Just show me where.'

He walked her to the start of the lane and pointed to the doorway.

'Is that where she actually died?'

'Maybe, we think she was walking from this end of the lane towards the doorway when he attacked her.'

'I need to retrace her steps.'

The look she gave him was so fraught he had to stop himself from reaching out and grabbing her arm to stop her.

'It's better if you wait here,' she said. She started to walk slowly down the lane. About twenty metres along she froze. Her back arched and she grabbed at her throat. Her knees buckled beneath her and she fell to the ground.

Ed ran over to her. Her eyes were open, staring. She didn't seem to be breathing. He started to panic and then suddenly she took a gasping breath and her eyes fluttered and focused on him. As his presence registered she shuddered and squeezed her eyes shut, tears seeping out from under her lids. He helped her to stand up.

Sorenson and Phil joined them and they stood there looking at Cass.

'What did you see?' Ed asked.

'Nothing, I didn't see anything ...'

His disappointment was unmistakable. He turned away.

'But I heard what he said. He said she was so much easier than the last one, and then he laughed.'

CHAPTER 7

He sat in his car a short distance up the road from Stuart Lane, within sight of the local police station. He'd been sitting there for nearly eight hours. The rage that had swept over him the day before had passed now, replaced by an intense, burning need to fix things.

Yesterday had been a disaster. Only once before had he come so close to being caught. He still couldn't work out what'd gone wrong. It should've been foolproof. He couldn't believe that someone had actually seen him. He was going to have to find Old Mick — he couldn't leave witnesses.

Stupid old bastard, he thought. Why the hell did he have to go and report it? Why couldn't he just shut his mouth, then the police would have been none the wiser, he would have the girl and Ginny would be happy.

She was hardly speaking to him at all today. He needed to fix things. He couldn't stand it when she was angry with him.

When he'd turned up with the van to collect the girl early yesterday morning he'd known straight away that something was wrong. There was a police detour set up and he'd had to go down Main Street instead of Jetty Street. As he drove slowly past Stuart Lane he could see that both ends were sealed off with police tape. Down the far end there was a cluster of police cars and other vehicles and small groups of people standing around talking.

He felt nauseous. Cold sweat had broken out under his arms and he'd nearly rammed into a car on the side of the road. That would have been catastrophic. Imagine getting caught because he crashed his van. He'd driven straight out of town, taken the van back to work and swapped it for his car.

When he'd returned to Jewel Bay, he'd been determined to find out what had happened and to work out what to do. He was worried the drugs would wear off and the woman would talk. Had she seen him? He didn't think so. How was he going to get to her? Was she in hospital? Did she have a police guard?

In the end he'd decided to go where he could listen to the local gossip. He'd pulled up outside of a café on Main Street and looked inside. It was barely 9.30 but the place was packed, full of people with their heads close together, relishing the drama.

He ordered coffee and found himself a table. Not long after, three people sat at the table next to him and started the conversation he was waiting for.

'It can happen anywhere.'

'But not here, surely. Jewel Bay isn't the sort of place where girls are found murdered,' said one of the women, shaking her head so vigorously that her body jiggled like a blancmange.

'Killed and stuffed into a crate, according to Mrs McCredie,' said another woman. She wasn't doing a very good job of disguising her enjoyment at being the one in the know.

'Does she know how she was killed?' asked the first woman.

'No, apparently the police haven't told anyone yet.'

There was a pause as their food was delivered.

'Did Mrs McCredie say how they found her?' their male companion asked between mouthfuls of bacon and eggs.

'She said someone anonymously called the police. Apparently Tess's boy was in here earlier. He was the first officer on the scene. Poor lad, and him only qualified for a few months. Anyway, he told Mrs McCredie that he thought it was Old Mick McKenzie that had called it in. Said he couldn't be sure but asked her to let him know if she heard anything about Mick's whereabouts,' the second woman said, licking her lips.

'Old Mick? How would he have known anything?' the man asked.

'Apparently he saw it happen.' This last titbit was delivered with relish, between bites of liberally buttered toast.

'Really? I hope the police have better evidence than that. Mick couldn't remember his own mother from one day to the next,' the man scoffed.

'Don't be so hard, he called it in, didn't he?'

'Yeah, and then he bolted I bet, straight down the neck of the next bottle. We won't see him around these parts again any time soon,' the man said, turning his attention to slathering marmalade on toast.

The eavesdropper tuned out. He'd heard everything he needed to know. Murdered? The drugs shouldn't have killed her. He never wanted them dead. They needed to be alive when he got them home.

He downed the rest of his coffee and left the café in a daze. One problem was solved but it had been replaced by another, bigger one. Someone had seen him.

That night the murder was reported on the TV news. The Jewel Bay police were appealing for the witness to come forward, and offering a reward. It was perfect. He needed to get to Old Mick first, and so here he was, sitting in his car with a clear view of the police station, watching, waiting and trusting his instinct that Old Mick would be tempted out of hiding.

He shivered. It had been a long and difficult day. He'd rescheduled the two services booked for that afternoon and the families were furious. He pleaded illness but it didn't seem to matter. He could still hear their angry voices in his head. They couldn't understand why there wasn't someone else who could just step in and do it.

The answer was simple: another person would snoop around. They might notice things. Still it wasn't good for business, having to shut up shop and spend the day just sitting here. If Old Mick didn't show up today he would have to come back tomorrow as

HINDSIGHT

well and maybe even the day after. That could be difficult. He had five more services booked for the rest of the week: two on Thursday and three on Friday including the two he'd cancelled today and rescheduled. He could imagine their reactions if he cancelled again.

Then there was the other problem. If he sat parked in the street two or three days in a row in the same car people might notice and start asking questions. He couldn't risk using the van with his logo on it.

The street lights flickered on. He looked at his watch — five fifteen. It got dark early at this time of year. He decided to call it quits. Sergeant Johnston had already gone. Only the young constable was left and he would probably go home in the next fifteen minutes. He started the car and looked in the rear-view mirror. A glimpse of someone moving through the gloom in the distance made him tense. He turned the car off and waited.

The figure got closer. Was that him? It could be; it was an older man, dressed in a shabby coat with the collar turned up against the bite in the wind. He wore a hat pulled down over his ears, its colour lost under years of grime and sweat. He shuffled along, casting anxious glances around him. When he reached the entrance to Stuart Lane he stopped and peered around the corner. It had to be Old Mick.

The watcher sank further down in his seat and pulled his cap down over his brow as the old man got closer and finally tottered past the car. He threw the door open, slid out and jogged around onto the footpath.

'Excuse me?'

The old man turned, fear widening his eyes. 'Yes?'

'Fairfield Police.' He flashed a fake badge, confident that it was too dark for the old man to tell the difference. 'Are you Michael McKenzie?'

The man turned away, looking down the length of the street, trying to decide what to do. 'Depends who's asking.'

'The Sergeant has already left for the day. He posted me here to keep an eye out in case Michael McKenzie decided to come in and assist us with our enquiries. If you're Mr McKenzie and you have any information that can assist us they have the reward waiting over at Fairfield Station.'

The old man's demeanour shifted so that his anxiety was tinged with eagerness.

'I came in to see if I could help, not for the money, like. How did you know it was me that saw it?' He shuffled his feet and rubbed his hands together.

'The officer who took the call on Tuesday night recognised your voice. Why don't you hop in the car? It's freezing out here. In less than half an hour we'll be in Fairfield, you can give us a quick statement and if the information is useful you can be on your way with your reward.'

Old Mick nodded. He shuffled towards the car. The other man walked back around to the driver's side and got in. Old Mick opened the door and then paused.

'What did you say your name was again?'

'Sorry, I'm Detective Richardson.'

HINDSIGHT

It was getting close to five thirty. Any minute the young constable would walk out of the police station and lock up for the night. If that happened the game would be up and he would have to either grab the stupid, old bastard and drag him into the car or drive off and leave Mick standing there. If he drove off that would be it, his chance gone forever. He clenched his teeth and plastered what he hoped was a reassuring smile on his face.

'I'm new in town. The Chief decided the other two detectives needed some extra help.' He smiled again.

Mick digested this for a few seconds. A sharp gust of wind whistled down the street, ruffling the wispy white tufts of hair that stuck out from under his hat. He shivered. Looking at the friendly face, he climbed inside and shut the door.

The driver pulled out from the gutter, accelerating down the street. He glanced in his rear-view mirror. The door of the police station opened and the constable stepped out. He smiled and sniggered softly. Mick stiffened. His head snapped around and he stared at the driver. His face contorted. He frantically scrabbled for the handle to open the door. It wouldn't budge.

The driver sniggered again. 'You can't open that door from the inside. Why don't you just relax, Mick, this won't hurt a bit.' And he thrust a needle into the old man's thigh, depressing the plunger.

Mick squealed in pain and fright, his hands grabbing for the syringe. He knocked it to the floor and sat there gasping. Within seconds his movements started to slow. He sat limply, staring straight ahead.

'Maybe it does hurt a little bit, but not nearly as much as what the next bit will.' He laughed, the sound filling the car and ringing in the ears of Michael McKenzie, who sat there, eyes open and staring at his hands lying useless in his lap.

CHAPTER 8

When the alarm went off it still felt like the middle of the night. I woke up tired and out of sorts. My eyes felt like someone had thrown a handful of sand in them and my arms and legs were leaden.

I'd spent most of the night tossing and turning and trying unsuccessfully to shut my brain down for long enough to fall asleep. Even Shadow gave up on me halfway through the night and went off on a night-time prowl instead of hogging the bed like he normally did.

All night the same images played through my mind like a movie reel stuck on a loop. I was walking down an alleyway holding a handbag, and wearing high heels that made it difficult to walk on the uneven surface. I wasn't feeling particularly nervous or anxious, just in a hurry. I didn't see anything out of the ordinary. I was mainly focusing on watching where I stepped, careful to avoid turning my ankle. I walked past a doorway and someone grabbed me from behind and forced their hand over my mouth and nose. I struggled but then there was a stinging in my neck and I started to feel weak. I could smell the man behind me. I could feel him. I tried to fight but then he put his lips next to my ear and whispered those words: 'You were so much easier than the last one.'

His voice was full of eager anticipation. Then he gave a soft laugh. Panic and fear started to overwhelm me; I felt a sudden crushing pain in my chest and then nothing.

It was frightening and frustrating. Every time it replayed I hoped to catch a glimpse of him; to see or hear something that might identify him. Every time there was nothing. I couldn't pull facts out of nothing. My talent wasn't like my mother's, I could only see and feel what Janet Hodgson had seen and felt — and she hadn't seen anything.

There was also the problem of Detective Ed Dyson. He was insufferable. First he'd looked at me as if I was a complete crank, inspecting me like some kind of weird zoological specimen. Then he topped it off by shrugging me off when I didn't instantly give him a description of the killer.

His partner was even worse. She obviously thought I was either a fraud or a fruitcake and I don't know which annoyed me more. What did I care what she thought? I did care what Ed Dyson thought, though, and that was really pissing me off. The fact that

HINDSIGHT

I found him attractive and wanted to make a good impression infuriated me.

Shoving the quilt back, I dragged myself out of bed. I walked over to the window and pushed back the blue velvet drapes. The sun wasn't up yet and the garden was still bathed in grey half-light. I thought I spotted Shadow cutting across the field, heading home for his breakfast. Crossing the room I unhitched my bathrobe from its hook behind the door and made for the bathroom.

I was still thinking about Ed Dyson as I turned the hot tap as high as it would go and started the usual manoeuvring with the cold tap to get the water just right. The old pipes coughed and spluttered.

Stepping into the shower I closed my eyes and conjured up an image of Dyson as the water cascaded over my back and neck. Tall, about six foot two, sandy hair, grey eyes with lines around them. Smile lines? No, more like hard knocks. He was no Adonis, he looked too careworn, too rough around the edges, but there was something that made my heart beat faster and made me feel awkward and schoolgirlish around him; embarrassing, but true. I wondered what he looked like without the rumpled suit, then quickly forced my mind away from that image. I couldn't fantasise about someone I was going to face in less than an hour.

I wondered what had etched the frown into his face. Probably working homicides was enough to do that to anyone after a while. I also wondered about his family. He wore a wedding ring but he didn't look well cared for: his shirt looked like he'd been sleeping in it for days. Maybe they didn't love each other any more and his marriage was falling apart. But why would he still wear the ring? Maybe he was still madly in love with her. That thought caused a twinge in my midsection. The thought of him in love with another woman wasn't very appealing. *Don't be ridiculous.* I gave myself a mental shake. I don't even like him.

I rinsed my hair and reached for my favourite conditioner; guaranteed to tame even the most unruly frizz and smelling like mangoes, it was one of the few ways I bothered to pamper myself. Massaging my scalp, I cast my mind back to the conversation from the day before.

I'd told them what the killer had said, those words that he whispered in Janet's ear. For what felt like much longer than the few seconds it must have been they all just stood there, looking at me. What I said was clearly not what they wanted to hear. Ed's partner, Steiner or something like that, was the first to have a crack at me. Her pale blue eyes bored holes in my head. 'Is that it? No details about what he looked like? No amazing revelations? Surely you must have seen something?'

What she meant was, if I could really see what Janet had seen I would have been able to give them much more.

'I could see what she saw for the last minute or so before she died but all I saw was the alleyway at night, no other people, then I was grabbed from behind. He put his hand over my mouth and nose, I felt a stinging in my neck and I started to feel weak. He whispered in my ear and I felt terrible pain in my chest and then nothing.' I gave the summary intending to sound matter of fact and not apologetic but only half succeeding. I was feeling wobbly and it took all my willpower to sound calm.

Detective Steiner gave a disgusted snort, turned and walked away, dismissing me without further comment.

Detective Dyson regarded me curiously, clearly at a loss. In the end he said nothing, choosing instead to walk off after his partner, leaving me standing there with Natalia, Chief Inspector Sorenson, who was clearly not impressed with her two detectives.

'I'm sorry, Cass. I apologise for the way they behaved. What you've told us wasn't what we wanted to hear. If what you heard is really what the attacker said, that suggests he's done this before.'

'Yes.'

'And that means that this case isn't a one-off.'

Natalia looked at her detectives, who were standing near the car, deep in conversation. 'Let's go over and join them. They're not that bad.'

I attempted a smile. Talking to those two was the last thing I felt like doing right then. I was tired and shaky after reliving Janet Hodgson's death. It had been a long time since I'd experienced a vision and I'd forgotten how exhausting it was.

We walked up to the two detectives.

'I am sure I don't need to tell you that if what Cass heard is correct, it means he's done this before. Cass, would you know the voice again if you heard it?'

'I'm not sure about the voice but I will never forget that laugh.'

Detective Steiner snorted again, 'Great, we just need to ask every likely suspect to have a good laugh.'

Natalia rounded on her. 'Detective Steiner, Miss Lehman is only trying to help and I, for one, am grateful for the assistance.' She glared at the younger officer. After a couple of beats she turned to Ed. 'Let's head back to Fairfield.'

The detectives were clearly unimpressed and as we passed the turn off, I wondered why Natalia wasn't dropping me at home. I wanted to ask her but she seemed to be lost in thought. Eventually she broke the silence.

'I think we should start looking at any other unsolved cases in the region where young women have been murdered. Would you be willing to help us, Cass?'

This was too much for Detective Dyson, who'd managed to bite his tongue until then.

'But, Chief, you're making a big leap. We don't even know that this guy is a serial killer, do we? So far it looks like he killed her unintentionally.'

He clearly couldn't see the point in prolonging my involvement. Part of me hoped he was right. To be honest, Natalia's question threw me. When I was busy making plans to help the police the day before I hadn't really thought of it as being any more than a one-time offer.

If I was honest, the Kerry Sampson case from back when I was nineteen was still nagging at my conscience. I felt guilty for not doing more. I'd thought about telling Natalia about it more times than I could count but something had always held me back and I'd refused to let Mum bring it up with her either.

With a blinding flash of clarity I realised that it wasn't that the police weren't ready for me back then; I wasn't ready for *them*.

Now that I'd finally decided to try and help I'd subconsciously assumed that helping once would wipe the cosmic slate clean. Clearly the universe had different ideas. Natalia glanced at Ed in the rear-view mirror, 'Like you, I have a bad feeling about this one. I don't want this to be part of the official investigation but it can't hurt to have Cass quietly look at any unsolveds to see if she can pick up on this guy.'

'Great, our very own episode of *Medium* meets *Cold Case*,' Phil muttered.

Natalia's jaw clenched. She glanced at me. 'Cass? What do you think?'

I looked out of the window at the passing coastline. 'I'm here because I believe I can help you,' I replied.

'Good, then we'll continue this tomorrow. Do you drive?'

'I can but I prefer not to, it's too risky, you know, with road fatalities. If I experienced a vision while I was driving …'

'Yes, I see. Detective Dyson will pick you up in the morning then, won't you, detective?'

He looked at Natalia in disbelief but his response was polite. 'Yes ma'am.'

Ed lived within walking distance of the station but she insisted on taking him home, telling him she wanted him fresh for the next day.

When she pulled up outside of his house I was surprised. I'd expected him to live in an apartment, or something that required little maintenance. Instead it was an older-style bungalow with a well-manicured lawn and a small garden bed across the front. Ed opened the door and climbed out. Before he shut the door he stuck his head back in.

'Miss Lehman? Eight o'clock sharp, at your place.'

His tone was faintly mocking. He slammed the door and sauntered across the road and up his pathway. We drove Phil back to her car at the station. Natalia grabbed a gym bag from her office, checked her messages and then we headed back to Jewel Bay.

Her motives for keeping me with her soon became clear. She grilled me all the way home, asking me repeatedly whether I was sure I was up for it. The more she pushed the more determined I became to help. Eventually I must have convinced her because she let it drop.

Mum and Gran pressed Natalia to stay for dinner and I was glad she did. The news that I was planning to continue my work with the police was about as well received as a fart in a lift. Mum was the hardest to convince. She knew what an emotional drain my visions were and she couldn't understand why I would want to subject myself to them by choice. The more she tried to talk me out of it the more I wanted to do it. I was ever the teenager in arguments with Mum. Natalia helped by being persistent.

'Anita, you know I wouldn't suggest it if I didn't think it was worthwhile. If Cass's talent is as powerful as yours then she's wasted sitting here at home when she could be helping others. Imagine where I would be if you'd decided not to use your gift?'

HINDSIGHT

Natalia wasn't a believer until she met my mother five years ago in the supermarket. Mum tripped over her own feet and Natalia reached out to help her up. The connection was enough for Mum to get an instant and blinding glimpse of a very short future. She told Natalia to wear a bulletproof vest for the next two weeks and to wear it not just at work but whenever she was away from home.

Natalia was sceptical but too afraid not to pay heed to such an adamant stranger — besides what harm could it do? Four days later she was shot in the chest by a ten-year-old at a petrol station. She'd walked in while he was trying to extract some money from the woman behind the counter. Natalia tried to reason with him but he panicked and turned what she'd thought was a fake gun on her.

She came away from it with a couple of cracked ribs and some hellish bruising but nothing more. If she hadn't been wearing the vest … She tracked down Mum and gave her the biggest bunch of flowers and box of chocolates she could find. They'd been firm, if unlikely, friends ever since.

Mum reached out and patted my hand. 'Yes, but I don't get killed every time I use my gift.'

'But you do feel pain when you see something terrible, and don't say you don't!' I said, thinking of all the times I'd found her staring out at the bay, looking tired and pale. 'Besides, you thought it was a good idea when I told you about it yesterday.'

'I thought you would help on the one case and then that would be that. I didn't think it would be an ongoing thing.' Mum sighed.

'I don't know, Cass, are you sure this is what you really want?' Gran asked quietly. 'It's a big risk.'

I looked at her in surprise. For some reason I'd expected her to be enthusiastic. She'd been quiet all through dinner, which was totally unlike her. When I'd broached the subject I'd fully expected Mum to find all sorts of reasons why I shouldn't do it but Gran was usually more open-minded.

'To be honest, Gran, I'm really not sure. I feel like I'm standing on the edge of a very deep pit and I'm not sure whether I want to jump or not.'

'Then why do it?' asked Mum.

'Because she can't spend the rest of her life living like a hermit with the two of us,' Gran said, before I could answer. 'Whether we like it or not, Anita, we have to let Cass find her own way. Natalia is right, she should be putting her gift to better use. What bothers me is how people are going to react. Up until now we've kept a tight lid on it. People are open to the idea of psychic readings and healing but Cass's gift is in a class of its own.'

Gran got up to make tea and we sat there lost in our own thoughts until she brought the cups and pot to the table. She poured and then passed around a plateful of her homemade burnt butter biscuits, one of my favourites.

As was so often the case, tea helped all of us to calm down. When Natalia got up to leave she looked at me questioningly. Mum and Gran left it to me to answer her.

'I'll see you in the morning,' I'd said.

HINDSIGHT

And so I found myself getting ready to do something that I really didn't want to, with a bunch of people who mostly thought I was a waste of space. I turned the water off and stepped out of the shower. I'd lost track of time and the bathroom was filled with clouds of steam. I stuck my head out and checked the clock.

Shit! Seven forty-five. I quickly brushed my teeth and fossicked through my drawers looking for some make-up that was less than ten years old. I gave up and settled for tinted moisturiser and a pale pink lip gloss. Just as I was starting to dry my mane of unruly hair I heard a sharp rat-tat-tat at the door.

Bugger! Ed was early. My hair was wet and I wasn't even dressed. I'd hoped to meet him at the door and avoid having to introduce him to Gran and Mum. I quickly donned my robe and stuck my head out of the bathroom but I could hear Gran already talking to him.

'I'll be down in a few minutes,' I yelled.

'Take your time dear, Mr Dyson is going to join us for some breakfast.'

Great, just the way I wanted to start the day, breakfast with the enemy.

After a minor crisis over what to wear I made my way into the kitchen. In the end I'd settled on black pants and a coffee-coloured turtleneck jumper that Mum said did good things for my complexion. I was still focused on my appearance and whether or not I should have put on the lip gloss when I walked through the doorway.

It was unusually quiet. Instead of the chit chat I was expecting, Ed, Mum and Gran were all seated at the table in silence. Mum's hand was resting on Ed's arm and he was staring at the table. In a flash I knew what had happened. Mum had read him. Judging by the look on his face, what she'd told him had really hit a nerve.

'Cass, you and I might just step outside for a few minutes and let your mother talk to Mr Dyson alone,' Gran said quietly.

Without a word I followed her out the back door into the small glass patio-cum-greenhouse attached to the back of the house. Gran waved me onto one of the benches bathed in morning sunlight.

'It seems Mr Dyson's pregnant wife went missing a couple of years ago. She hasn't been seen since. When your mother shook his hand she got one of her flashes and she told him she was sorry about the passing of his wife and unborn child.'

'Oh no.' I felt sick.

'She didn't realise that he didn't know.'

'He didn't know?'

'He didn't know they were dead. Not for sure.'

'Oh my God, is he OK?'

'I don't know, dear. Your mother realised as soon as the words were out of her mouth when she saw his face. It's best we let her deal with him.'

We sat silently. I looked out across the field behind our house. There were still patches of frost on the grass. The scattered trees were mostly bare of leaves except for the copse of evergreen conifers that acted as a windbreak against the sea breeze. Years of

HINDSIGHT

wind had made them lean at a strange angle, off kilter. Eventually the murmur of voices inside stopped and all we could hear was the sound of magpies calling to each other from the gum tree on the side of the house. Mum came out a minute later. She looked terrible.

'He's gone ... I'm so sorry, Cass. I thought he knew. He had the aura of someone carrying great sorrow and I just assumed it was over their death.'

I was prepared to be angry with her for being so careless but the look on her face froze my tongue. I sighed. 'It's OK, Mum. I didn't even know that his wife was missing. How come we didn't read something in the papers?'

'I remember it,' said Gran. 'It was in the papers but I think she went by her maiden name.'

'Didn't Natalia tell you anything about it, Mum?'

'Natalia doesn't ever talk about work with me.'

'Her disappearance must have been investigated?' I asked.

'It was but there was no evidence of any foul play or any suspect arrested from what I remember,' Gran said.

'That must have been terrible for him to live with for two years.' I tried to imagine not only losing someone I loved but having to live with the uncertainty of not knowing what had happened to them.

'Yes, it's taken its toll. I could feel that very strongly the minute I met him,' Mum said.

'So how did he cope with your reading? Did he believe you?' I asked.

'I'm not sure. He was shocked and angry. I think part of him didn't want to believe me and the other part was relieved to finally be told something definite. I think in his heart he's known for a long time.'

CHAPTER 9

Ed walked out of Cass's front door into the cool winter sunshine. He stood there for a few seconds, staring into space, not seeing the riot of plants in the front garden, not seeing the sparkling blue of the sea stretching off into the horizon.

He didn't know what to do. The knot of pain in his chest was threatening to overwhelm him and sink him to his knees. He drifted over to his car and opened the door. He slid in behind the wheel and started the engine, letting it idle while he tried to work out where to go. He needed somewhere he could just think. He didn't want to go home. He couldn't even contemplate going into the office.

The stupid thing was that if anyone had suggested that he seek the help of a psychic when Susan went missing he would have ridiculed them. He believed in the world he could experience through his own five senses and he found the idea that some people were born with a sixth sense ludicrous. The problem was that up until now his experience of people with those kinds of abilities was limited to tarot card readers at country fairs and the shows on TV. He'd never met anyone like Cass or her family before. Years of interviewing suspects and witnesses had given him a knack for picking up on lies and deceit and nothing about Cass, or her mother, told him they were frauds.

Then there was Sorenson's insistence that Cass could help them. He was more than a bit surprised at the Chief's conviction. Until yesterday he would've sworn that she had the same attitude to these things as he did. Of course Phil wasn't about to be convinced any time soon. She'd continued to voice her thoughts on the subject after he got home last night. The phone rang ten minutes after Ed walked through the door and he knew instantly who it was.

'It's a crock of shit. She might be a first-class actress but I don't buy it for a second. She just wants her fifteen minutes of fame like every other crazy out there. What better way to do it than to suggest there is a nutcase out there who's attacking women?'

Ed listened to this and more, offering the occasional grunt. Eventually Phil ran out of steam.

'Don't tell me you actually believe her?'

'I didn't say that.'

'Yeah but you aren't saying much to the contrary either. All I'm hearing from you is the sound of silence.'

HINDSIGHT

'I'm just not sure.'

'You're kidding, right?'

'No, I think she actually believes in what she does.'

'Great, so she's delusional.'

'I'll reserve judgement until I see a bit more. Plus, she knew stuff, like the needle in the neck.'

'Sorenson must have told her,' Phil said and ended the call.

He'd decided that he was going to be more civil with Cass and give her the benefit of the doubt.

He was surprised when he'd pulled into Cass's driveway that morning. Despite all his years in the region he'd never come across the place before. It was well outside of town and sat on top of a slight hill. The house was surrounded on three sides by fields. At the front of the house was a cottage garden, barely contained by a white picket fence that desperately needed a paint. Beyond the garden was the road, beyond that a sheer cliff and then nothing but ocean. The views were breathtaking. The nearest neighbours were a couple of miles down the road. It was stark, isolated beauty.

The house was a two-storey Cape Cod style with the addition of a large veranda on the front. It had three dormer windows in the roof and bay windows on the ground level. The front veranda was obviously well used, cluttered with chairs, cushions, and a couple of rockers and clear blinds to block out the wind.

When he knocked on the door he'd expected Cass to answer. He was momentarily disappointed when an older woman answered; her grandmother, he realised.

She was a striking woman. At first glance she looked nothing like her granddaughter. Her hair was silvery white of course, but it was her complexion. Unlike Cass's, it was a warm olive and her eyes were so dark they were almost black. They were beautiful eyes, deep sparkling pools. Given Cass's age, he guessed she would have to be somewhere between seventy-five and eighty-five. She looked closer to seventy but he suspected that she was one of those women who carried her age very well. First impressions over, his eyes took in more of her face and he realised that she did in fact share a lot of features with her granddaughter. They had the same mouth and nose, the same delicately arching brows.

She gave him a few moments of contemplation, obviously used to people regarding her in this fashion, before she reached out her hand.

'I'm Gwen Carmichael, Cass's grandmother. You must be Detective Dyson. Please come in. Cass isn't quite ready yet. You look like you could use some breakfast. I've just made some pancakes and a fresh pot of tea if you'd care to join us?'

Ed shook her hand, registering surprise at the strength and warmth of her grip. Her manner put him instantly at ease and he found himself accepting her breakfast invitation.

He followed her across a small entrance foyer, past the staircase and an ancient hall table that was threatening to subside under the weight of all the hats, coats and scarves that were heaped on top of it. A multitude of paintings and old photos adorned the walls. This was a home, not a house. Walking into it he realised how little his own place felt like a home. In the weeks after Susan's disappearance he'd systematically removed nearly all the pictures and photos. The reminders were too painful.

He followed Gwen into the kitchen, pausing in the doorway. It was an old farm-style kitchen with work benches along two walls, an enormous stove that looked like it predated the industrial era and a big solid oak dresser on the third wall. In the centre of the room was a large wooden table surrounded by an odd assortment of chairs that didn't match but didn't look out of place either. Jars, pots and crockery were clustered on every available surface. On the far side of the room was the back door and next to it, with its face firmly planted in its bowl, was the biggest black cat Ed had ever seen.

Sitting at the table was the third woman of the household, Anita Lehman. Ed didn't know what he'd been expecting but the woman in front of him wasn't it. She had a mass of curly red hair that rioted around her face defying all attempts to tame it. Her eyes were pale blue and her skin the translucent white that only true redheads seem to possess. He looked from one woman to the other, trying to work out how the two of them could possibly be mother and daughter.

Anita rose to greet him, smiling at his confusion. 'I'm Anita Lehman, Cass's mother. I look like my grandfather, a throwback,' she said, answering his unasked question.

He stepped forward and offered his hand. She hesitated ever so slightly and then grasped it firmly, as her mother had done. A heartbeat passed where she looked intently into his eyes and then the smile slid from her face and she spoke those words.

'Mr Dyson, I'm so sorry for your loss. It's a terrible thing for a young woman to die, especially when she is expecting a child.'

He stood there, the words bouncing around in his head for a few seconds, trying to make sense of what she'd said.

'I'm sorry, you have it wrong. My wife is missing.'

The look on Anita's face changed from sorrow to horror as she realised what she'd done. 'Oh, God, I'm sorry. I thought you knew ... I wouldn't have said anything if I'd realised.'

'Realised what?' he said.

'That you didn't know. Please, sit down, let me explain.'

He stood there, trying to decide what to do. One voice inside his head was screaming at him to walk away, that this woman didn't know what she was talking about. Another was telling him to sit down and hear what she had to say.

He sat down. Anita and Gwen did the same. Gwen poured them cups of tea. It was at that point that Cass walked in, only to be gently shepherded out the back door by Gwen. And so he sat at the table with Anita and listened to the words that he'd dreaded hearing for so long. Never in his wildest dreams had he imagined that someone like Anita would be the one to tell him.

She told him that his wife had been dead for a long time. She told him that he needed to let her go, to get on with his life and to stop blaming himself.

He asked how she'd died but Anita just shook her head.

'I'm sorry, I can't see that. There's something stopping me. I just know she's no longer with us.'

HINDSIGHT

'Did she suffer?' The words were ripped out of him. It was a question that had tormented him in the darkest hours of every night since she'd disappeared.

'I don't know, I'm sorry. She's at peace now,' Anita said quietly.

And with that he'd stood up and walked out of the kitchen. He was afraid that if he sat there for another second he would break down.

So he ended up sitting in his car, staring at nothing, trying to work out what to do and where to go. He needed space and time to think. He couldn't decide where to go so he just drove, barely aware of the passing scenery.

His phone started ringing a few minutes later and he looked at the number on the dial. It was Sorenson. Anita Lehman had probably called her. He ignored it. A couple of minutes later the phone went off again, Phil's number this time. Again he let it ring out. He couldn't find the words to talk to anyone, not even Phil. He turned the phone off and drove along the coast until he reached a dead end, then pulled onto a gravel verge that had become an unofficial lookout. He got out of the car and stood on the edge, looking out at the sea.

He'd been steadily climbing as he drove and the ocean was close to one hundred metres below him now. Waves crashed on rocks eroded into weird formations after centuries of pounding. Every time a wave hit, white foam spewed into the air then oozed over them like custard over a Christmas pudding.

The wind had picked up and it was slowly turning the flesh on his face numb. He wished it could turn the rest of him numb as well.

He looked down. It would be easy to step over the edge and end the pain. Losing Susan, when she first went missing and now, made him understand how people could kill themselves. He'd grieved when he'd lost his parents to a car accident, but at least once the grieving was over he could move on. With Susan there had been no moving on.

He'd always thought that suicide was a total cop-out, for the mentally unstable. Now he understood that sometimes it seemed like it was the only way to end the pain of loss. Maybe that made him a nutcase, but there it was.

He sat down on the gravel and let his legs dangle over the edge. Time slid away. Oblivious to the cold he lost himself in memories of Susan.

It was the chattering of his teeth that brought him back. Clamping his jaw shut he got up and went back to the car. He knew what he needed to do. He had to find out how she'd died and mete out his own brand of punishment to whoever was responsible, but for now what he needed was a hot shower and a stiff drink.

CHAPTER 10

After Ed left, I went back into the kitchen with Mum and Gran. Normally, I was the only one who struggled with conversation first thing in the morning but today we were all lost for words.

Mum grabbed the phone off the wall and dialled Natalia's number. Gran and I sat there listening to one side of the conversation.

'Nat? It's Anita. Yes, he was just here … No, she didn't. Look something happened … No, nothing like that. It was my fault. I shook his hand … Yes, I did. I told him I was sorry that his wife had died … No, I didn't realise … Yes, I'm so sorry. I am sure … No, I don't know how or where … He left about ten minutes ago … No he didn't say … OK, will you let me know?'

'Well?' Gran asked.

'She's worried. She said she'd try to get hold of him.'

Gran nodded. She filled the kettle and switched it on. Mechanically she rinsed the tea pot, added new leaves and put out three clean cups.

'Do either of you want something to eat?'

'No thanks, Mum.'

'Not hungry, Gran.'

'No, me neither.' Gran sighed.

Gran brought the pot over to the table. I didn't even feel like my normal morning coffee. Somehow tea seemed the only thing to be drinking right then. Gran poured and we sat there, sipping. All I could hear was the sound of the kitchen clock tick, tick, ticking away.

'It's best to let Anita and his friends help him now. I don't think we could do anything to make things better,' Gran said.

'I'm sorry, Cass,' Mum said. 'I've ruined your plans for today.'

I sighed. Mum had thrown a serious spanner in my plans to put my talent to better use. I couldn't help wondering if I was ever going to find a life for myself outside of this house. Maybe it wasn't meant to be. Gran was watching me and must have picked up on my thoughts, or read my face as she so often did.

'Cass, this doesn't mean you should chuck it in, you mustn't give up so easily.'

'I doubt he'll want anything to do with me now.'

Mum looked even more upset.

'You don't know that,' Gran said. 'Once he gets over the initial shock you might find he's actually quite relieved to know.'

HINDSIGHT

'Maybe. I think I'll go upstairs and finish editing that manuscript. I told the client I'd have it to him by the end of the week.'

The energy I'd felt earlier had evaporated and my legs felt leaden as I dragged myself up each step. Part of me was angry at Mum. It wasn't the first time she'd suffered from psychic Tourette's and blurted out a vision. It was fine when it worked out like it had for Natalia but more often than not all it did was make someone hostile. Some of the townsfolk who were in the cross-the-road-to-avoid-us category hadn't started off there — they'd been pushed there by Mum giving them some piece of unwelcome news.

Gran, ever the peacemaker, tried to explain it to me in terms of my own talent. She told me that sometimes Mum's visions were so strong that she felt compelled to tell the person what she'd seen, just as I couldn't control mine. I wasn't so sure. I still thought Mum had a choice but there was nothing I could do for the people I had visions about.

When I got to my room, I threw myself on my bed and laid there, letting my anger run its course. Maybe I was just making excuses for myself. I could do something for some of the people I had visions about. Maybe helping to find their killers was my responsibility. Maybe I was actually worse than Mum. Instead of simply misjudging how to help others, I'd been guilty of completely shirking my responsibilities for years. The thought was not a comfortable one. If I'd been given this talent to help people then I'd failed miserably so far.

I jumped off the bed and walked over to the window. The ocean was a deep azure blue today, dusted by flecks of white where the wind whipped up choppy waves. There had to be a reason why I was given such a god-awful ability. It was time I started trying to find it. Gran was right. I couldn't let one setback stop me.

I made a decision. I would go and see Ed. I would try to comfort him and offer whatever help I could with the current case and his wife's death. I knew Gran and Mum would try to talk me out of going to see him. They would tell me I needed to give him some space. My gut was telling me differently. I needed to go and find him, now.

It was easier said than done though. The problem with living with your mother and grandmother is that you get to know each other too well. Add the extra level of perceptiveness that comes with all of our talents and you get a situation that makes it virtually impossible to pull the wool over anyone's eyes. Plus, I wasn't a good liar at the best of times.

It was much easier than I'd expected. Gran was out in the garden when I went back downstairs and it was only Mum sitting in the kitchen, looking a bit lost. I instantly felt terrible for being angry with her. I went up to her and gave her a hug.

'Don't worry, Mum. I'm sure it will be all right.'

'But what about you and your plans?'

'I'll wait for the dust to settle.'

She nodded, looking a bit brighter.

'I can't seem to get into my editing today.' That much was true.

HINDSIGHT

'I thought I might head back into town and keep going with the research I started.'

'Great idea! I'll drop you in,' she said, standing up.

'No, I'd really like to drive myself.' I held my breath waiting for her reaction. She looked at me steadily for a few seconds before replying.

'All right, if you think it will be OK.'

I tried to mask my surprise. I was ready for her to hurl all sorts of arguments at me about how dangerous it might be if I had a vision while I was driving.

'I think it will be. I only stopped driving as a precaution. I've never actually had a vision in a moving car.' Only in a parked one at the lookout with Michael Jenkins.

'How were you yesterday in the car with Natalia?'

'No problems at all.'

'Well it should be OK, then, especially since you're only going as far as town.'

She gave me a very direct look as she said this and I wondered if she suspected that I was up to something, but she didn't say anything. I think she was still feeling bad about mucking up my plans with Ed.

'I think I'll make a day of it if you don't need the car?'

'Gran and I don't have any plans.'

'I'll see you tonight then.'

I grabbed the keys and my handbag, gave her a peck on the cheek and went off in search of Gran. I found her in the conservatory, re-potting some plants.

'I'm off into town to do some research, Gran.'

'Are you? Is Anita going too? I thought she was going to help me harvest and dry some herbs today.'

'I'm going to drive myself.'

She looked up at me, 'You be careful, Cass.'

I knew she meant more than the driving. I hurried over and gave her a quick hug before walking around to the garage and getting into the car. My stomach was in knots and I could feel my pulse racing. It'd been a very long time since I'd driven anywhere. Hell, who was I kidding? I couldn't even remember the last time I had gone anywhere by myself unless it was just a walk to get some fresh air. When Shadow was around I didn't even get to go to the toilet by myself.

I started the car and reversed gingerly out of our driveway and then I was off. As I got further from home my nervousness was replaced by exhilaration. I turned the radio on, switching from Mum's favourite talkback to the music station I listened to. I cranked it up and rolled the window down, enjoying the icy breeze on my face and how good it felt to be out and about, by myself, doing something as normal as driving.

The bubble burst when I reached the turn-off for Fairfield. Why I was doing this came back into focus. The tension got worse the closer I got to town.

I was in a state by the time I managed to find my way through the back streets, trying to remember the way to Ed Dyson's house. As I pulled up out the front, I felt a mixture of relief that I'd found it and dread at how he might respond to my invading his privacy.

HINDSIGHT

I jumped out of the car before I could have any second thoughts and strode up the pathway. I gave the old-fashioned brass bell a quick ring and waited. No answer. I rang again; still no signs of life from within. I walked over to the bay window and peered inside. I could see the lounge room and a doorway through to what was either the kitchen or dining room. There was no sign of anyone. It was too cold to sit on his veranda chairs; I would just have to wait in the car.

The minutes dragged by. I wondered if maybe he'd gone back to work or if he'd gone somewhere to think. I decided to give it another half an hour before heading back to Jewel Bay and actually going to the library. Wouldn't that just suck? I would have gone through all the angst of lying to Mum and Gran only to end up doing exactly what I'd told them I was going to do.

Twenty minutes passed and I was starting to think I would need to leave sooner rather than later. Nature was starting to call in no uncertain terms and the cold wasn't helping. Just as I was about to chuck it in and start the car, I saw a charcoal-grey sedan pull around the corner into the street. As it got closer I could see that it was Ed. He looked straight at me but his expression didn't change and he didn't seem to register my presence.

I waited for him to get out and then jumped out of my car and hurried across the road. I walked up to him and put my hand on his shoulder just as he was putting his key in the door.

'Detective Dyson?'

I thought I'd made enough noise to wake the dead as I walked up the gravel path, but apparently not because he just about leapt out of his skin. He jerked around and thrust his hand inside his jacket, drawing his gun as he did so.

'Jesus Christ, woman! Never, ever sneak up on an armed police officer like that! I could've bloody shot you.' He put his gun back in its holster, glaring at me and breathing heavily.

The speech I'd been carefully rehearsing seemed to have disappeared into the deepest realms of my brain never to be found again. I stood there looking at him.

'Well? What do you want?'

'Can I use your toilet?' I squeaked.

'You came all the way here to use my toilet?'

'No, but I really need to go. Can we go inside, please?'

He stared at me then grunted and turned back to open the door. He headed inside, leaving the door open behind him. I stepped inside and shut the door behind me, following at a half run to keep up. I followed him into a large, modern kitchen.

'Bathroom's back through that doorway and across the hallway.'

'Thanks.'

I hurried through the doorway he'd pointed at and for a while all I could think about was the relief of emptying a bladder that was so full that it had been a very near thing when he pulled his gun on me. I tried to imagine what his reaction would have been if I'd peed all over his tessellated tiles. It didn't bear thinking about. I finished up, and stepped back into the hallway. I could hear him on the phone in the kitchen.

Not wanting to intrude on his call, I walked into a large sunny room that spanned the back of the house. Bookshelves lined the

HINDSIGHT

walls. At one end there was a billiard table and a couple of leather couches. At the other end was a large oak desk and chair. It was what was behind the desk that caught my attention.

A large whiteboard was set up. Stuck on it was a collection of photos of women and under each one there was a name and a date. I went over and stood there staring at all the faces. There were probably about twenty of them. They weren't police photos. They were family photos; smiling faces of people having fun. I looked at them, trying to work out what connected them.

They were all so different. Some were old, some young. There were brunettes and blondes and the occasional dark-haired woman or redhead. Some looked well groomed, others not so much. A few were very pretty but many were quite ordinary. As I stared a few started to stand out. My eyes were drawn to four of the pictures.

At first I couldn't work out why those women were pulling my focus and then I realised; it was their eyes. They had the most stunning green eyes. It wasn't obvious at first glance because their overall appearances were so different. One was quite young with strawberry blonde hair and freckles. Another was late twenties or early thirties with dark, honey blonde hair and porcelain skin. The third and fourth were both middle-aged. One was thin and had greying brown hair and the other was a redhead, good-looking in a well-preserved and cosmetically enhanced kind of way.

What they shared was a set of extraordinary green eyes. I pulled the four photos off and stuck them together along the bottom of the board, putting them side by side to better compare them. I was so engrossed I didn't realise that the murmur of Ed's voice in the background had stopped. I didn't hear him come up behind me and so for the second time that day he nearly gave me a heart attack.

'What the hell do you think you're doing?'

I turned around with my heart pounding, wondering whether Detective Dyson actually got pleasure from frightening the hell out of me.

'Um, while I was waiting for you on the phone I just thought … I didn't want to eavesdrop … I didn't mean to …' I let the words trail off, feeling annoyed for sounding so pathetic. He stood there glaring. The silence stretched on.

'Who are they?' I finally asked.

I could almost hear the cogs in his brain whirring as he had an internal debate about whether to answer me or just tell me to mind my own business and get the hell out of his house.

'They're all the women who've gone missing in this region in the last ten years and haven't been found.'

'Wow, that's a lot.'

'That's just the women.'

'Oh.'

'Why have you got those four picked out?'

Suddenly, I felt silly. He was this experienced detective who had, no doubt, considered every possible link between these women and I was about to tell him four had similar eyes. He was going to think I was being ridiculous.

'Well?'

'Um ... it's their eyes. They all have the most incredible green eyes.'

He stepped up to the whiteboard and leaned in, studying the pictures closely. Eventually he turned and walked over to the window, looking out over the back garden. I stood fidgeting, wondering what to do next.

Finally he turned back and looked at me. His expression was blank. He'd pulled down the shutters on whatever he was feeling.

'Why did you come here today?'

It was a question I'd been expecting but it still took me a couple of seconds to unglue my tongue from the roof of my mouth. 'I felt terrible about what happened this morning and I wanted to offer to help; with this new case or any old cases, or with your wife's death — whatever you need.'

'I don't see how you could possibly help.' He forced the words out between clenched teeth. 'What I need is for you and your family to leave me the hell alone. Don't you think you've done enough damage for one day?'

It was clearly my cue to leave but I'd come this far and I wasn't going to give up. 'I just can't do that. What Mum told you this morning is terrible, and I can't begin to imagine —'

'No, you can't.'

'... No, I can't, but I do know that I might be able to help you find out how she died. All we need to do is work out where it happened.'

'That's it, is it? Simple! You do realise she's been missing for nearly two years? If I knew where she went missing from don't you think I might have found her by now?' he shouted.

'I don't know.'

'And I suppose you just randomly pulled her picture down off the whiteboard along with the other three?'

'What?'

'The second one! It's my wife. But you knew that didn't you? This is all just part of some grand plan you have to fuck with my head! Did you come to the station yesterday and offer to help just so you could get to me? Are you some weird, crazy, bunny-boiling, fucking stalker?' he roared, his eyes bulging, opening and closing his fists by his sides as though he wanted to wrap his hands around my neck and strangle me.

I backed away, shocked by the violence of his reaction and feeling more than a little frightened. I was about to turn around and head for the safety of the hallway when I heard the front door open and close. Ed and I both turned toward the noise.

'Ed, are you here?'

It was Phil. Great. Just what I needed, Detective Dyson in an apoplectic rage and his best buddy Phil, who already thought I was a pain in the arse, about to join us. I didn't think she would take too kindly to my causing Ed further upset on what had already been one of the worst days of his life.

Phil took in the scene with one swift glance. 'What the hell are you doing here? Can't you just leave him the fuck alone? Hasn't your whack-job of a mother done enough damage? Did you think you'd better come here and finish the job?'

I felt the blood rise to my cheeks. It was one thing for someone to have a crack at me but I was very sensitive about people criticising my mother or grandmother. Mustering as much dignity as I could, I looked her straight in the eye and answered coolly, emphasising every word.

'My mother is not a whack-job. She's a psychic, and a very talented one. It is not my fault that you choose not to believe in what she does. I am sorry that she upset Detective Dyson but she meant no harm. I came to offer any help that I could give. Clearly you don't want my help. I'm leaving now.'

I walked up to her and stared her straight in the eye. We were about the same height but I didn't like my chances if she decided to take me on. I waited for her to move out of the doorway so I could pass. She glared at me, clearly wanting to say more.

'Let her go, Phil,' Ed said, sounding weary.

She stepped aside and let me pass. I hurried down the hallway and out the front door into the pale sunshine and cold air. Shutting the door behind me, I took gasping breaths. My heart was pounding and my hands were shaking. I walked quickly across the road and got into the car. I sat there for a few minutes, collecting myself.

I drove home slowly. My grand plans to forge a life for myself, to find a niche and some independence, had gone up in a puff of smoke. There was no place for my talent in the real world. I'd been foolish to think Ed Dyson would want my help. Our worlds were poles apart and it would be better for both of us if they stayed that way.

PART TWO

To have the gift of seeing but never to be believed.
Apollo's Curse

CHAPTER 11

When Cass left, Ed felt relieved but guilty as well. He hadn't meant to lose his temper with her and accuse her of being a — what was the term he'd used? A bunny-boiler. He didn't really think she was a stalker. She was definitely a bit strange, but when it came down to it he believed that she really did want to help. Phil, on the other hand, was convinced she was a danger to the public and should be locked up.

'What the hell was that crazy bitch doing here?'

'She came to see if she could help me.'

'You're kidding right?'

'No.' He sighed heavily. 'She was feeling bad after what happened at her place this morning.'

'And what was that? Sorenson was a bit bloody tight-lipped about it. All she said was that Cass's mother told you that Susan was dead. When I asked how the hell she'd know when the rest of us have been working our arses off to try and figure it out for the past two years she didn't want to tell me.'

'Apparently Anita Lehman's a psychic. When she shook my hand she told me how sorry she was that Susan was dead. At first I thought she was just someone who had the wrong end of the stick but when she saw the shocked look on my face she apologised and said she thought that I knew.'

'Knew what?'

'That Susan was dead and had been for a long time.' It hurt just to have to say it.

'Shit, Ed, just because some old witch who reckons she can read tea leaves thinks she knows something doesn't make it true.'

'I know, but I believe her. I think I've known for a long time. There's nothing that would've made Susan run away with my child inside her.'

Phil looked at him, trying to decide what to say. In her gut she'd felt the same thing for a long time. 'I'm sorry.'

'Yeah, I really didn't need a psychic to tell me what's been obvious.'

'I don't know what to say.'

'There's nothing to say,' Ed turned back to the whiteboard and reached for Susan's photo where Cass had stuck it at the bottom.

'So what's the deal with the three others?'

Phil was as familiar with the whiteboard as Ed. They'd spent many long evenings together trawling through the case files trying to find even the slimmest connection.

It had been a tedious and fruitless task; a complete long shot. Sorenson would never have allowed them to do it on work time. Nothing suggested a serial killer. Missing persons who turned up dead were usually killed by someone they knew.

'I didn't find anything. It was Cass. She came in here while I was on the phone. She reckons these four all have the same green eyes.'

'Green eyes? What's so special about green eyes?'

'All four have very intense green eyes. I should know, it was one of the things I loved the most.' The words stuck in his throat as a vivid image of Susan, eyes shining, flashed through his mind.

Phil came up next to him. She took the photo of Susan from him and studied the four women.

'The eyes are the same, but the type of woman is totally different. Serial psychos normally have a particular type.'

'Yeah, normally.'

'So she's suggesting that not only do we have a serial killer but we have one that doesn't go for a particular type of woman, just women with green eyes?'

'She didn't suggest anything. She just put them together and told me they all had the same eyes. I bit her head off before she had a chance to say anything much.'

'Yeah, I guess we both gave her a hard time, but honestly, if I never saw her again that would be too soon. I just want to get on with the job without some weird freakin' psychic medium tagging along.'

'She's not a medium,' Ed corrected her.

'Whatever, anyway, now that I've found you and you haven't chucked yourself under the nearest bus, Grace is insisting that you come for dinner tonight.'

'The boss has spoken, hey?'

'You know it and I know it.'

Ed laughed in spite of himself. He really didn't feel like company but if he declined the offer Phil would get her head chewed off and Ed would never hear the end of it. Besides he knew what he'd end up doing if he didn't go. The bottle of single malt in the cupboard was calling him. If he stayed home he would end up at the bottom of it.

'So … do you feel up to heading back to work or not?'

'Yeah, I guess. If I stay here I'll just spend the day feeling sorry for myself. I suppose everyone knows?'

'Nah, Sorenson and I kept a tight lid on it. The others think you're out investigating a lead. You won't have to face the Spanish Inquisition when you get back.'

'Thank God.'

'The CS clowns have requested a meeting this afternoon. Not sure what they have.'

'Something implicating Janet's former in-laws?'

'Stranger things have happened.'

'I'll grab my coat and keys.'

HINDSIGHT

As Ed headed for the kitchen, Phil's mobile chimed with a text message. Ed's followed a few seconds later.

'It's Sorenson,' Phil called out. 'Something's up. Will you ring in or will I?'

'I will.' He hit the speed dial and waited for a connection. 'It's Ed.'

'Hi, how're you doing?'

'I'm fine.'

'Are you sure? If you need to take some time then I can bring someone in from Noarlunga to cover for you.'

'No, really, I'm fine. So what's the story?'

'A body's been found on the side of South Road in a ditch. A cyclist found it. It looks like it's Old Mick.'

'What makes you think it's him?'

'Sergeant Johnston from Jewel Bay got the call and he was the first on the scene. He reckons the body's in a bad way but he's pretty sure it's him.'

'Any idea what killed him?'

'Yep, looks like he was hit by a truck.'

Flashing lights indicated the traffic diversion, blocking off the southbound lanes. Cars were filing past at a slow crawl, the faces of the drivers and passengers automatically turning to see what was happening.

Ed and Phil pulled up then climbed out and walked over to Sergeant Johnston and Constable Forsyth.

'Reg, Alex.' Phil nodded at them. 'Not often that we have the pleasure twice in one week.'

'Trust me, this is no pleasure. He's over there.' Reg pointed to the tent that was set up to shield the scene from the eyes of passing motorists.

Ed and Phil walked over and stepped inside to look at the remains. They both looked a bit grey when they returned to talk to the two uniformed officers.

'What makes you think it's Mick? There's nothing left of the face,' Ed asked.

Forsyth jumped in, eager to contribute. 'The age, build and type of dress all fit. The coat and hat are similar to the ones that Mick is always seen in.'

'What do you think happened?' Phil asked.

The young man looked confused. 'He was hit by a truck, ma'am.'

'Yes, I can see that. What I mean is, how do you think it happened?'

'Oh, um ...'

'Reg?' she asked, not in the mood to be patient.

'It looks like he might have stepped out in front of the vehicle. He was a hopeless alcoholic so there's a good chance he was drunk at the time.'

'Where's Sonya?' Ed asked.

'She's on her way.'

'Guess we'll know more once she's had a look.'

'I can't see how it could be anything except an accidental death,' Phil said. 'We never identified him as the witness in the news broadcasts.'

'Unless someone let the cat out of the bag.' Ed said it casually but there was a question under the surface.

Reg bristled. 'Not me, I didn't say a word to anyone. I looked for him around his usual haunts and asked a couple of people if they'd seen him but I didn't mention that it was in relation to the murder. I wouldn't be so daft.'

They all turned and looked at Alex, who'd gone white and was shuffling his feet.

'Did you tell anyone, son?' Reg asked. 'Come on, speak up.'

'Um, I'm sorry, sir. I did tell Mrs McCredie I thought it was Old Mick that'd phoned it in and asked her to let me know if he showed up. She always gives him a free feed if he's in town.'

'Christ,' Phil muttered.

'Mrs McCredie? Who's she?' Ed asked.

'She owns the café on Main Street,' Reg said. 'She's got a mouth the size of the *Titanic*.'

'Ah, yes, she's the woman who was asking us questions over lunch yesterday, Phil. She's probably told every second person who's been into her place about Old Mick.' Ed glared at the young officer.

'I'm really sorry, I didn't think. I just thought she might be able to help us find him,' he stammered.

'No, you didn't think did you?' Phil snarled.

'There's nothing to be done about it now,' Ed said. 'What's done is done. The important thing is to try to work out exactly what happened here.'

'I never did like coincidences,' Phil said. 'We'll just have to wait until Sonya has a look at him. We'll know more then. Either way, we've just lost our only witness.'

'Yes, whoever killed Janet Hodgson is either very clever or very lucky,' Ed said.

'Let's head back. We need to get our shit together before the CS boys lob on our doorstep,' Phil said.

Back at the station, Senior Constable Samuels was chafing at the bit. 'CS guys are in Interview Room 2. They didn't look too pleased about having to wait.'

'Well, next time we'll just ask the victim to hold off being killed until it's more convenient, shall we?' Phil asked, giving Samuels a look that wiped the smirk off his face.

'Hey, don't shoot the messenger.'

'If only we could,' Ed muttered as they walked down the corridor and into the interview room.

Rawlinson was seated at the table reading through some papers. Byrnes was pacing backwards and forwards. He looked up as they walked in.

'Have a seat.' He waved at the chairs on the other side of the

HINDSIGHT

table. Ed and Phil walked around and sat down. 'You're late. Our meeting was scheduled for 2 PM.'

Ed saw the blood suffusing Phil's neck and face, making her look like a beetroot with ginger fluff on top. He jumped in before she could say anything.

'We had to see about a road fatality —'

'Surely someone else could have handled that?' Byrnes interrupted.

Ed took a breath. 'If you'd just let me finish? It looks like the victim was Old Mick.' Seeing their blank looks, he went on: 'You know, the probable witness to Janet Hodgson's death.'

'The homeless, unreliable witness who might have seen the killer through his drunken haze?'

'It was the best lead we had,' Phil muttered.

'Well it's just as well we have something more promising then isn't it?' Byrnes beamed. 'Fill them in, John.'

Rawlinson stood up and handed them each a sheet of paper with a mug shot of a man, probably in his late fifties. He had a sallow, olive complexion and his face was sullen and pockmarked. His long, greasy hair was tied back in a ponytail.

'That is Joseph Liberetti, hired gun. Lives in South Australia, supposedly retired here to be close to his grandkids. We believe he's responsible for at least eight hits, all eastern seaboard, but we haven't been able to pin any of them on him to date. Our sources tell us that he was hired to track down and kill Janet-slash-Alicia. He has no alibi for the time that she was killed and best of all —' he produced another piece of paper with a flourish, '— we have him filling up his white van with petrol in Reynella on the day she was killed. That's pretty close.'

'That's not enough for a conviction,' Ed said.

'No, of course not, but it's enough to pull him in for questioning and with a bit of luck we might be able to convince a magistrate to give us a search warrant for his van and his house. We've had him under surveillance since our intelligence came in. We're just waiting for the nod from up above to move in and arrest him,' Byrnes said.

'But why would he knock her out and leave her there to collect later? That's not the sort of thing those guys do,' Ed said.

'We think he must have been told to find out what she knew before he killed her,' Byrnes said.

'What, you think he planned to take her somewhere and torture her for information?' Ed asked, shooting Phil a look of disbelief.

Rawlinson looked at him coolly before answering. 'Yes, something like that.'

'Jesus, this is Australia we're talking about, not downtown Chicago,' Phil said.

'We wouldn't expect you to come across this sort of thing too often but with the cases we work it's not unheard of, especially when drug families are involved,' Byrnes said.

'If you say so.' Phil shrugged.

'We do, and given this development, we spoke to Detective Chief Inspector Sorenson when we arrived. The link to organised crime makes it a Tier 3 case and she's agreed to our taking full responsibility for the remainder of the investigation.'

HINDSIGHT

'Now, hang on a minute —' Phil stood up, scraping her chair back.

'You're off the case. Speak to your boss if you have an issue with it,' Rawlinson said, looking pleased with himself.

'You —'

'Leave it, Phil,' Ed interrupted before Phil said or did something she might have to apologise for later. He stood up and started to move out of the room. He paused with his hand on the door knob.

'I don't suppose you know where your boy was last night do you?' he asked, looking at Rawlinson.

'As a matter of fact we do,' he said, ruffling through some papers. He shot Byrnes a quick look and received an almost imperceptible nod to go ahead.

'Surveillance had him at the casino last night and then in a city hotel with a couple of hookers afterwards. Must've been a lucky night on the tables.'

'So there's no way he could have been involved in Old Mick's death then?' Ed asked.

'Surely you don't think his death is related? He was a drunk. He probably just staggered out in front of the truck and never knew what hit him.'

'Yes, more than likely, but we need to be thorough.' Ed gritted his teeth and smiled at them, mustering all his willpower to stay civil.

'There's no way it's related to the Hodgson case. If it was Liberetti who killed her he was a very busy boy last night,' Rawlinson said.

'Good luck with the case boys.' Ed propelled Phil out the door, feeling the hostility emanating from her.

They walked back to their desks. Phil barely made it before she exploded.

'I can't believe those fucking wankers have just waltzed in here and taken the case off us without even having the courtesy to let us know first. Jesus they're a couple of arrogant pricks.' She thumped the desk for emphasis.

Everyone else in the room stopped what they were doing and stared at her. Samuels had a grin on his face, clearly enjoying the show. Ed grabbed Phil's arm again.

'Come on, let's go get a coffee.'

By the time they got to Enzo's, her colour was back to normal and she'd stopped huffing. Ed ordered them both double shot flat whites and they sat down at their usual table, tucked into a corner away from the handful of other patrons sitting near the windows. The barista knew them well and they had their coffees within a couple of minutes.

'There you go; I was beginning to think I wasn't going to see you today. Hard day?'

'Yeah, not a good one, Steve,' Phil answered. 'Thanks.'

They sipped in silence. It was Ed who finally spoke.

'You were right. It's too much of a coincidence for Mick to turn up dead just after he witnessed a murder.'

'Do you think whoever had Janet killed sent someone else to kill Mick?'

HINDSIGHT

'Why spend the time and effort getting rid of a witness that one of their high-class lawyers could discredit in five minutes?'

'So what, then? You think someone else killed both of them?'

'Maybe. I'll reserve judgement until we hear from Sonya.'

'I doubt she'll have anything for us today.'

'Yeah, but there's something else I want to ask her.'

'What's that?'

'What colour eyes Janet Hodgson had.'

CHAPTER 12

I drove out of Fairfield and away from Ed Dyson's house in a daze. To say that I felt like a failure would be an understatement. Phil's scorn didn't really bother me. I didn't really expect anything else from her. She'd taken a dislike to me from the moment we met. I'd been hoping for more from Ed though.

Instead of being grateful for my help he thought I was some kind of freaky stalker. He thought I'd come to the police station and offered to help on the Janet Hodgson case with the express purpose of getting up close and personal with him. The uncomfortable thing was that he was sort of right. I had asked Sorenson if I could work with him.

Then there was the whiteboard. It hadn't even occurred to me that one of them was his wife. How stupid am I? Why else would he have set up a whiteboard with all the women that had gone missing in the last ten years? He was looking for links and hoping there might be something that would help him to find her. He'd probably been staring at it night after night for the last two years and there I went, waltzing in and telling him that four of the women had the same eyes. No wonder he'd snapped.

I was so busy beating myself about the head that I wasn't focusing on where I was going. I was almost at the turn-off for our house. I needed to decide whether to go home or head into town and hide out for a while. If I went home I would have to 'fess up. Mum and Gran would know that something was wrong; they wouldn't expect me until dinnertime and it was barely midday.

I decided to seek the refuge of the library. I parked the car on Main Street, making a complete dog's breakfast of reverse parking. I got out of the car, bracing myself for the inevitable encounter with Mrs Jones. Sure enough, she was at her usual post, ever vigilant, glasses perched on the tip of her nose so she could peer over the top of them with just the right note of disapproval.

'Cassandra, twice in one week after such a long absence, what a surprise.'

'Hello, Mrs Jones. Yes, I enjoyed doing my research here the other day. I thought I would repeat the experience.' I forced a smile, battling to be polite and not tell her to mind her own bloody business.

'Will your mother be stopping in again too?'

The question seemed innocent enough, but as was always the way with her there was a criticism as well. What she really meant

HINDSIGHT

was would my mother be coming in and would we be loud and thoughtless again. My smile started to feel like it might crack at any second.

'No, I'm here by myself today, Mum stayed at home.'

'Ah, well, you enjoy your quiet time then.'

I headed for the computers and local history files. I wanted to sit and think for a while. My plans from earlier in the week to map out safe routes in Fairfield and other neighbouring towns seemed pointless if there was nothing meaningful I could do with my talent.

What I really wanted was to replay that morning's dreadful conversation. I thought about Ed's reaction to my offer to help with his wife's disappearance and death. I got the impression he was pretty angry with himself as well. It must have been hell to be a detective used to solving crimes yet be unable to solve the one that was most important to him. I'd borne the brunt of two years' frustration.

I tapped into one of the computer terminals and typed in *Fairfield police officer, wife missing*. I got a whole bunch of hits straight away. One of the first ones I clicked on was an article from the Adelaide *Advertiser*. It had a large picture of Susan next to the article.

She was attractive: long blonde hair and a peaches and cream complexion. It was her eyes that really did it. They sparkled with a deep enjoyment of life.

The article outlined the facts about when she went missing. It explained that Ed had been ruled out as a suspect early on.

He'd been working a case and hadn't been alone for more than five minutes. Neighbours had seen him leave for work and wave goodbye from the front door. She was alive when he left and gone when he got home.

I clicked on a few other links. Mostly they were appeals for information. Without any new developments or salacious details to keep the readers interested, the media interest died down pretty quickly.

I looked at my watch. It was coming up for 1.30 PM and I hadn't had anything to eat all day. My stomach was protesting so loudly that I half expected Mrs Jones to tell it to be quiet. My head was starting to pound too — probably caffeine withdrawal.

I headed for the doorway hoping to sneak past Mrs Jones, who had her back to me sorting through a pile of returned books and putting them in order. I got within ten steps of freedom before her voice stopped me in my tracks.

'Leaving so soon, Cass?'

She really was a nosy old cow. 'Yes, I can't seem to get into it today.'

'Hmm, perhaps the peace and quiet isn't for you.'

I decided to let that one go. With a quick nod and half wave I bolted for the door. Stepping out into the light and air, I breathed deeply, relieved to be away from her overbearing ways. I strode briskly down the street to Mrs McCredie's.

It was reasonably busy, as always, and I nodded to the few people who recognised me. Not too many; a testament to my reclusiveness. As I waited to order I heard a couple of older

HINDSIGHT

women over by the window clucking over the terrible way someone had died. Over near the drinks fridges, a young bloke was asking his girlfriend not to walk home but to catch a cab to be safe. The conversations weren't the usual run-of-the-mill things people talked about in country towns. Still, people were bound to be twitchy.

Mrs McCredie brought my food over. She paused after she'd deposited the plate, licking her lips, a sure sign that there was something she wanted to tell me. I waited patiently. She was a kind person and over the years she'd visited our home regularly for readings from Mum and herbs from Gran.

'So you've heard the news then?'

'About Janet Hodgson?'

'No, about Old Mick.'

'What about him? Has he given the police a description of the person who attacked her?'

'Oh no, nothing like that. He was hit by a truck last night on South Road and killed.'

'Killed?' The word came out as a squeak.

'Police are saying that he must've been drunk and walked in front of a semitrailer. If you ask me it's too much of a coincidence: one day he sees a murder and the next day he turns up dead? I don't think so!' She tutted a few more times and then left me to my meal.

I sat there staring after her. My mouth was probably hanging open. People didn't just go around pushing old men in front of trucks, did they?

I mechanically forked the food into my mouth. My appetite had disappeared again. I could've been eating chaff for all it mattered. After a while I gave up and put my knife and fork down. I looked around me. All the worried faces and concerned conversations made sense. Everyone in here knew what'd happened and most of them would be thinking that it was no accident.

I took a few half-hearted slurps of my milkshake to wash down the lump of food that seemed to have lodged itself in my throat, picked up my bag and keys and headed for the door. There was only one place that I wanted to be.

When I got home I couldn't get inside fast enough. I stood in the warm dimness of the hallway and let the familiar smells and sounds envelop me like an embrace.

'Is that you, Cass?' Mum called.

'Yep, it's me.' I threw her keys into the bowl on the hall stand and headed for the kitchen. I pushed my way in, smelling blueberry muffins baking. My stomach growled, announcing the return of my wayward appetite. I walked over and put the kettle on and then slid into my chair with a sigh.

'Don't tell me you've been baking, Mum?' Blueberry muffins were one of the few things that Mum could cook. The fact that she was baking was a sure-fire sign that something was bothering her. She was standing at the sink washing dishes and had her back to me.

'Yes, I was worried about you, Cass.'

'You didn't have to worry, Mum, I'm fine.'

She turned around, wiping her hands on her apron. She looked

HINDSIGHT

at me for a few seconds then sat down. 'No, you're not,' she said quietly. 'Do you want to tell me what happened when you went to see Detective Dyson?'

I gave her a twisted sort of smile. 'You knew then.'

'I didn't know for sure; let's just say I was pretty certain. You really are a terrible liar, Cass; you go all blotchy and wring your hands. It's a dead giveaway. You've done it ever since you were a little girl.'

'I really need a cup of coffee and one of those muffins and then I'll tell you what happened.'

'OK, the muffins are nearly ready. Can you call Gran?'

'Do you know where she is?'

'I think she's upstairs in her sewing room.'

I stuck my head out of the door. 'Tea's ready!'

Mum sighed. 'I could have done that. I meant for you to go and get her, not to yell like a fishwife.'

It was a familiar remonstrance from Mum and, after the morning I'd had, even being told off by her felt soothing.

'I knew that had to be you, Cass. There was no way your mother would be yelling for me like a banshee.'

'Sorry, Gran.'

'That's all right, sweetheart. You look wrecked. Things didn't go very well, then? Was he still angry?'

I barked out a short laugh. 'You too, hey? And there I was thinking I had been so clever and devious.'

The timer on the oven went off and Mum got up and took the muffins out. I made a pot of tea for them and a bucketful of coffee for myself. When we were all sitting again I suddenly felt at a loss where to start.

'So you went to see Detective Dyson?' Gran prompted. 'How was he?'

'He certainly wasn't thrilled to see me. He had this whiteboard set up with all these photos on it.'

'Photos of what?' Mum asked.

'Photos of all the women who've gone missing in the last ten years. I couldn't help myself, while he was on the phone I went up to look at them. I noticed that four of them had these incredible green eyes so I pulled them off and rearranged them together so I could have a better look. He was really pissed off. One of the pictures was of his wife and I came out with this lame statement about them all having the same eyes as if he wouldn't have thought of it himself. It just went from bad to worse then. I offered to help him find his wife and he accused me of being a stalker.' I felt myself getting all teary at the memory.

Mum reached out and took my hand.

'Never mind, Cass, you meant well,' Gran murmured. 'He might realise that once he calms down a bit.'

'I don't think so, Gran. I think he's made up his mind about me. He made it pretty clear that if he never saw me again that would be too soon.' I couldn't hold it any more. The embarrassment and horribleness of it swept over me and I covered my face and cried like a big baby.

Mum and Gran wisely waited for me to calm down before either of them said anything. Mum just pushed the box of tissues in my direction. Eventually the tears stopped and I pulled myself together with a good nose blow and a few shaky breaths.

'Sorry,' I mumbled.

'That's all right. Better to let it all out. So, why does he think you're a stalker?' Gran asked.

'He thinks that the only reason I offered to help the police was so I could work with him. I guess going to his house today was a stupid idea.'

'I'll have a word to Natalia,' Mum said.

'No, please don't,' I said quickly. 'I feel embarrassed enough without having to drag her into this. Let's just leave it for now, please, Mum? Anyway, the scene with Ed was only the beginning of my bad day. I didn't want to come straight home afterwards, so I went into town —'

'You didn't have a vision did you?' Mum asked anxiously.

'No, nothing like that, I went to Mrs McCredie's to get something to eat and she told me about Old Mick.'

'Old Mick?' Gran asked.

'Yes, everyone thinks he was the one who witnessed Janet Hodgson being killed. Mrs McCredie told me he was killed last night. She said that he got hit by a truck on South Road.'

'That's terrible! The poor man,' Mum cried.

'Oh, how awful.' Gran's hands flew to cover her mouth.

'That's only half of it, Mrs McCredie seems convinced that it was no accident. She thinks he was killed because he saw the killer.'

'What have the police said?' Gran asked.

'I don't know.'

The ticking of the clock marked out the seconds as we sat there, lost in thought.

'So what do you want to do, Cass?' Mum asked quietly. Her words sliced through the silence.

'Do? What do you mean?'

'Well, I assume you think you can help the police work out who killed him?'

I let the implications of that sink in. Call me stupid, but I'd been so busy focusing on the dog's breakfast I'd made of my visit to Ed's that it hadn't even occurred to me that I might be able to help the police with Mick's murder. The thought of it made me feel physically ill. The only way I could possibly help the police would be to go to the scene where Mick had died and experience his death for myself. If he was murdered I might see who did it but I would also experience the full horror of being flattened by a semitrailer. I sat there staring at the table, not sure what to say.

'No one could expect her to do that, Anita,' Gran said eventually.

'No and I wouldn't want you to, Cass. You don't know what experiencing a death like that might do to you.'

'It would stay with me for the rest of my life. Besides, Detective Dyson would rather eat crushed glass than set eyes on me again.'

'I could always read for you,' Mum said.

It was said as a statement but it was more of a question. For years I'd resisted any attempt by Mum to nose around in my future.

Normally I would've just said no without hesitation. This time though, things were different. I felt lost and in need of direction. Despite my almost overwhelming loathing at the thought of reliving Old Mick's last moments, there was also a voice in my head whispering that I was being selfish; telling me that if I could help in any way then I should, no matter what the personal sacrifice.

'OK.'

Mum looked startled. Gran stood up and rested her hand on my shoulder.

'There's no shame in not helping, Cass, and just remember, you might not like what your mother sees.'

'I know.'

'Well, I'll leave you to it.'

She left the kitchen, shutting the door behind her. Mum and I sat there looking at each other. This was uncharted territory for us. Mum took my hand and stroked it.

'Close your eyes, Cass. Try to relax. You're going to need to totally let go if you want me to be able to read you.'

I shut my eyes and focused on the ticking of the clock. I felt a strange pressure behind my eyes. My first instinct was to block it but I took a few deep breaths and imagined opening a door to my inner self. Mum said nothing for a while. I could hear the magpies warbling outside. We had a resident family that Gran had been feeding for years. The adults were calling to each other and every so often last season's youngster would try it on, squawking like a newly hatched baby in hope of a free feed from one of his parents. Eventually Mum let go of my hand and I opened my eyes. She was sitting there staring at me, tears in her eyes.

'What is it?' I asked, panicked.

'I won't lie to you, Cass. It's not going to be an easy or pleasant road. I can't get a totally clear reading, even when you want to let me in, I can't quite get everything. I saw you working with Detective Dyson. Apart from that all I got was fear and visions of fire. For some reason fire kept coming up.'

'Great! Well, that makes it easy then doesn't it? If helping Detective Dyson leads to fear and suffering then I won't help him. You've said yourself that the future isn't set in stone. Look at what you did for Natalia.'

'Yes, that's true, but it's not always that simple. Sometimes fate will have its way no matter what we do.'

'Well it's not going to have its way with me,' I said.

CHAPTER 13

'You're kidding right?' Phil looked at Ed like he'd suddenly sprouted an extra head. 'You don't seriously think that kooky Miss Raising-the-Dead might actually have hit on something?'

'Look, right now I'm willing to give anything a shot. If Janet Hodgson had green eyes …'

Phil looked at him, her jaw clenched. It wasn't the first time they'd been down this path. Over the last two years they'd followed so many false leads they'd lost count. Phil had put up with it in good grace, being a friend and lending a hand because it genuinely seemed to help Ed. But this latest development was testing the boundaries of her tolerance.

'I know you don't want me to do it. I'm not asking you to help. All I'm asking is that you turn a blind eye,' Ed said.

'You know you've got to stop doing this eventually don't you? If there was something there — if there really was a link between any of those missing women — don't you think we would have found it by now?'

'Yeah, true. And I guess that CS would have found anything there was to find, especially with their high tech databases and systems. I'm sure if there were links and patterns they would've picked them up,' Ed said.

'CS? You reckon? If Byrnes and Rawlinson are anything to go by I wouldn't be putting too much faith in that mob of clowns.' Phil snorted her disgust. 'C'mon then, let's go back and find Sonya. While you're talking to her, I'll give Reg and his rookie a call and let them know that CS have taken over the world again.'

They stepped out of the café into the cold. Even though it was barely 4 PM the dampness was already creeping into the air. They hurried the short distance back to the station, their breath creating puffs of steam.

When they walked back into the squad room Phil slipped behind her desk and picked up the phone.

Ed headed for the lift and took it to the basement, where Sonya and her team had their autopsy suite and facilities. The lift doors opened and Ed's nostrils were assaulted by the smell of chemicals and disinfectant. It was like a hospital but not quite; the silence was all wrong. It was unmistakably a place of death, not life. Ed walked down the corridor and peered through the glass into the autopsy suite. Sonya was bent over Old Mick's body.

Ed rang the buzzer. Sonya glanced up and, seeing who it was, stepped over and pushed the button to unlatch the door with her elbow, gloved hands held aloft. Hearing the faint buzz and click, Ed pulled the handle and stepped inside.

'Gowns and masks are over there if you want to come and watch.'

'No thanks, I'm happy to keep my distance. I've already seen what the truck did to him. I don't really want to see it again.' Ed walked over to the bench that ran along the wall furthest from the autopsy table, pulled out a stool and sat down.

Sonya turned back to the body on the table. 'So what can I do for you?'

'I want to know what colour eyes Janet Hodgson had, and your preliminary thoughts on Old Mick here.'

Sonya stopped what she was doing and looked at Ed.

'How is her eye colour relevant? Word is that CS took over the case because it was an organised hit.'

'It's just a long shot and if you could do me a big favour and not let Sorenson know I asked, that'd be great.'

'I won't lie for you, but unless she asks me whether you're still investigating the Hodgson case I won't go out of my way to mention it, deal?'

'Deal.'

'Just let me finish what I'm doing and I'll hop onto the computer and have a look for you.'

'So what's your feeling about Mick?'

'You know I don't deal in feelings, Ed, only in facts, but the facts are quite interesting. His liver has advanced cirrhosis.

He also had emphysema. He was a fairly heavy smoker, or had only recently given up. He'd eaten not long before he was killed. None of that is remarkable. What is interesting is the trauma he suffered.'

'I thought he looked pretty much like he was hit by a semitrailer.'

'Well, yes and no. If a person walked out in front of a semitrailer generally most of the trauma would be from about knee high upwards due to the height of the vehicle off the ground. This body shows severe impact trauma from about shoulder level.'

'So what does that mean?'

'Two possibilities, either the vehicle was exceptionally high off the ground or the victim wasn't standing at the time he was hit.'

'I can't think of any vehicles that would be that high. So if Mick wasn't standing what was he doing — lying on the road?'

'No, that doesn't fit either. He was in some position that made his shoulders level with the grille of the truck, kneeling maybe.'

'I can't imagine why he would have been kneeling on the road.'

'No, and it doesn't look like he was facing the oncoming vehicle either. Most of the impact was on the right side.'

'So what do you think?'

'It's possible he was pushed in front of the truck.'

'Pushed? Someone hurled him in front of an oncoming truck?' Ed felt sick.

'Yes, like a sack of potatoes, but don't go off half-cocked. You need to wait for the official report. I'll have it for you tomorrow. I need to finish examining him and get the blood work back.'

'Thanks, Son,' Ed muttered.

'You wanted to know about Janet Hodgson?'

He nodded.

Sonya took her gloves off and walked over to the computer in the corner. She clacked on the keyboard for a few seconds, tapping her foot impatiently as she waited for the file to load.

'Let's see, Janet Hodgson: hair colour — dark blonde, natural; eye colour — green. She had green eyes,' Sonya said.

Ed felt like all the air had been sucked out of the room. His heart started to beat faster and he felt faintly nauseous. *Don't get ahead of yourself. It doesn't mean anything yet. It could still just be a coincidence.* He realised Sonya was looking at him curiously. He decided it was better to say nothing, just in case Sorenson started asking questions.

'Hmm, I thought they were blue. Thanks, Son.' He tried to sound normal and almost succeeded. He could tell Sonya was disappointed he wasn't willing to say more. He felt a pang of guilt; she was probably justified in feeling hard done by when he hadn't reciprocated the sharing.

He walked back to the lift thinking about the two cases: Janet and Old Mick. If Cass Lehman had somehow managed to find a link between missing women, if there was a serial killer out there killing women with green eyes … His thoughts went to Susan. He felt like his heart had been ripped out of his chest and fed through a shredder.

Today he'd started with Anita Lehman annihilating the faint hope that Susan was still alive and ended it with the possibility she'd fallen prey to some fucked-up psycho with a thing for green eyes. And then there was Old Mick, the poor bastard. Was it the same killer tidying up loose ends? The brutality of it sent fingers of ice down Ed's spine. Phil wasn't going to like it one bit.

She was waiting for him in the squad room. She took one look at the expression on Ed's face and sighed heavily. 'Oh no, don't tell me …?'

'Yes, she did, and there's some other stuff as well,' Ed said.

'Fill me in on the way home. You know how Grace feels about having her dinners ruined.'

Ed had forgotten about dinner. The thought of a cosy get-together was about as appealing as root canal therapy, but he knew from past experience that he could only get away with excuses for so long. Grace would eat him on toast if he didn't show up and that would be nothing compared to the misery she would inflict on Phil.

What he really wanted was to go home and start comparing the cases of the five women: Susan, the three others that Cass had pulled off the whiteboard and Janet. If they really were victims of the same person then the killer had to be picking them out somehow. There had to be something they shared as well as their eye colour.

If he could find it, he would find their killer.

CHAPTER 14

Thursday morning dawned frosty and clear. He felt good. Ginny was happy again and he could get on with business as usual. He needed to finish preparing for five services. Two were open casket. They were nearly ready, he just needed to add some finishing touches. Doing the faces was his specialty. He was an artist — people said they always looked so alive, like they were just sleeping. He turned on one of his favourite symphonies by Mozart and let the waves of music assault him, revelling in the feelings of relief and elation now that Michael McKenzie wasn't going to bother them any more.

He smiled broadly. It will be a closed casket funeral, that one. He wondered briefly about the man. Where exactly did he come from? Was it Jewel Bay or Fairfield? He'd got the impression from the snatches of conversation he'd overheard that the man was itinerant. He must have come from somewhere though. Maybe he has family in these parts, maybe even in Clifton. That'd be ironic; he might end up cleaning up his own mess after all. He sniggered. *Well, I do prefer to clean up after myself. I did with all the others.*

Not all of them, Ginny would remind him. Before Janet Hodgson there had been one other that the police had found. It happened the first year after he and Ginny were married. He remembered the night well. It was the closest he'd ever come to getting caught, up until now. He'd wanted to take the girl earlier, like he did now, but Ginny insisted that he wait until the eve of their anniversary and do it as part of their celebrations.

It was a bad move. There was no time to watch and wait for the best opportunity and he couldn't *not* do it. If he'd waited it wouldn't have been in time for their anniversary and that just wouldn't have been right.

He remembered every detail of that night. He'd been such an amateur then. Everything that could have gone wrong did. The girl heard him coming and turned around. She recognised him from the expo. Then he'd tried to use chloroform to subdue her and she'd fought back. It was a disaster. She'd nearly got away. He'd ended up having to kill her within metres of the security guards patrolling the university campus. He closed his eyes, replaying it. It had taught him a lot.

He'd driven straight home and told Ginny. She was angry he'd taken such a risk. Still, when he gave her the gift she forgave him. It was perfect. For the first time in ages she looked at him and told him how much she loved him. Those few days each year after their anniversary were the best days. They were better than the best Christmas, better than any birthday.

He put his tools down and peeled off his gloves. The corpses looked as good as he could get them, probably better than they'd looked in real life, and he couldn't afford to spend any more time on them. He still had to work out what he was going to do this year. The girl he'd chosen was dead; the police had found her and he didn't have Ginny's present. There was only a two-hour window before the first service. He'd better get cracking.

He selected a key from his keychain and unlocked the door leading to the basement. Turning on the light, he headed down the narrow staircase into the dim room below. It was his special room, the place where he kept all his records and plans. It was also the place where he emptied out the furnaces after a cremation. Along one wall were four shelves holding a selection of urns. The bottom three shelves held empty urns, spares for clients. The top shelf held his private collection; three identical urns in top-of-the-range black marble.

He ran his hand gently over each. There should have been four by now with another to come next week. It irked him that they were missing. By rights they were his and they should be here with the others.

He walked over to the side of the room furthest from the furnaces. Up against the wall there was a desk, a filing cabinet and bookshelves full of medical reference books.

He selected another key and unlocked the top drawer to his desk. Taking out a small box he opened it and took out yet another key to open the filing cabinet. He pulled out a ledger, flicked on the desk lamp and sat down to start reading. Each page contained meticulous records of the people he'd seen at expos over the last twelve months. Every year there were four main events he attended. Three were held in late spring or summer, one in June. It meant he had to write off four weekends a year but it was worth it.

He ran his finger down the page, pausing as he got to each entry highlighted in green. There were not many. Depending on which part of Australia you were in only about fifteen per cent of the population had what he was looking for. As he got to each entry he reviewed what he'd written. Over the last year there had only really been three possible candidates. Janet Hodgson was one. He still remembered the thrill he'd felt when she'd sat down and removed her sunglasses.

He looked at the other two. One was a mother of two. She'd had her youngest child with her when she came to see him. The baby had grizzled through most of their session, distracting her and making the session hard for him. By asking a series of careful questions disguised as friendly chit chat he found out that she was a stay-at-home mum and had another child who was three and a half.

He didn't like mothers of young children. Chances were that she would have them with her nearly all the time. He didn't want to have to deal with a child as well. Plus the frenzy would be much worse if a child and its mother went missing.

HINDSIGHT

He looked at the last entry. He remembered her well. She was older, close to fifty and had recently divorced. Her children were grown up and had left home years before. He'd chosen Janet above her because Janet lived in Fairfield whereas this other woman, Rita Hoffman, lived in Adelaide. It was much further and more risky too.

Since the fiasco at the university he'd avoided targeting people who lived in the city. There were too many people out and about, even in one as sleepy as Adelaide.

He looked at her address. She lived in one of the new multi-storey apartment blocks. A lot had security cameras. Still it might be worth a drive to check it out. Time was ticking and he couldn't afford to be too choosy. He looked across the page. He had a phone number. He picked up the phone and dialled.

'Hello?'

'Hello. Can I speak to Rita please?'

'Sorry she's not here. Who's calling?'

'Brian, I'm an old school friend. When will she be back?'

'Not for another three months yet. She's in Europe. Would you like me to take down a message to give her next time she checks in?'

'No, don't bother, thanks. I'll make a note in my diary and give her a call when she's back.'

He rang off and sat there thinking. He opened one of his desk drawers and pulled out an almanac. Flicking through the pages he found the entry for the coming weekend. There wasn't that much on. It was the middle of winter, after all. There was one event that might be a possibility. The Medieval Society was holding a winter festival in McLaren Vale. There was still time to ring the organisers to arrange a stall. He didn't have any services booked for Saturday or Sunday. No need to piss off any more families. If he found someone he could take them before his and Ginny's anniversary on Monday. It was tight.

He felt a buzz of energy start to build in the pit of his stomach. Hunting was always exciting. He jotted down the number of the Medieval Society and put the almanac and his ledger away, carefully locking the filing cabinet and the desk. He turned off the desk lamp and stood up, surveying the room. In the middle of the room, gleaming under the light, was a stainless steel surgical table, identical to the one upstairs. He'd made a few modifications to this one, though. Strong leather straps were bolted to it at the top and bottom and in the middle. No need for straps upstairs. He hadn't had a customer try to get up and walk out on him yet. He smiled. He walked past the table, running his hand over it as he did so. Still smiling, he headed upstairs to tell Ginny the good news.

Ginny was anxious to know what was happening. He loved the fact that she worried about him so much.

CHAPTER 15

After Mum read for me I needed the sanctuary of my room. Shadow's considerable bulk was spread out across the bedspread. I gently pushed him to one side, receiving an indignant look from under half-closed lids.

'Sorry, puss, but it is my bed,' I said. I stroked under his chin and was rewarded by loud purring and copious dribbling.

I threw myself onto the bed and closed my eyes. I'd reached sensory overload; my head was pounding and I felt drained. I thought back to the morning. I'd been so excited. Embarrassment sent a rush of blood to my cheeks as I remembered the silly thoughts I'd had about trying to look good to impress Detective Dyson.

Who was I kidding? He didn't see me as a woman, he saw me as a nuisance, and now he won't be seeing me at all. Images flashed in front of my eyes; the faces of the four women, especially his wife's. A wave of self-pity hit me. Would anyone ever love me like that? Based on my efforts over the last two days I was destined to live a life of solitary spinsterhood.

I cried into my pillow, sobs that shook my shoulders. I was crying about what had happened and the destruction of my plans, but more than that, I was crying about the injustice of being born with a talent that was more of a curse than a gift. Ten years of isolation suddenly got the better of me and for the first time in a long time I was bitter about it.

Shadow came over to see what all the fuss was about. He rubbed his head against me and then I felt the roughness of his tongue chafe my cheek. I sniffed and smiled through my tears.

'What would I do without you, puss? Just promise you won't eat me if I drop dead. I can handle being a crazy cat lady but I draw the line at being eaten, OK?'

A knock on the door interrupted my wallowing.

'Come in,' I sniffed.

Gran poked her head around the door to survey the scene and then stepped into the room. 'It's just me, I could hear you crying and I thought I'd better make sure you weren't about to chuck yourself out the window.'

'No, not today, Gran, your geraniums are safe.'

It was a standing joke between us. When I was a teenager I'd had a huge fight with Mum about whether or not I could go to a disco in Fairfield. Mum didn't want me to go. She thought I was too young. For once her reasons had nothing to do with my talent and that enraged me even more. I thought she should be more lenient with me because I'd been dealt such a bum rap. She thought that my talent had nothing to do with anything and that I should be treated like a normal teenager as much as possible.

Gran had come into the kitchen when I was in full flight, yelling at the top of my voice. I told them both that they didn't really care about me and that I might as well just chuck myself out my window and be done with it. It was a fine moment of teenage melodrama. Without missing a beat, Gran told me to go ahead but asked if I could wait until she'd moved her geraniums.

I'd stood there looking at her with my mouth hanging open for a couple of seconds and then suddenly I'd seen the funny side of it and we all erupted into laughter. I still didn't get to go to the disco.

'I'm glad to hear that I don't have to move them today. It's freezing out there.' She smiled as she said it but she was busy scanning my tear-ravaged face. She walked over and sat on the bed next to me and started to stroke my hair. It was something she'd done ever since I was a little girl and her touch instantly made me feel like a burden had been lifted.

It's part of her talent. By laying her hands on someone she can help to heal them mentally or physically or both. She's not the second coming. She can't make blind people see or help people in wheelchairs to walk again, but if someone can be healed she can speed up the process. Her talent is like any other though and comes with its downside. When she helps to heal someone it's like she takes on some of their pain and hurt; somehow it transfers to her. When she used her talent more regularly she would often come home looking like she'd aged ten years in one afternoon.

'It's all right, Gran. I'm just feeling sorry for myself. I feel ripped off. I thought I might finally have found a way to use my bloody talent. I was feeling scared but excited to be doing something useful and now it's fallen in a big hole. I think I might be destined to be stuck in this house forever.'

'Well, thanks a lot you for making living with your mother and me sound so appealing!'

'You know what I mean. I love you both but you won't be here forever and I need to find a life of my own, a purpose, maybe even a partner and children one day.'

Gran sighed. 'Yes, you do. Your mother and I both know it, although I think it suits Anita to have you right here under her nose where she can keep an eye on you.'

'I know Mum wants to keep me from feeling pain but I can't live like this forever. I feel like my life is on permanent pause. I haven't done any of the things most women my age have. I haven't travelled. I haven't even had a serious relationship.'

'Well, only you can change that. You don't have to do anything you don't want to, but sometimes you don't gain anything unless you're willing to take some risks and feel some pain along the way. Maybe you've been wrapped in cottonwool for too long.'

'Maybe.'

'You don't need to make any decisions now. You've had a really rough day. If you give yourself some time to digest everything that's happened you might find that a path opens up.'

HINDSIGHT

'You always know the right thing to say, Gran. Will I ever be as wise as you?'

'The wisdom is nature's compensation for the wrinkles. Why don't you come downstairs and help me get some dinner ready? It looks like puss wants his dinner as well.'

Sure enough my hoover-cat was patiently waiting by the closed door for us to finish talking and get down to the serious business of filling his bowl.

'That cat needs to go on a diet,' Gran said.

'Shhh, don't mention the D word, he knows what it means!' I laughed. 'Besides, you know what the locum vet said.'

Shadow's an exceptionally large cat, both tall and long and his normal vet is used to his panther-like proportions. The last time we'd taken him to the vet a locum was filling in. When the young man popped his head out and called my name I huffed and puffed my way into his surgery. Approaching the table I heaved the cat carrier up and plonked it down with an audible whoosh of breath. The vet looked at his booking sheet and then looked at me.

He was clearly wondering what was wrong with me if I couldn't even carry a cat without breaking into a sweat. Then he opened the door to the carrier and started the usual routine to try to get Shadow to come out from its depths.

I cut to the chase. 'Have you got any liver treats?' I asked.

'Um, yes, somewhere,' the young man muttered, surprised that his bedside manner wasn't working.

'He responds well to food.'

'Ah, OK then, let's give that a try.'

He produced a liver treat and sure enough Shadow emerged a few seconds later, all nine and a half magnificent kilos of him. The young man's eyebrows shot about halfway up his forehead.

'Is he friendly?' he asked. I could see him doing mental calculations about how much damage those extra-large paws could do.

'He's a big softie.'

Sure enough Shadow behaved impeccably and suffered the usual indignities of thermometers and prodding with nothing more than a nervous purr. Then came the moment of truth. The young man picked him up and put him on the scales. I held my breath. The last time I'd visited I'd been sent away with a bag of diet cat food and a flea in my ear, metaphorically speaking.

We both watched the scales flitter backwards and forwards. It was like a weigh-in episode of *The Biggest Loser*. Finally the scales stopped moving and the digital readout flashed 9.56 kilos. I felt a flush of embarrassment start to creep up my neck and ears. The vet looked at me out the corner of his eye. He picked up Shadow, who gave him a smooch, asking for another treat.

He turned to me and looked me straight in the eye. 'He's got very heavy fur,' he said, reaching into his pocket for another treat.

The memory, coupled with Gran's magic touch, wiped out the last of my bad mood. I followed Shadow and Gran out the door and downstairs. Mum was in her study doing a reading for a client and she had another booked straight afterwards, so the three of us headed for the kitchen and fell into the comfortable rhythm of getting a meal ready. Gran took the lead, I peeled and chopped and Shadow got under our feet.

Mum came in an hour later, looking tired but pleased, which told me that both readings had gone well. She didn't look like the weight of the world was on her shoulders and that meant that neither client had any dark clouds in their immediate future.

Gran put piled plates in front of us. We were having a family favourite, beef and Guinness pie with mashed potatoes and green beans. Mum opened a bottle of shiraz and with each sip I felt my sense of wellbeing return. I've long since resigned myself to the fact that I am a comfort eater. It's hard not to be when you have someone like Gran in charge of the kitchen. Peach cobbler with cream followed for dessert and then I got up and made us a pot of tea.

We sat there, full and content, sipping our tea. Then I pushed my chair back and took in the two women who were my whole universe. I was struggling to remember why it was that I wanted something different from this. My self-pity party of the afternoon seemed ridiculous now.

CHAPTER 16

By the time Ed got home from Phil's house he was wrecked. It had taken everything he had to hold it together through dinner. Phil pressed him to stay for a nightcap but he refused, pleading a pounding head. His brain felt like it was being squeezed in a vice and the pain was ricocheting around behind his eyes every time he made a sudden move.

He walked through the front door and straight to the medicine cabinet. He rummaged around looking for the last of the pills the doctor had given him when he fractured some ribs in a fight with a drunken lout a couple of years ago. He finally hit pay dirt and threw them down with a mouthful of water straight from the tap, then stepped back out to the hallway to head for the bedroom. Pausing mid stride, he looked at the door to the back room.

Trying to ignore his pounding temples he walked into the room, flicked on the light and made a beeline for the whiteboard. He looked at the photos Cass had picked out. He stared at their eyes. The colour was the same, that deep, sparkling green. It was so simple that it had never even occurred to him. He'd looked for physical similarities; similar features, similar age and similar build. The idea that someone could be choosing victims based on eye colour alone was weird. As if there was such a thing as normal with these psycho bastards.

He thought back to the scene with Cass that morning. He'd been pretty hard on her. He'd been totally incensed by what he saw as her intrusion into his home, his life and his grief. He didn't really believe that she was stalking him. She was an odd one. He guessed she was somewhere approaching thirty but she acted much younger. She lacked the self-confidence of most women her age. From what he knew about her it was not very surprising. Sorenson had said something about her living like a recluse because of her gift. Some gift; if that's what it's like to have a sixth sense, she could keep it. The fact that she had come stampeding over to offer to help him without even giving him a chance to draw breath suggested that she wasn't used to interacting with people. Most people would've realised that he needed time to digest the morning's events without another full-frontal assault to add salt to the wound.

Still, he felt a bit like he'd kicked a puppy. Phil hadn't made the situation any better either. Her sledgehammer approach had sent Cass running from the room with her tail between her legs. She

HINDSIGHT

was probably at home vowing never to help anyone ever again and he was largely responsible.

He looked at the photos of Susan. His heart clenched and he felt tears well in his eyes. He didn't know what was worse: the thought that she had left him, the thought that she had been in some terrible accident, or this latest version of hell, the idea that some freak had taken her and done terrible things to her. He forced his mind away from these thoughts. The only thing down that path was madness.

He put the photos back in their places. His headache was starting to ease but the combination of painkillers and exhaustion meant he could barely focus. He would sleep and then look at things again tomorrow.

He dragged himself down the hallway and into the bedroom. He tore his clothes off and let them drop to the floor as he walked. Without turning on the light he threw himself onto the bed and tugged the quilt over himself.

The alarm next to his bed was buzzing furiously. He cracked one eye open. It felt like he was deep under water. The effort to wake up was huge. He raised a leaden arm and thumped the clock, managing to hit the snooze button. He lay there, half asleep, until it went off again ten minutes later.

He sat up, throwing back the quilt and swinging his legs over the side of the bed. He did a stocktake on how he was feeling. The headache had gone, all that was left was bone weariness.

He shuffled into the ensuite and spent twenty minutes standing under a pounding shower, letting it needle him awake. Eventually the water started to turn cold and he reluctantly got out. He wiped the steam off the mirror and surveyed the damage. His eyes were bloodshot, stubble decorated his chin, and his hair, unruly at the best of times, was sticking up at impossible angles. *You're not going to break any hearts today, sunshine.*

He gave himself the once-over: quick shave, teeth brushing and combing hair into submission. By the time he was done he was starting to feel better. His stomach was demanding food. He threw some boxer shorts on and headed for the kitchen.

His mobile chirruped; new message. Phil. She'd phoned while Ed was in the shower, checking to make sure he was still alive and functioning. He flicked the kettle on then grabbed the phone and pressed the speed dial, holding it to his ear while he rummaged through the pantry and freezer looking for something to eat that was approximately within its use-by date. Phil answered on the second ring.

'Hey, I was in the shower.'

'Good, I was just about to come over and make sure you were still with us.'

'Don't worry, if I was going to top myself I would have done it before now and saved you from having to kick my arse back into shape.'

'Well you sound a bit better. Grace was really worried. She said she couldn't remember the last time you turned down her banana caramel pie.'

'I had a splitting head, I just needed some sleep.'

'Yeah, I was hoping it was that and not any plans you might've had to dive into a bottle.'

'Nope, no whisky, just a couple of painkillers and bed for me last night. Hey, I need a favour.'

'Am I going to like it?'

'Probably not, I need you to cover for me. Tell Sorenson I had a migraine and I'll be in late? I want to spend a couple of hours going over some of the missing person files.'

There was a long pause followed by a whoosh of expelled breath. Ed fished a frying pan out of a draw and cracked in a couple of eggs that he hoped were still fresh enough to eat. He shoved two pieces of ice-crusted bread into the toaster.

'Let me guess, the ones that little Miss Pain-in-the-Arse picked because they had green eyes?'

'You have to admit, the fact that Janet Hodgson had green eyes too might mean she's onto something.'

'It might mean jackshit too, I don't know how many people have green eyes but it's got to be quite a few.'

'Maybe.'

Phil sighed again. 'If you have to, you have to. What time will you be in?'

'Ten thirty at the latest.'

'You'd better be, we've got a mountain of calls and paperwork and I ain't doing it all by myself.'

Ed focused on his breakfast preparations. He had a burning desire to get started, but he had to eat first. The toast popped and he grabbed it, burning his fingers. He was no Jamie Oliver, that was for sure. Before Susan had disappeared he wouldn't have been able to find a frying pan. The kitchen was her domain — he was relegated to menial tasks like dishwashing and taking out the rubbish. She'd been a sensational cook: in the first two years after they got married he'd gained ten kilos.

He slathered margarine on the toast and slid the eggs on top. Remarkably, they were still roughly the right shape and colour. He spooned instant coffee into a mug and poured boiling water on top. No point looking for milk; any milk in his fridge would have been there for so long it would have its own ecosystem. He stuffed a forkful of eggs into his mouth. They tasted OK — hopefully they wouldn't be back to prove him wrong.

With plate and mug in hand he headed for the back room. He plonked them on the desk and pulled open the filing cabinet drawer. Over the last two years he'd compiled his own files on each of the missing women. Each contained copies of key documents from their official files as well as information he'd pulled together by conducting his own quiet investigations.

He'd been limited in what he could and couldn't do. The Crime Service handled all missing person cases and they weren't amenable to sharing. If they'd known he was snooping around there would've been hell to pay. He also couldn't contact the family and friends of the missing.

If he started approaching them they were likely to ask why yet another officer was interviewing them. Given that most were already in a fragile state, any approach might have antagonised

HINDSIGHT

them into filing a complaint or making a phone call to the CS and then the jig would've been up. He'd spent the last eighteen months looking for patterns and links, looking for something that others had missed. The hours he'd burned didn't bear thinking about and it wasn't just him. Phil was there at his side a lot of the time as well. It was no wonder that he'd just about ripped Cass's head off when she waltzed in and started talking about green eyes. It was so obvious that they hadn't even considered it.

The eggs were turning into a gelatinous mess as they cooled so he stuffed a couple more forkfuls in his mouth then shoved the plate to one side. He took a slurp of coffee, scalding his tongue, then pulled out the four files and spread them on the desk. He plucked the photos off the board and placed each above its file. For the next hour he sat there, first reading the files one by one and then opening each of them simultaneously and comparing the information recorded on official reports.

The first victim, Virginia Hope, went missing back in 2008. She'd moved into a new house in Clifton a few months earlier from inner city Adelaide. She'd moved for two reasons: to get away from an ex-boyfriend who was physically abusive and to buy her own house. Clifton was a place where housing was still relatively affordable.

Her new life was pretty straight forward. She didn't know many people. She'd been friendly with an old lady who lived next door to her but the woman had died shortly before Virginia went missing. She'd also joined a local tennis club and was seeing a man she'd met there. He was interstate on the day she disappeared so there was no reason to look at him too closely.

Most of the investigation focused on her ex-boyfriend, who had no alibi for the time she went missing. He'd been hauled in for questioning on three separate occasions but there was no proof of anything, no physical evidence at his home, in his car or at his workplace. Innumerable police hours were spent looking for forensic evidence. They found nothing.

On the day she went missing she went to work as usual, catching the bus like she always did. She caught it home again and got off at her normal stop and that was the last time anyone saw her.

The second victim had disappeared in 2010. Angela Bingham was thirty-eight, whereas Virginia was only twenty-three. Physically she was very different. Virginia had strawberry blonde hair and freckles and a natural, fresh look about her. Angela was a fiery redhead with porcelain skin but she looked like she worked hard at keeping herself beautiful, well preserved. She lived in McLaren Vale and was single but led a very active social life. She was a board member of two charities and ran her own PR company. Her life was full of cocktail parties, black-tie dinners and other schmoozing opportunities.

The Crime Service was kept very busy interviewing the multitudes who featured in her life. All their enquiries eventually ran dry and they were left with nothing. There was no evidence that she'd met with foul play; no blood traces, no signs of a struggle, no one who seemed to have a grudge against her.

HINDSIGHT

The third woman was Susan. She'd disappeared in 2011. He didn't need to read her file. Every page of it was imprinted on his brain. His beautiful Susan. She was radiant. He looked at the photo of her he kept on his desk. He felt like a knife went through him. She was so full of life. Her head was thrown back a little and she was laughing. He'd taken it on their first wedding anniversary. He'd surprised her by walking into the bedroom wearing nothing but his hat and utility belt and twirling his handcuffs. She was shocked initially but then erupted into fits of giggles. He remembered his chagrin; he'd meant to turn her on, not make her laugh so hard she cried. Once she'd calmed down, they'd made love slowly and with such tenderness that it made him ache just thinking about it. Afterwards they'd gone out for lunch and she'd been teasing him about his newfound adventurous streak when he snapped her photo.

Missing woman number four was Simone Blakewell. She was forty-five and had greying brown hair. She was thin to the point of being bony. Unlike the other three women, she was quite plain — the only beautiful thing about her was her eyes. She was a single mother who didn't have much of a social life at all. Her two children were aged nineteen and twenty-one. They both still lived at home when she disappeared.

The kids were looked at but quickly ruled out as suspects. There was no motive for them to want her gone. In fact, their lives were considerably less comfortable without her around. The ex-husband was also investigated but he was remarried and no matter how hard they looked they couldn't find either a motive or any evidence to suggest he was involved in her disappearance.

Ed sat back, stretched and looked at his watch. Time had flown — it was nearly ten o'clock. He was going to have to get going soon or risk facing Phil's wrath. He stood up and flipped the whiteboard over so that he had a blank surface. He put up the four photos and wrote their names and the dates they'd gone missing. Then he wrote in Janet Hodgson's name. He stood there for a few seconds looking at it and then it hit him. If you ignored 2009, the women had gone missing in consecutive years. He felt his gut lurch. It was more than that. The women had all gone missing in either June or July. There it was, staring him in the face, the pattern he'd been trying to unlock for nearly two years.

So what had happened in 2009? Was there a missing woman they didn't know about? He stood there, his heart racing. No, she wasn't missing; people didn't disappear without someone noticing. Either the killer had skipped a year or there was another Janet Hodgson, another one they'd found dead. He ran out of the room and down the hallway, grabbing his keys and jacket on the way through. If there was another dead victim she might be the key to finding the killer. And Susan.

CHAPTER 17

Ed walked into a squad room so taut with nervous tension it was palpable. Phil wasn't at her desk so he threw his jacket over the back of his chair and picked up the phone to check his messages. Samuels spotted him from across the room and made a beeline for him. Ed sighed and replaced the receiver. As much as he found the man irritating there was no faster way to find out what was going on.

'Afternoon shift started then has it?' Samuels asked with a leer.

'What's up?' Ed didn't bother to acknowledge the snide remark. There was no point. A reaction was what Samuels wanted.

'Results are back from the lab on the Michael McKenzie case.' Samuels paused, waiting for Ed to ask the question.

Ed gritted his teeth. He was going to have to play the game if he wanted to find out anything. He looked around, hoping Phil might appear and save him from the charade. No such luck. He took a deep breath.

'So what did they find?'

'The blood results indicate that he was nowhere near drunk enough to walk in front of a truck or pass out on the road.'

'Really?' Ed tried to mask his distaste at Samuels's relish over the details.

'Yes, and there's way the truck hit him.' He paused again for dramatic effect. 'Sonya thinks he was pushed or thrown in front of it.'

'So it looks like a homicide?'

'Yep, but I haven't told you the best bit.'

Ed just waited, looking at Samuels and trying not to let his impatience get the better of him. Aside from the alcohol reading, Samuels hadn't told him anything he didn't know. He just wanted to be done with the conversation to get on with a search for female homicide victims in 2009 and see if anything stood out.

'They found traces of the same muscle relaxant in his bloodstream as they found in Janet Hodgson's.' Samuels watched Ed's face, delighted at being the one to deliver the bombshell.

'So the two are definitely linked?'

'Seems that way. Anyway, Phil is in the conference room with Sorenson. They're on a conference call with CS now giving them the news.'

'Thanks, Bill.' Ed headed straight for the conference room. He wanted to be a party to whatever decision was made. If there was even the slightest chance that Janet and Mick had been killed by the person who had killed Susan, he wanted in.

He gave a cursory knock then walked in. Sorenson was talking and Phil was looking red and sweaty, which told him that things weren't going smoothly. He looked at the screen on the phone. The call had only been going for eight minutes. He felt a twinge of irritation. If Samuels had just got to the point he wouldn't have missed much.

'... and given the likelihood that the killer is probably from this region —'

'That's not definite,' Byrnes interrupted. He sounded really pissed.

'Yes, but it's highly likely. You have to agree that the traces of the same muscle relaxant having been found in both victims clearly suggests they were killed by the same person?'

'Yes, it appears that way.'

'Well, the most likely way the killer would have found out the identity of the witness was through local gossip. Unfortunately, a young officer in Jewel Bay asked one of the local business operators about his whereabouts and let slip that he was the likely witness.'

'That doesn't mean the killer's a local. He could have been hanging around and overheard the chatter,' Byrnes said

'If he stayed around after we found the body,' Phil said.

'Killers like to revisit the scene,' Rawlinson chipped in.

'Maybe, but I think the local angle is more likely. Besides, even if the killer isn't local, both victims were, and you said yourself that your suspect couldn't have killed Michael McKenzie,' Ed said.

'Yes, that's correct,' Rawlinson said.

Ed could almost imagine the look Byrnes would've been giving him right at that moment.

'It doesn't mean that it's not an organised hit. Even if it wasn't Liberetti, they could have had multiple contracts out on Janet,' Byrnes said.

'Have you got any leads on another suspect?' Sorenson asked.

'No, until ten minutes ago we were comfortable with Liberetti.' The tone of his voice made it sound like the Fairfield police were personally responsible for the fact that they had the wrong person in custody.

'Well, given the situation I would like my detectives reinstated on the case,' Sorenson said.

There was a pause. Eventually Byrnes answered. 'I'll need to speak to DCI Fisher.'

'I've already spoken to him. He asked me to brief you.'

More silence, then, 'Fine, we need to sort things out down this end. We'll come down first thing in the morning.'

'Good, we'll continue with the investigation and see you then.'

They terminated the call and the three of them sat for a few seconds before anyone spoke.

'So you're up to date with what happened this morning, Ed?' Sorenson asked.

'Yes, Samuels filled me in.'

'Good.' She stood up to leave the room and then stopped. 'How's the head?' She looked at him closely.

She's looking to see if I look hung-over, Ed thought. 'Much better thanks. I'm keen to get on with it. I want to catch whatever crazy bastard thinks it's OK to throw an old man in front of a truck.'

'Yes, I want you and Phil to work out what your next steps are and fill me in on your plans. This room is booked until twelve — you might as well stay here and do it. Ed, come and see me when you're finished.'

'Yes, ma'am,' Ed said.

She closed the door firmly behind her, leaving them to it.

'So?' Phil asked.

Ed knew the question wasn't about where he thought they should start their investigation. 'So it looks like Cass might have been on to something.'

'You're kidding, right?'

'No, I reckon there's a pattern. Each of the missing women disappeared in consecutive years starting in 2008 and they all disappeared in either June or July. There's only one problem: there's a missing year.'

'A missing year?'

'Either the killer skipped a year, there's someone missing that we don't know about or there was another Janet Hodgson.'

'Another body?'

'Maybe.'

'Which year is missing?'

'Oh-nine.'

Phil thought for a while. 'I don't remember any unsolved homicides around here in 2009.'

'No, me neither, but I still need to check. Maybe it wasn't in our region.'

'You want to check before we say anything to Sorenson?'

'Yeah, I'd like to have the full picture before we do. If there are five in a row, all missing or dead at around the same time of year, all loners, all with green eyes, there's no room for any doubts.'

'All right, we'd better come up with a plan for Sorenson. Once we've got something I'll write it up while you do a database search.'

'Thanks Phil, I owe you one.'

'One? You owe me a shitload more than one. I've lost count of the times I've covered for your sorry arse.' She snorted and ran a hand through her cropped hair, making it stick up at crazy angles.

'So what's the plan for Old Mick? We could try to find the truck driver. If we canvass the trucking companies and try to find out which drivers were on South Road at that time we might be able to find him.' Ed got out of his chair and started to jot down notes on the whiteboard.

'Yeah, if we can find the driver he might remember seeing a car parked by the side of the road and give us a description.'

'Yep, and what about Janet?'

'We need to go back over her phone records and see if anything stands out. This guy is into eyes. Maybe he's an optician?' Phil said, only half joking.

'We should be so lucky. I don't want to tell Sorenson about the eye thing yet so if you're serious about checking out her optician then let's keep that out of the official plan, OK? What about her friends and colleagues?'

'She didn't have any friends but we should reinterview her colleagues. I might do some quiet crosschecking with the friends, relatives and associates of those other missing women.'

'Thanks, Phil, you're a champ.'

'I know, I'm a diamond in a box full of coal. You can thank me on Friday by buying me a beer. I'll go back to my desk and start writing up an action plan for Sorenson. I'll list off who we're going to interview and why. You know we're gonna have to tell her about the possible serial sooner rather than later, though. If there really is someone out there picking off a woman every year he might decide he wants to have another go at snatching a victim this year.'

'Yeah, I know. We'll have to tell Sorenson by the end of the day and let her make the call about what to tell CS.' Ed sighed.

'She'll want to tell them. If we have a serial killer on the loose then it's automatically their case.'

'Yeah, I know.'

'And you know that Sorenson won't want you working it if Susan was one of the vics?'

'I know that too.'

'Well, let's get to it then.'

'I'll go and see what Sorenson wants and join you back in the squad room,' Ed said as they walked down the corridor.

He stopped at the door to Sorenson's office and gave a quick knock before sticking his head around it. She was on the phone but waved him into a chair.

He sat down and waited for her to finish, letting his eyes wander over the bits and pieces she had dotted around: a couple of pot plants that looked in need of a drink; her degrees, framed and hanging on one wall; and bookshelves crammed full of textbooks and journals. She'd come to them from one of the metropolitan stations in Adelaide five years ago. She'd had a pretty hard time of it at first; some of the old school types were sceptical about working for a woman, others were naturally suspicious of anyone who wasn't from Fairfield and then there were one or two who thought that the only education worth having was one gained through hard knocks.

She was a tough but fair boss and she knew a lot more than what she'd learned from text books. It wasn't uncommon for her to decide to come out on a case with them and more often than not she contributed some insight. Over time even the most hardcore officers had developed a kind of grudging respect for her.

She finished her call and turned to Ed. Her pale blue eyes locked with his and she studied him for a few seconds before she spoke.

'Do you want to tell me what happened with Cass?'

Ed sighed. 'She called you then?'

'No, her mother did. She called to tell me that Cass has decided she doesn't want to help us with our investigation after all. I asked why she'd changed her mind but Anita wasn't exactly forthcoming.'

'She came to see me after her mum dropped the bombshell about Susan. She reckons she wanted to see if I was all right. She caught me at a bad time. I didn't behave very well.'

'What did you say?'

'I accused her of stalking me.'

'Why would you do that?'

'I thought it was a bit strange that she turned up here asking to work with me one day and then showed up at my home the next and started going through my things while I was on the phone.'

'She went through your things?' Sorenson's eyebrows shot up in genuine surprise.

'Well, sort of, I had some information about Susan's disappearance written up on a whiteboard and while I was on the phone she went for a wander and started studying it and offering ideas.'

'She was probably just trying to be helpful. She isn't very good with people. She's spent most of her adult life locked away in that house with only her mother and grandmother for company. I can promise you she isn't a stalker. I've known her and her mother for nearly five years and they are lovely, genuine people.'

'Yeah, once I simmered down a bit I realised that she probably was trying to help but she's just not very good at it. How did you meet them?'

Sorenson paused. From the look on her face he could tell she was debating whether or not to tell him. 'Anita Lehman had a vision that saved my life.'

'That time you got shot by that kid in the petrol station?'

'The very same.'

'None of us could work out why you were wearing a vest.'

'Now you know. I'd prefer if you didn't share it with anyone else.'

'Sure.'

'So you can understand why I have a lot of time for Anita and her family. As far as I'm concerned they're the real deal.'

'What do you want me to do?'

'If you think you owe Cass an apology then I'll leave it to you to make it right.'

'Do you still want her to work with us?'

'I honestly think she might be able to help in some way. She might be able to shed some light on the Michael McKenzie death if she can see what he saw just before he died.'

Ed pondered this before he answered. It was true that they were back to square one with their only witness dead. If Janet Hodgson's killer had also killed Old Mick, which seemed highly probable, then what Mick had seen before he died became incredibly important. It could be the key to finding the killer.

It hadn't occurred to him that Cass might be able to see the killer through Old Mick's eyes. He'd been so swept up in his own quest that he hadn't even thought about asking Cass to help with the Michael McKenzie case. How slow was he? He realised that Sorenson was looking at him curiously, trying to work out what was taking so much mental effort.

'Sorry, I was just trying to work out how to approach her.'

HINDSIGHT

'If you're going to ask for her help then you're going to have a tough battle on your hands. In the time that I have known her I've found her to be a fairly single-minded young woman. Once she's made her mind up about something she doesn't change it very easily.'

'Great, sounds like I'm really going to have to eat humble pie.'

'Several servings.'

'I'll talk to Phil about it. She's working on our plan now.' Ed stood up to leave.

'I want to be organised before the CS Detectives arrive tomorrow.'

'Yes, ma'am,' Ed said and headed for the door.

'Oh, one more thing.'

'Yes?'

'If you're going to go and see Cass, leave Phil behind, OK? I don't think she'll be much help to you.'

'Yes, ma'am.'

Ed left her office for the squad room. He had plenty of thinking to do. Sorenson was right. If Cass was legit then she really might be able to identify Old Mick's killer and that meant finding Janet Hodgson's killer and the killer of four or five other women, including Susan. The thought gave him a rush of nervous energy.

Phil was hard at it when he got back to his desk. A classic two-fingered typist, she was pounding away at her keyboard. Ed decided to save the conversation about Cass until he'd done some searching for the missing victim. Convincing Phil that they needed Cass's help wasn't going to be an easy or quick conversation.

He logged on and started by double-checking missing persons from 2009. None were women with green eyes.

He turned to the homicides from that year. There weren't many still unsolved and only three were women. He skimmed the details about each. He didn't have to go very far before one leapt out at him: a woman found murdered on the Adelaide University campus. What got his attention was one crucial fact: her eyes were cut out. His gut clenched. This had to be it.

He opened the case file, searching for a photo of the victim or a description that would tell him what colour her eyes were. At last he found it, a thumbnail picture of her. He blew it up on his screen. The photo wasn't great but there was no mistaking it, her eyes were a vivid green, just like Susan's — just like all the other women.

'Who's the chick?' Phil asked.

Ed nearly jumped out of his skin. He was so engrossed in what he was doing that he hadn't realised that Phil had stopped typing and was standing directly behind him.

'I think she's the missing link,' Ed answered.

'Two thousand and nine?' Phil asked.

'Yep, she was murdered and her eyes were cut out — her green eyes.'

'Oh God, I remember that one. It happened at the uni, right? CS worked it for ages but never got anywhere. There was no forensic evidence to speak of.'

'Yeah, I remember it too. It made a lot of people very nervous. They were all wondering if it was the beginning of something. When no other vics with missing eyes turned up they heaved a sigh of relief. Looks like it was something more, it's just the killer changed his MO and went country.'

'Yeah, right into our backyard, lucky us,' Phil said.

Ed stared at her. Phil realised it was a bad choice of words as soon as it was out of her mouth.

'Jesus, I'm sorry, I didn't mean to sound flippant.'

'Yeah I know, it's just — to think that if someone had been paying more attention they might have caught on sooner and Susan might still be here …'

'I know,' Phil said.

They both sat there in silence, contemplating what might have been.

'OK, I'll print this out. Let's go get a coffee. You can fill me in on what you've put together for Sorenson and I can run something by you as well.'

'Something Sorenson said?' Phil asked.

'Yeah.'

'I'm not going to like it, am I?'

'Nope.'

They headed to Enzo's. Ed waited until they were settled at their favourite table before he launched into it.

'Sorenson wanted to talk to me about what happened with Cass yesterday.'

'Oh yeah? Did she go running to Sorenson and tell her we didn't play nice?'

'No, the opposite actually, she went home and decided we could pretty much go to hell and she didn't want to work with us.'

'Suits me just fine,' Phil said.

They paused as their coffees arrived.

'Yeah, I thought you'd say that,' Ed said.

'But there's more to it?'

'Cass's mother was the one who rang Sorenson to let her know what had happened. Sorenson actually wasn't that pissed about it. She seemed to understand why we had issues with it all.'

'Issues? There's not an iceberg's hope in hell that I'll ever believe that she can do what she says she can do or want her help.'

'Hmm, well, that's gonna be a problem,' Ed said with a sigh.

'Oh shit, don't tell me Sorenson still wants us to work with her?'

'Sorenson just thinks that she might be able to give us something on Old Mick's killer.'

'And Old Mick's killer is the same person that killed Janet Hodgson and all the rest.'

'Yep, although she doesn't know about the rest yet.'

'Jesus, why doesn't she just issue us with a Ouija board and be done with it? I just don't understand where all this is coming from. I would never have picked Sorenson as someone who believes in all that mumbo jumbo, she's so freakin' down the line and letter of the law with everything else.'

'Something must have happened that turned her into a believer,' Ed said, skating as close to the truth as he dared.

'Yeah, I'd love to know what. It must have been something important. So, what are we supposed to do? It doesn't sound like Cass wants to work with us any more than we want to work with her after yesterday's little scene.'

'Sorenson thought maybe I should go and talk to her and see if I could change her mind,' Ed said.

'Let me guess, she told you to leave me behind.' Phil sounded annoyed but she had a wry smile on her face.

'Yeah.'

'I guess she knows me pretty well. So when are you going, and more importantly, when are you going to tell Sorenson about the others?'

'The sooner, the better with Cass. If I have to go and apologise I would rather just get it out of the way. I don't know about telling Sorenson though. What do you reckon? Should I tell her now or after?'

'Now. If Cass agrees to help then she can do her voodoo with both Old Mick and the girl from 2009,' Phil said.

'I hadn't thought of that, of course, she could visit both places. We know where both of them died so it doubles the chance of our getting an ID on the killer. You're a fucking genius, Phil!'

'I try. Besides, you can't ask Cass to work on a murder that Sorenson doesn't even know we're looking at, not with the mother having a hotline straight to her — she'd be bound to find out. Then there's the added bonus that if Sorenson thinks Cass'll only work with you then there's a better chance she'll leave you on the case.'

'Yep, true, OK, I'd better go see Sorenson. This'll be interesting.'

'I'll come too, we still need to fill her in on our plan for the case, although it's about to change anyway. Something tells me she'll be pissed off that you didn't go to her yesterday when you first started to suspect a serial,' Phil said.

'Yeah, not to mention how she'll react when she finds out I've been quietly researching missing persons for the last eighteen months.'

'Yep, you're gonna get you're arse kicked.'

'Big time.'

They walked out into the southerly whipping off the sea, bringing fingers of ice from Antarctica. They hunched their shoulders against its bite and quickened their pace. Ed had a feeling the reception waiting for him inside wasn't going to be much warmer.

CHAPTER 18

Sorenson was on the phone when they got to her office. Ed took a seat and Phil paced around looking at the books and anything else in the room that caught her attention while they waited for the call to end. When it did, Phil took the seat next to Ed.

'So, you have a plan for the McKenzie and Hodgson cases?' Sorenson asked, giving them her full attention.

'Yes we do, but there's something we need to talk to you about first,' Ed said. He drummed his fingers on his knee.

'Is it about the case?' she asked.

'Yes it is.' He took a deep breath. 'We think there is a good chance that Janet Hodgson and Old Mick were the latest victims of a serial killer who has been operating in the region for the last six years.'

She sat there in silence for a few seconds. Her face was impassive; she didn't look shocked or even startled.

'You have some basis for thinking that?'

'Yes.' He took another deep breath; this was the bit he'd been dreading. 'I've been reviewing missing persons' cases for the last eighteen months for any possible patterns. When Cass came to see me yesterday she identified a link between four women who've gone missing in the last six years.'

'Cass did?' This clearly surprised her.

'Yes, she noticed that four of them had the same eye colour.'

'Eye colour? So let me get this straight, you have sensitive case information about missing persons at home without authorisation and you showed it to Cass Lehman?'

'Um, sort of, it was just pictures, but I didn't show her, she found them.'

'So they were lying around?' She sounded both annoyed and incredulous.

'I have a whiteboard with pictures of all the women who have gone missing and not been found in the last ten years. I've been reviewing the cases looking for links.' He sat back, feeling some kind of relief now that he'd come out with it.

Sorenson sat staring at him.

'Did you know about this?' She looked at Phil, her eyes boring into the younger woman's.

'Yes I did, I've been helping him. None of it has been done on work time.'

'It's not the time I care about, although I am glad to hear

it. It's the fact that the two of you have been looking into cases that we have no jurisdiction over for the last two years, and that sensitive information about those cases has just been casually lying around Detective Dyson's house where anyone can stumble across it. What the hell were you thinking?' she yelled.

'I was just trying to make sense of Susan's disappearance,' Ed said quietly.

Sorenson sighed heavily. 'You're lack of judgement is understandable, but Phil, I expected more from you.'

'Yes, ma'am, I worked on it because I genuinely thought it was helping,' Phil said.

'All right, forget all that for the moment and go back to the idea of a serial killer. You've got to be kidding, right? Don't you think the CS would have noticed a serial killer operating for the last six years?'

'We think they missed it because the killer isn't after a particular type, he's after women with the same eye colour.'

'You said four victims in six years? What makes you think that's a pattern? It could just be coincidence.'

'I thought so at first too, but we think there's actually six,' Ed said in a rush, keen to convince her. 'The pattern's definitely there. It started in 2008. Four of the vics are missing persons but two have turned up as DBs, one in 2009 and Janet Hodgson. This is the 2009 case.' He slid the case printout across her desk.

'And the only thing connecting them is that they had the same eye colour? Lots of people have the same eye colour.'

'Yes, that's true; this is a very unusual shade of green though. Not that many people have eyes that colour but that's not the only similarity. There's the fact that they all led pretty solitary lives and the timing of each disappearance,' Ed said.

'Timing?'

'Yes, each of them disappeared within a two-week window in either late June or early July. So we have one victim a year starting in 2008, all with the same unusual eye colour, all missing or dead at the same time of year.'

Sorenson processed this information for a few moments. 'And this is the file for the 2009 case?'

'Yep, and look at the autopsy report. The eyes were removed.'

Her eyebrows shot up. 'And when did you work all this out?'

It was another question Ed had been dreading. He'd hoped that in the excitement of it all she might not ask. No such luck.

'I started to wonder yesterday, but I hadn't found the 2009 case then. I only just found that.'

'We weren't sure there was a pattern and we needed to be more certain before we came to you. As soon as Ed found the 2009 vic we came straight to you,' Phil said, trying to rescue Ed from the hole he was digging himself.

'You should've come to me the minute you suspected you had a serial.'

'Yes, ma'am,' Ed said. What else could he say?

'And you think the Hodgson case is the latest?'

'Yes, she had the right colour eyes and the time frame fits.'

'But he didn't take the eyes.'

'No, but when he put her in the crate he probably thought she was still alive and would be there when he came back,' Phil said.

'So why did he leave the 2009 vic behind?'

'I don't know, maybe he was interrupted?'

Sorenson sat there, thinking.

'So if he's collecting eyes, doesn't that mean he doesn't have this year's to add to the set?' she finally asked.

'Yep, that's what we're worried about. He might be out there right now looking for another vic,' Phil said.

'The latest any of the vics has been taken or killed is the fifteenth of July. That was the 2009 case,' Ed said.

'It's the tenth today,' she said.

'Yes,' Ed said.

They sat there looking at each other.

'Is there anything else I need to know?' Sorenson asked.

And there it was, the question he'd been dreading.

'Susan was one of the vics,' Ed said.

Sorenson pushed her chair back and stared at him, then she stood up and walked over to the window that looked out over the street. It was a grey day and specks of sleet had started to hit the glass, leaving long exclamation marks of water in their wake. The weather was as grim as Sorenson's expression, reflected back at her in the glass.

She sighed. 'I'm sorry to hear that, Ed.' She turned and looked at him.

He couldn't think of anything to say to her. For some reason her sympathy was the last thing he wanted. It made it more painful.

'You realise that I have to tell CS? It'll be their case?'

'Yeah, we know,' Phil said.

'And Ed, you know I can't let you work the case if Susan was one of the vics? If we managed to catch the guy and you were one of the lead detectives a good defence lawyer would make mincemeat out of our case in five seconds flat.'

'Yeah, I was hoping I could still participate in an unofficial way,' Ed said.

'You really can't be anywhere near it. What did you have in mind?'

'It's about the conversation we had earlier, about Cass.'

'What about it?' Sorenson asked.

'I still want to go and see her and ask her for her help. There are two vics she might be able to help with now, Mick and the victim from 2009. If she gets anything on the killer we might get the jump on the CS guys.'

Sorenson thought about this for a while before she answered. 'I can't sanction it as part of the official investigation but I won't stop you from trying to talk Cass into helping. If she agrees and she gives you something we'll decide what to do then. I'll tell CS about the possible serial but not about Cass's involvement. The sooner you go and see her the better.'

'I'll go now.'

When Ed and Phil walked out of Sorenson's office, he felt like he'd been in there for hours. Looking at his watch he was surprised to see that only half an hour had slipped by. It was lunchtime and the squad room was relatively empty. Phil looked at him, trying to read his expression.

'You OK?'

'Yeah, a bit wrung out.'

'So, what now? Do you want to grab a bite?'

'I just want to get on with it. I'll head straight over to the Lehman house and see if I can convince Cass to help us.'

'Good luck,' Phil said then barked out a short laugh. 'Shit! What am I saying? I can't believe I'm wishing you luck to go and talk that crazy woman into working a case with us.'

'Yeah, who'd have thought it?'

CHAPTER 19

I blinked my eyes against the sunlight and vaguely wondered what had woken me. I looked at the clock and then had to look again. Unbelievably it was nearly 2 PM. I climbed out of bed and headed straight for the bathroom.

Sitting on the loo, I heard the doorbell ring and realised it was what had woken me. It wasn't a polite ring either; it was someone who had been trying to get attention for quite some time. It was followed by a sharp rapping on the glass around the door. I finished, flushed and washed my hands then threw on a robe and headed downstairs.

'Gran? Mum?'

There was no answer, just more knocking on the glass.

'All right, all right, I'm coming,' I bellowed, heading for the door.

I hastily fastened the robe over my pink flannelette pyjamas that sported pictures of frolicking cartoon cats and threw open the door. There, looking more than a little annoyed, was Detective Dyson.

'Yes?' I said. It wasn't very polite but I'm not a morning person. Of course it wasn't morning but I had just woken up so as far as I was concerned it was the same thing.

'Hello Miss Lehman. I didn't wake you up, did I?' His sweeping gaze took in my bleary eyes, out-of-control hair and less than flattering attire.

'Yes, you did as a matter of fact.'

'It's nearly two o'clock.'

'Not all of us work regular hours, you know,' I said, still snarly.

'You work?'

'Of course I work.'

I could tell he was trying to figure out what kept me up all night. I was tempted to tell him we ran a brothel but I was afraid he might believe me. In the end his curiosity got the better of him.

'So what do you do?'

'I'm an editor. I do a lot of work at night. It's nice and quiet.'

'Ah.'

We stood looking at each other. It was a miserable day and the winter chill was starting to seep into my bones, particularly my bare feet, but I wasn't about to break the silence. He'd come to see me, he could bloody well tell me what it was he wanted, I wasn't going to ask.

'Can I come inside?' he asked, looking uncomfortable.

The petty side of me wanted to say no and leave him standing on the doorstep but I thought better of it. 'Do you need to use our bathroom?'

He looked at me blankly for a few seconds, then cracked a smile, remembering my predicament the day before. I liked his smile. I don't think I'd actually seen it until that moment. It was crooked and very sexy. I dragged my mind away from that line of thought; there was nothing but quicksand and crocodiles down that path.

'No, but I could murder a cup of coffee.'

I capitulated. 'Yeah, me too, come in and I'll put the kettle on.'

I turned around and he followed me down the hallway into the kitchen. He eased his large frame into one of the bentwood chairs while I put the kettle on and reached for the plunger and my special stash of single origin beans from Brazil. It was a relief to have a minute or two with my back to him to collect my thoughts and tame the butterflies running riot in my stomach. The downside was that I caught a glimpse of myself reflected in the kitchen window. I was a fright. My hair looked like a bird had nested on my head and I had bags the size of suitcases under my eyes. I made a half-hearted attempt to smooth some hair behind my ears, knowing it was futile, and turned to look at him. I was surprised and embarrassed to find he was staring at me. He'd been watching my every move.

Once the coffee was steeping, I grabbed milk, sugar and mugs and dumped them on the table with the pot. I also grabbed the cake tin. A muffin for breakfast would do the trick nicely. I sat down, poured the coffee, pushed a mug towards him and offered the muffins. He shook his head. We sat there sipping in silence for a minute or two.

'Thanks, that's great coffee. Look, I just want to apologise for the way I behaved yesterday. I said some things that weren't very fair and I feel bad about it.'

'What, you mean the bit where you called me a freak or the bit where you accused me of being a stalker?' I mumbled through a mouthful of muffin.

To his credit, he looked sheepish. 'All of the above. I realised as soon as you left that I was too hard on you and that you were only trying to help.'

'I was, I felt bad about what happened with Mum.'

'Your mum isn't very subtle, is she?'

'No, when she sees something she tends to just come out with it. It's a compulsion.'

'She knocked me for six.'

I wasn't sure what to say. I didn't want to upset him by saying the wrong thing about his wife so I decided to just say nothing. He changed the topic.

'What you said about the women and their eyes, did you get some special vision about that or something?' he asked.

I had to laugh. He really wasn't comfortable talking about

HINDSIGHT

anything supernatural. His tone told me he still couldn't quite take it seriously.

'No, nothing like that, my talent is quite narrow. I only see something if I'm standing where someone has died and only if they suffered a violent or sudden death.'

'So how does it work? You don't talk to the dead person?'

'No, I see through their eyes. It's as though the events that led to their death have left an echo that only I can hear.'

'What's it called?'

'Retrocognition.'

'I've heard of precognition.'

'Yeah, precognition, or ESP, is the sexy one, the ability to predict the future and save the world. What I do isn't that cool.'

'How long have you had it?' He made it sound like a disease.

'Since I was eight.'

'So what happens if you accidentally come across a place where someone has died?'

'You saw what happened the other day. While I'm having the vision I can't see or hear anything else. Mum and Gran have both seen me do it and they tell me that I freeze and kind of switch off until the vision has passed. If it's a really bad one it leaves me feeling terrible afterwards.'

'So you see and hear what the person who died saw and heard?'

'Yes, but it's not just sight and sound. I feel what they felt.'

I looked down at my hands, which were clenched in my lap. It was hard to even talk about it without remembering some of the horrible ones. I could feel Ed's eyes on me. He was processing this last bit of information and trying to decide what to make of it.

'You mean if they were shot you would feel what it's like to be shot?'

'Yes. I've never felt that, though.'

'So how do you go if you're out and about and you get one of these visions?'

'I don't really leave the house much. Yesterday was the first time I'd driven in years.'

I looked at his face. Suddenly I got it. He wasn't just here to say sorry. He wanted something. All the questions had a point. I should have realised he wasn't just making casual conversation, he was a detective after all. A hot flush crept up my neck and over my cheeks. Yesterday he and his bitchy partner had sent me packing after making me feel about two inches tall and now he was here because he wanted my help.

'Forget it,' I said.

'Forget what?'

'I'm not going to help you.'

'Why not? Isn't that what you wanted to do yesterday?'

'I've changed my mind.' I folded my arms across my chest.

'I don't understand. Yesterday you were falling all over yourself to work with me and now you don't want to?' He pushed his chair back and rubbed his hands through his hair in frustration.

'I was hardly falling all over myself, Detective Dyson. Trust me, it's not that much fun,' I said with all the dignified frostiness I could manage.

'Just call me Ed, OK? Look, I've said I'm sorry and I mean it. I really do want your help. I don't know if you've heard but our only witness turned up dead yesterday. Just between you and me, we think he was killed by the same person who killed Janet Hodgson.'

'Half the town knows that.'

'They do?'

'Yes, I was in Mrs McCredie's yesterday and she was convinced he was murdered.'

'Mrs McCredie again? That woman has a mouth the size of a front-end loader.'

I had to smile. It was a pretty accurate description.

'The problem is that we have no leads. We were hoping you would give us a hand and see if Old Mick saw the killer before he died.'

'You're kidding, right? Yesterday you couldn't get rid of me quickly enough and now you're asking me to throw myself in front of a semitrailer for you?'

'Um, yes, I suppose I am, in a manner of speaking.'

I just sat there and looked at him. The guy had balls. 'I don't really see why I should. Surely you have something else?'

'Nothing concrete. Look, I'm going to be up front with you and this bit really does have to stay between you and me. We think that Janet Hodgson might have been the latest in a series of murders. When you picked out those missing women from the board the other day you actually gave us a connection. We think there are six victims, seven if you include Old Mick. All of them except for Mick were women with green eyes.'

I gaped at him. Surely he was taking the piss? How could someone like me have found a link when they couldn't? It didn't inspire much faith in their detecting abilities.

'We think the killer has been taking one victim a year in a two-week period from late June to early July,' he added.

'So if he's killed this year doesn't that give you a whole year to work out who he is before the next victim?' I asked.

'Yeah, it's possible but unfortunately we think he's taking these women because he wants their eyes. He didn't mean to kill Janet Hodgson straight away. He was coming back for her. She died of a heart attack brought on by stress. That means he didn't get a chance to take her or her eyes. We think there's a good chance he's going to try again.'

I started to feel ill. Some sick, perverted person was out there snatching women so he could collect their eyes? It wasn't something I wanted to spend any time imagining. It was the sort of thing you saw on American TV shows, not something that happened in sleepy little towns like this one.

Ed reached for the coffee pot and poured us both another coffee. I sipped and tried to sort out how I felt. Did I want to know what it felt like to be run down by a semitrailer? Nope — not now, not ever. Did I feel like I should help to stop a serial killer if I could? Yes, unfortunately.

I glared at him. He wisely decided to say nothing.

'You know I can't refuse, don't you?' I said, sounding crabby even to my own ears.

'I realise how hard it must be for you.'

'Do you? Do you know what it feels like to die? No, I don't think you do, so keep your platitudes to yourself and while we're at it, let's get something straight. I'm going to help you because I don't want another person to get hurt, not because I have some weird desire to get close to you.' I spat the words out.

'OK.'

'Is there anything else I need to know?' I said.

'Yeah, as a matter of fact there is. He killed and left behind one of the other victims. He took her eyes. That's the main reason we think we've got a serial killer who's collecting eyes.'

I stared at him in shock. 'So you're telling me you want me to look at not one but two murder scenes?'

'I am.'

'Did he take her eyes before or after she died?' It came out as a whisper. For some inexplicable reason the thought of experiencing having my eyes cut out was even more horrifying than the thought of being hit by a truck. I didn't think I could do it.

'The pathologist said it was done afterwards.'

'Thank God.'

I wrapped my arms around myself. I felt terribly cold despite the warmth of the kitchen. For as long as I could remember my main aim in life had been to avoid having visions. The result had been almost ten years of self-imposed exile. Now I was actually contemplating having two visions in a row by choice. It was insane.

'I don't know if I'm strong enough to do it.' Fear made my voice waver.

He studied me carefully. He would've had to be blind and stupid not to see how scared I was. 'I'll be there with you.' He reached out and took my hand in his.

His words slid over me. They didn't do anything to calm the pit of anxiety in my stomach. I snatched my hand back. If he had meant to soothe me with his touch he had achieved the exact opposite. It was at that moment that Gran came barrelling into the kitchen through the back door. She stopped dead when she saw the two of us sitting there. A smile flitted across her face then disappeared as she took in the scene before her.

'Hello, Detective Dyson, Cass. Is everything all right?'

'No, not really, Gran,' I said.

She looked at me waiting for some kind of explanation but when she didn't get one she turned her attention to Ed.

'Detective Dyson?'

'I've just been asking Cass to help. It involves her experiencing the deaths of two murder victims.'

'Cass? You don't have to do it you know.'

'I think I do, Gran.'

She walked over to me and put her arm around my shoulders, kissing the top of my head.

'You do what you think you need to, dear. Detective Dyson, you will need to look after her if she does this for you.'

'I will,' he said.

'No, I don't mean in the conventional sense. I mean you really have to look after her. When she has a vision she's unaware of anything else around her. You need to make sure nothing happens to her. After it's over she's weak and disoriented and very distressed. She'll need a quiet place where she can recuperate before you start asking her any questions.'

Gran sounded so unlike her normal, easy-going self as she barked out instructions that I almost smiled in spite of myself. Ed sat there like a small boy being told off by a school marm, nodding as she fired off instructions.

'When did you want me to do it?' I asked.

'Today.'

'What, both of them?' I squeaked.

'Yes, one in Adelaide, so we probably won't be back until later this evening.'

I blinked in shock. I hadn't considered that he might want me to do it straight away, but there was never going to be a good time.

'I'd better shower and get dressed then.' I stood up and glanced at Gran. Going by the expression on her face — knitted brows and lips of string — she had a few more choice things she wanted to say to Detective Ed Dyson. Good. He deserved it.

CHAPTER 20

Ed drove in silence. Cass was lost in her own thoughts. She hadn't taken very long to get ready, much to his relief. He was still smarting from the chewing out her grandmother had given him. She'd told him in no uncertain terms that his behaviour of the day before was not acceptable. She'd told him she was sorry for his loss but that it did not excuse boorish behaviour and that he basically needed to grow up, get over himself and learn to recognise when someone was being genuine. He sat there, eyes downcast. He couldn't even feel very annoyed about it. Everything she'd said was true.

Ed looked at Cass out of the corner of his eye. She was wearing a moss-green jumper and jeans. She didn't look like she was wearing any make-up; she didn't need it anyway, she had perfect skin. When she'd opened the door to him dressed in a daggy dressing gown and ridiculous pink pyjamas he'd almost laughed out loud. It was the look on her face that stopped him. She was so grumpy about being disturbed that any smart comments on his part weren't going to get him very far.

'Which one are we going to first?' she asked.

'I thought we'd go where Old Mick died first. Better to do South Road while it's still daylight. Less chance of us getting run over.'

'Tell me about the other one. Who was she and how did she die?' Cass asked.

'Her name was Marcy Lucas and she worked at Adelaide University. She was attacked on the way to her car one evening. We think the killer meant to take her with him like the others. Initially he knocked her out with some chloroform but then he must have changed his mind so he killed her and took her eyes.'

'How did he kill her?'

'He broke her neck.'

'Oh.'

'Would you experience that if she was already unconscious?' Ed asked.

'I don't think so. It would be like the Janet Hodgson one. I only experienced it to the point where she passed out.'

'So it shouldn't be too bad for you then?'

'I suppose not if you think being attacked and having a chloroform-soaked rag held over your face is not too bad,' Cass said.

HINDSIGHT

'Point taken, I just meant that compared to Old Mick's, it shouldn't be as horrible.'

'Yeah, great, let's save the nice murder for later.'

'I can't say anything right, can I?'

'Nope.'

Ed sighed. He was trying really hard but she wasn't making it easy. After his performance yesterday he couldn't blame her. He decided to change tack and try to take her mind off what was ahead.

'Tell me about your family. Is it just the three of you?'

'Yeah, none of us has a great track record with men. My granddad died of cancer, my dad up and left and I'm heading for spinsterhood at a rapid rate.'

Ed grimaced, so much for putting her in a better frame of mind.

'Sorry, I didn't mean for that to sound quite so snarly. My granddad was a lovely man and he and Gran were very much in love. Gran just hasn't been interested in anyone since he died. With my dad there was nothing very unusual; he and Mum just weren't suited. Her talent was only part of the problem. As for me, I've just never met the right person. I don't really get out and about enough.'

'Socialising might be risky with your particular talent. It might freak people out if you had a vision in the middle of a party. Has that ever happened?'

'Not at a party but it did happen when I was in a car with a date once. For some reason I never saw him again.' Cass laughed.

Ed relaxed a fraction. She had a great laugh and it lifted the mood in the car.

'So does your gran have a talent too? Is it something that all the women in your family have?'

'Yeah, we think it started with the German side of the family about three hundred years ago. We're not sure though because back then they had to be a bit careful about telling people in case they got labelled witches. Gran's a healer.'

Ed's eyebrows shot up, 'I'm surprised that everyone isn't flocking to her door.'

'She doesn't really do it much any more, not for clients anyway. Besides, she's not the messiah. She can't perform miracles. What she does is speed up the healing process. If someone can be healed, then she helps.'

'So if someone is dying she can't help them?'

'That's right; she tried to help Granddad and nearly died herself in the process.'

'So how come you all have different talents? Isn't that a bit weird?'

'What and all of us having the same talent would be less weird?' She laughed again. 'Let's face it, we broke the mould when it comes to weird. I do know that these things tend to run in families. We're a bit unusual though because we all have really strong talents and it hasn't skipped any generations yet. The way I understand it is that, genetically, we're geared to be psychically sensitive. For each of us it manifests itself in a different way.'

Ten minutes later they turned onto South Road. Two

kilometres further on, Ed pulled over to the side of the road and stopped the car. Cass sat there staring out of the windscreen before throwing open the car door and stepping outside. Ed followed and stood just behind her. Cars and trucks whizzed past her creating a backdraft that whipped her hair around her face. The grass on the verge was sodden and their feet sank into the ground. Ed shivered and tried to stamp his feet, creating a wet sucking sound as the mud reluctantly let go of each foot. He rubbed his hands together, trying to keep his circulation going.

He watched Cass look around. It was a desolate scene. Empty farmland stretched from both sides of the road. There were no animals in sight, just muddy fields dotted with the occasional tree, twisted and gnarled by battering from the wind.

After a few moments he walked up beside her and gently put a hand under her elbow. She flinched at the contact but didn't move away.

'It's over this way. How do you want to do this? Do you want me to walk with you or just watch?'

'You need to walk with me. If I have a vision I'll lose sight of everything except what I'm seeing in my head. You'll need to make sure I don't really walk in front of a truck.'

She walked over to where he'd indicated. The grass had been churned up by traffic, leaving a quagmire. Taking one careful step at a time, she walked into the muddy mess. Ed walked close behind her, holding his breath as he waited to see what would happen. She walked onto the edge of the road and stopped.

'Cass?'

She didn't answer him. She just stood there, swaying slightly each time a truck whizzed past. He walked around and looked at her face. What he saw made him wish he hadn't. Her eyes were enormous, the pupils so large her eyes looked black. She stared sightlessly, without blinking. Her pale skin had gone almost blue with the cold and her mouth was hanging open in fear. He wanted to reach out and touch her but he didn't dare. The seconds dragged past with excruciating slowness. Without warning, Cass took a sharp rasping breath then gave a long, gut-wrenching scream. She swayed and Ed thought she was going to fall. Instinct took over and he grabbed her. A sudden jolt of agony shot up his arms as he touched her. Then it was over. She blinked and wobbled and her knees gave out.

Ed held her, supporting her weight. She leant heavily against him, resting her head on his shoulder. She shook violently and cried with deep, uncontrollable sobs. He half carried, half walked her back to the car and helped her inside. Running around to the other side he started the engine and turned the heater up full bore. He sat there, watching her anxiously, rubbing her back as she cried. His heart was pounding in his chest and his gut was clenched with anxiety. That scream had scared the crap out of him and the sudden pain he'd felt was like a massive electric shock. Fishing around behind the passenger's seat he found an old and battered box of tissues and passed it to her. He felt completely helpless. He knew now why Cass's grandmother had been so adamant that he look after her.

Gradually Cass started to regain control. She took deep shaking breaths. After another five minutes she slowly turned her head and looked at him. Her face was puffy and blotchy.

HINDSIGHT

'Are you OK?'

She looked at him. Her eyes held so much pain he had to look away.

'I don't think I'll ever feel OK after that,' she whispered.

'Can you talk about it yet?' He didn't want to press her but he really wanted to know what she'd seen.

'Start the car and find me a place that sells coffee. I need a few more minutes and a hot drink first.'

The car was so hot that sweat was starting to run into his eyes. He didn't dare turn the heat down, though; Cass was still blue. He wasn't sure if it was from fear or cold but either way, the heat seemed to be helping.

A short time later they were tucked into a booth in the petrol station diner, mugs of steaming coffee clasped in their hands. Cass took a few sips then slowly put the mug down and looked at him.

'It was the same person; the same killer.'

'How do you know? What did you see?' Ed had so many questions he hardly knew where to start.

'The vision started in a car. I couldn't move. I was looking at my hands in my lap and trying to move them but I couldn't. The man sitting next to me said something about it hurting a bit but not as much as the next bit would, then he laughed. It was the same laugh.' She shuddered as she said it.

'The same as Janet Hodgson's killer?'

'Yes.'

'What did he look like?'

'I couldn't turn my head but I could see him out of the corner of my eye and he had brown hair, I think, and fair skin. He was wearing a cap so I could only see bits of his hair poking out. He didn't seem overly tall or big but he was sitting down.'

'What was his voice like?'

'Australian — I mean, he didn't have an accent.'

'Anything else about him you can remember? What was the cap like? What was he wearing?'

'The cap was dark blue. He was wearing a khaki jacket and jeans. I think he had sandshoes on but I can't be sure. Oh, and he was wearing a wedding band.'

Ed blinked in surprise. It wasn't unheard of for serial killers to be married but it was unusual.

'So what happened?'

Cass took a long sip before she responded.

'We pulled over to the side of the road. It was dark by then and he came around to my side of the car and lifted me out. He dragged me round to the front of the car and propped me up against the bumper bar. Then he sort of crouched in next to me and waited.' Cass paused and swallowed a few times, tears started to run down her cheeks at the memory. 'He waited for a truck to come and then he grabbed me and just tossed me out in front of it.'

She covered her face with her hands. Ed stared at her. He felt sick. He reached out and patted her shoulder, trying to comfort her. She uncovered her face and looked at him.

'He was so afraid. You have to catch the bastard that did this.'

'I'll do my best, Cass.'

HINDSIGHT

'I haven't helped much have I?'

'Every bit helps, at least we know it was the same person and we know a bit more about him. With a bit of luck we might get more at the next one, that's if you're OK to keep going?'

Cass looked out the window at the cars pulling in and out of the petrol station. The last thing she wanted to do was have another vision. Every time she closed her eyes she saw the semitrailer bearing down on her. The fear was worse than the pain. The pain of the impact had seared through every nerve in her body but it was over in an instant, leaving only the nothingness of death. The fear was something she would never forget. It would haunt her dreams. A person who could cause that much fear and suffering couldn't be left free to hurt someone else.

'I want to keep going. I need you to catch this guy.'

Ed let out a long breath he hadn't realised he'd been holding. They finished their coffee and got back in the car. Ed pulled out of the station and they headed for Adelaide. Cass closed her eyes. She went quiet for so long that Ed assumed she was asleep until her voice interrupted his silent stewing.

'So how long have you been a police officer?'

'Since I was eighteen, nearly twenty years.'

She wanted to know what it was like to be a police officer. He told her some of the funnier situations he'd found himself in over the years. Before he knew it they were pulling into the car park where Marcy Lucas was killed.

Ed glanced over at Cass. Her expression was unreadable but she'd gone white again and her hands were clenched in her lap. Ed parked the car and they both sat there for a few moments. It was approaching five o'clock and there were only a few people around. 'Her car was parked over there in the space next to the blue van. We think he attacked her as she was walking to her car.'

'Where did she actually die?'

'She was found lying behind her car.'

'OK, let's get on with it,' Cass said.

She strode over to the car space and started to walk around its perimeter — Ed had to break into a jog to keep up with her. This time she got a hit almost straight away. The minute she reached where the car would have been she stopped. Ed just stood behind her and waited. He didn't want to see her face again. Once was enough.

He was expecting her to stand frozen to the spot but it was different this time. After a few seconds she threw her hands up and started to struggle with an invisible opponent. Ed had to step back to avoid being battered by her flailing arms. Then she threw her hands up to her throat and fell to the ground, gurgling and gasping, her legs kicked out as she struggled to breathe. Ed started to panic; could she actually suffocate?

A couple of students noticed the commotion and came over to see what was going on. They looked on nervously, whispering to each other.

'Should I call an ambulance, mate?' one of them called out.

Ed had been so focused on the battle Cass was having at his feet that he hadn't noticed that they had an audience. He suddenly realised how strange it must look.

'No, she'll be all right in a minute. It's a type of epilepsy,' he lied.

This was met with doubtful looks. One of them pulled out his mobile and started to dial.

'I'm a police officer,' Ed said. He fished around in his pocket for his badge and flicked it out. The young man with the phone came over and had a look. He didn't seem satisfied but he stepped back.

While he was sorting out the onlookers, Cass went still. He looked down. She was staring sightlessly at the sky. Another surge of panic hit him. He knelt down and lifted her head and shoulders off the ground, resting her against his legs. He felt for a pulse. The steady throbbing against his fingers was a huge relief. He looked at her chest, it was rising and falling almost imperceptibly as she took shallow breaths. 'Cass? Cass, can you hear me?'

He picked her up and carried her over to their car. Struggling to balance her weight, he managed to open the door and slide her inside. He wound the seat back so that she was lying down and ran around to the driver's side and climbed in, puffing from the effort. He cranked up the heat again then sat there helplessly, stroking her hand, waiting for her to come back from wherever she was. He was still sitting there when a police car pulled into the car park and stopped in the space right next to them.

'Shit, shit, shit,' he muttered, watching the two officers climb out and come around to his side of the car. Their eyes took in the prone form of Cass next to him and he could tell he was going to have to do some serious explaining.

He wound down the window. 'Hello officer, I'm Detective Dyson, from Fairfield.' He handed over his badge. 'This is my friend Cass. She wanted to come and see the university grounds but unfortunately she's had a fit, she's epileptic.'

'You're a long way from home, Detective Dyson. I'm PC Glen Noakes and this is PC Julia Harding.'

'Are you all right, miss?' PC Noakes called.

While Ed had been focused on the two officers, Cass had finally come to. She was dazed and shocked but aware enough of what was happening to realise that she had to hold it together.

'I just need to rest,' she whispered.

The two officers looked at her closely. She managed a thin smile.

'I'll be fine. Ed will look after me.'

'OK, we'll just go over and speak to those students. If you could wait please?' Harding said.

Noakes stood by the car while Harding went over to the students still huddled next to the blue van.

'They're just making sure. They're worried that I might have hurt you and you're too afraid to say anything,' Ed said under his breath. 'Don't worry, we'll be out of here in a couple of minutes.'

Harding finished talking to the students and walked back to join her partner. She leaned in the window.

'Sorry, detective, just had to be sure. You look after her now. She looks like she needs some rest.'

'No problem, you have to do your job. If there's nothing else we'll be on our way?'

HINDSIGHT

'Yes, that's fine, have a safe trip.'

Ed started the car and they pulled slowly out of the car park. He watched the two officers return to their car. Harding picked up the radio as soon as she got in.

'They're still checking. She'll be radioing in my details and rego right now just to make sure I'm legit. Can't blame her, I'd do the same thing.'

Cass nodded mutely.

'What can I do, Cass? Do you need another coffee?' Ed asked.

'No, just take me home. I'll fill you in on what I saw then. Right now, I just need to rest.' She leant back and closed her eyes. Ed pulled over to the side of the road and took his jacket off. Gently, he laid it over the top of her.

'Thanks,' she whispered.

Ed drove through the city, navigating what was now peak-hour traffic. He'd just hit the beginning of South Road, which was bumper to bumper, when Cass startled him by speaking. He'd assumed she was asleep.

'It was the same man, and she recognised him,' she murmured.

He waited for her to say more, but she didn't. When he had a chance to look at her she still had her eyes closed and a minute later he heard her gently snoring. She slept and he drove, pondering what this new development might mean. If the vic knew the killer then there was a good chance they might be able to track him down.

'We're gonna get you, you sick fuck,' he hissed through clenched teeth.

PART THREE

Agamemnon: *The gods fail not to mark*
Those who have killed many.
The black Furies stalking the man
Fortunate beyond all right
Wrench back again the set of his life
And drop him to darkness.
Aeschylus, *Agamemnon*

CHAPTER 21

After we left Adelaide I could barely keep my eyes open, I was so exhausted. I'd never had two visions in one day and the aftermath was crushing. I couldn't think, I couldn't move and I could barely speak. I was too exhausted even to cry.

As soon as we left the campus I let the exhaustion take over. I muttered something to Ed, God only knows what, and the next thing I knew he was squatting next to me with the door open, shaking my arm. We were in my driveway.

'Cass, are you awake?' He sounded so anxious I guessed he must have been trying to wake me for a while.

I groaned and blinked a few times, trying to shake myself out of the fog.

'I don't know if I've got the energy to move,' I mumbled.

Something in my expression must have told him I wasn't kidding. I really didn't know if my legs would hold me. He just nodded and, in one swift movement, bent over and lifted me out of the car. Even in my daze I couldn't believe how strong the guy was; he made me feel like some dainty little wisp of a thing, and with all Gran's good food I am certainly no featherweight. He slammed the car door with his butt and carried me to the front door. I gave in and just rested my head on his shoulder. It felt so good.

Gran must have heard the car pull up because she was waiting at the door, lines of worry etched on her face. 'Is she all right?'

'I think so, just exhausted.'

'Bring her into the lounge room and I'll make a pot of tea, she needs something restorative.'

I felt like I should say something, remind them that I was there too, but I just couldn't be bothered. The warmth of Ed's body was making me sleepy again and I wanted to shut my eyes and go back to sleep. I must have done that because the next thing I knew I was lying on the couch and Gran was waving a cup of tea under my nose and stroking my brow.

'Drink this, Cass.'

'I just want to sleep, Gran,' I complained.

'I know, dear, but Detective Dyson needs to know a bit more about what you saw before you can go to sleep again. He has to know if you saw anything about the killer that might help identify him.'

'Where's Mum?'

HINDSIGHT

'She's in the study with a client. She'll be finished soon.'

I sat up reluctantly and took the cup from her. I looked over in the corner. Ed was sitting quietly in Grandad's old armchair. I was surprised to see him there. Normally Gran ushered visitors towards the settee. Gran wasn't sentimental about many things but that chair embodied some of her happiest memories of when she and Grandad used to sit in this room at the end of the day, talking or just enjoying each other's company. Ed had obviously moved up in her estimation quite dramatically.

Our lounge room was a cosy room of no particular style. All three of us were bower birds, inclined to buy pretty things to line our nest. The result was a room filled with brightly coloured silk cushions, tapestry throw rugs, a couple of Persian carpets and a varied collection of lamps and knick-knacks. It was a very female space but, surprisingly, Ed didn't look uncomfortable or out of place.

I took a long sip of tea and involuntarily screwed up my face. The taste alone was enough to shake me out of my comatose state. I could pick out a few of the herbs she'd put in: a touch of peppermint, some rosemary and ginseng but that was where my knowledge of herbs hit a brick wall. I had no doubt that there were other things as well but I just concentrated on trying to hold my breath while I drank it because even the heavy-handed addition of some honey hadn't made it very palatable.

'Would you like a cup, Mr Dyson? I'm sure you've had a difficult day too.'

Ed had been watching my face while I struggled to swallow each mouthful.

'No thanks, I'm fine, really.'

'You're not thirsty then?' She had a twinkle in her eye as she asked the question. She knew damn well that he was probably gasping for a cup of coffee but was too polite to say so. 'I've got some coffee brewing in the kitchen if you would like a cup?'

Ed gave an audible sigh. 'I'd love a cup, thanks.'

Gran left to fetch his coffee and we sat there looking at each other over my cup of tea. I was starting to feel more like myself and images of what I'd seen at the uni were beginning to crowd into my head.

'Thank you for looking after me.'

'To be honest, you scared the crap out of me. When you collapsed at the uni and I couldn't wake you up, I actually thought you might be dead.'

'I never remember any of that but other people who've seen me have a vision have been pretty freaked out.'

'Yeah, well, your grandma did warn me, but being told isn't the same as experiencing it firsthand. Let me tell you, the scream you gave at the first scene was enough to scare ten years off my life.'

'I screamed?'

'Loud and long and ear shattering.'

'That must be why I have a sore throat.' I smiled thinly. It was an attempt at humour but really there was nothing funny about it. Gran chose that moment to come back in with a tray laden with coffee, milk, sugar and two enormous plates of apple pie and ice cream. She put the tray down next to Ed and passed each of us one of the plates.

'I don't think I really feel like eating, Gran,' I said feebly, knowing that resistance was futile.

'Nonsense, I bet you haven't eaten since lunchtime!'

'No, we haven't,' I said.

'It does look good, ma'am. It's been a long time since I had homemade apple pie,' Ed murmured, the spoon already halfway to his mouth.

'Well then, eat, you'll both feel better. I'll leave you to it. Give me a yell if you need anything, I'm just going to be in the kitchen. I have some herbs I need to bag up. I'll tell Anita not to disturb you.'

'Thanks, Gran.'

Silence followed her exit as we both sat there and wolfed down her divine apple pie. Nobody on earth could possibly make better pie than she did. I was three-quarters of the way through devouring my serve when I heard a contented sigh and the clatter of spoon on china from the other side of the room.

'That was fantastic! Does she cook like that all the time?'

'Yep,' I muttered through a mouthful.

'If I lived here I'd weigh three hundred kilos. I'd be one of those people you see on TV who has to be lifted out of the house with a crane.'

'Welcome to my pain. I gave up on being thin a decade ago. I couldn't deal with the deprivation.' I let out a sigh of my own as I placed the spoon on my spectacularly clean plate and leant back against the couch. It was a remnant from the seventies, covered in donkey-brown velvet and stuffed with feathers that tended to sink after a while. I squirmed against the cushions, trying to mould them to my back.

'You look just fine. I hate really skinny. Women should have curves.'

A gold star for Mr Dyson, I thought. He just keeps getting better. Enough idle chit chat though, the pie was over and I needed to tell him what I'd seen. The food and tea had been a welcome distraction but now it was back to business. With a deep breath, I got down to it.

'Marcy Lucas was at her car when she was attacked by a man who came up behind her. She heard him coming and turned around in time to see him. That was when she said, "Oh, you're the guy from the expo, aren't you? What are you doing here?"'

Ed sat up straight. He looked at me eagerly. 'Was that exactly what she said?'

'Yes, exactly. Then he jumped on her and tried to hold a cloth soaked with something horrible over her mouth but she managed to fight him off. I think she might have hurt him, but she wasn't quick enough. He grabbed her again and started to strangle her.' I put my hands up to my throat at the memory and tears filled my eyes. I'd been fighting for breath, terrified, my heart pounding and unable to force any air into my lungs, which were screaming for oxygen. 'Then he put the rag over my — I mean, her mouth again and everything went black.'

'Is that where it ended?'

'Yes, she must have died before she regained consciousness.'

'And it was definitely the same man?'

HINDSIGHT

'Yes, I'm as certain as I can be. It was very dark. The light near her car wasn't working. I saw his face. He was probably in his twenties with brown shortish hair. He was pretty average looking, medium build, not overly tall. He was the sort of guy you wouldn't look at twice in the street.'

'So what makes you so sure it's the same guy?'

'It was the way he talked. I heard him talk to Janet Hodgson and Old Mick.' I shuddered at the memory. 'There was something eager in his voice. He enjoyed what he did. He seemed more nervous about Marcy. With Mick and Janet he was a lot surer of himself, almost cocky. You have to catch him, Ed. He really enjoyed killing Old Mick.' The last few words came out as a whisper and all of a sudden the apple pie was sitting like a stone in my stomach. I felt physically ill at the memory of the killer's laughter as he'd taunted the old man.

Ed was looking down at his hands, which were clenched so tightly into fists that the knuckles almost glowed white. In a flash I remembered that his wife was one of the victims too. How hard must it be to know that someone so perverted had taken his wife? I couldn't even begin to imagine how that must feel.

'I'm sorry, Ed.'

'Sorry?' He looked confused for a few seconds until he got my meaning, then he sighed heavily. 'Cass, you have nothing to be sorry for. You're the only person who has given me anything that might help to find Susan and the man responsible for taking her away from me.'

He looked at me with a fierce burning in his eyes.

A gentle knocking on the French doors broke the tension.

'Yes?' I called.

'Cass, it's me,' Mum said. 'Are you both all right in there? Can I get you anything?'

Typical Mum, Gran would have told her to leave us alone but worry would have got the better of her and she just had to make sure I was OK. She poked her head in.

'Come in, Mum, I think we're pretty much finished.'

Mum came into the room and sat on the couch next to me, looking at my face and reading the weariness.

'Was there anything else, Cass?' Ed asked.

'No, nothing that I can remember right now. If you like I'll spend some time tomorrow writing both of them down for you, just to make sure I haven't forgotten to tell you anything.'

'You don't mind?'

'No, it helps to get things out of my head if I put them down on paper.'

'You look exhausted, Cass,' Mum said. No points for subtlety there. Ed took the hint and stood up.

'I'm going to get going. Cass, I'll ring you from work tomorrow to see how you are, OK?'

I smiled tiredly. My temporary burst of energy had worn off and the lead was creeping back into my limbs. I had to get to bed. I looked at the clock — it was only 9 PM. It felt like the middle of the night.

HINDSIGHT

Ed headed for the door and Mum saw him out. I heard her bid him goodnight and then the sound of the door closing solidly behind him. A few moments later Mum came back in.

'Let's get you upstairs.' She helped me up from the couch and, like a person looking after someone very old and infirm, she walked me up the stairs. Every step took supreme effort. I honestly don't think I would have made it if she hadn't been there with her hand under my elbow, propelling me on. I got to my bedroom and collapsed on the bed. Mum gently took off my shoes, socks and jeans, peeled back the bedclothes from one half of the bed and eased me into it, tucking me in like a small child. She smoothed back my hair and gave me a tender kiss on the forehead.

'I'm proud of you, Cass. You did a good thing today.'

I don't think the door was even shut behind her before I slipped into a deep, dreamless sleep.

CHAPTER 22

Ed left Cass's house full of nervous energy. It'd been a full-on day, but Cass's revelations about the killer had fired him up. He wanted to get the guy and he wanted to do it now. He thought about calling Phil but he didn't want to disturb her down-time with Grace. He couldn't bear the thought of going home; sleep was out of the question.

He decided to head to the station. He wanted to look back through the case files and see if there was any mention of the other women attending expos. What he needed was the women's diaries, if they kept them. The Marcy Lucas case was a no go, all the evidence would be in Adelaide. Janet Hodgson's and Susan's were local though. Any evidence on their cases would be boxed up in the evidence room.

He remembered Phil picking up something that looked like a diary when they searched Janet's flat. Hopefully she was a religious user of it. He also wanted to check back through Susan's diary. Hers was definitely boxed with other bits and pieces that the investigating detectives thought were relevant. Thinking back, he was sure that she'd gone to some sort of fair or expo in the summer with one of her friends from work, but he couldn't remember what it was.

He drove away from Jewel Bay to Fairfield barely aware of his surroundings. For the first time in a long time he actually felt hopeful that he might find an answer to Susan's disappearance. It was not knowing that ate away at his insides night after night. For months he'd woken up at three in the morning and stared into the darkness, wondering. He'd played out so many scenarios in his head to explain what had happened — including Susan being the victim of a serial killer.

Now it was almost a certainty, he felt strangely numb. It was weird; facing his worst fears, surely he should feel horrified and appalled, not detached, like he was wrapped in cottonwool and it was happening to someone else. Maybe he'd expended all his sorrow imagining the worst so that there was nothing left to feel now? No, it wasn't that. One thing he knew for sure was that sorrow could be infinite.

Cass was partly responsible for him feeling like he'd suddenly fallen down a rabbit hole. He still couldn't believe that he was working with a psychic — it beggared belief. Hard facts and good detective work were the keys to solving crimes. There just wasn't room in his universe for the intangible, airy-fairy world of sixth sense mumbo jumbo — until yesterday.

Anita Lehman had started the unravelling process and Cass had finished it. Any skerrick of a doubt he had left had been blown away when he witnessed her visions firsthand. He was more than a bit shocked at how the visions affected her. Now he got it. He understood how a bright and attractive young woman like her could lock herself away from the world. She wasn't a nutcase, she was cursed. He felt a deep compassion for her.

She also brought out a fierce protective streak in him. He'd felt like some old-fashioned hero rescuing a damsel in distress when he'd picked her up and carried her back to his car, and a big part of him liked playing that role. It wasn't too often that he got to feel heroic these days.

Ed pulled into the station car park and swiped his access card. He took the lift up to the squad room. There was no one around. He looked at the roster on the wall; Samuels and Matthews were on-call tonight. The Hodgson case had ground to a halt until the CS landed back on their doorstep in the morning and Sorenson would have sent everyone else home to rest up while they could.

He booted up his computer. He liked working at night when there were no distractions — no phones ringing, no Sorenson looking over his shoulder asking what he was doing. He started by doing a search for expos held in 2009. The word 'expo' was what Cass had said and it was pretty specific. He thought it was unlikely that the vic would have used that word randomly.

There were plenty: cars, house and garden, handyman, caravan and camping, sex and adult products, mind and body, and psychic. Although it was possible the vic was interested in cars, camping or handyman stuff, Ed ruled those out as less likely. From what he'd read of Marcy's file he also thought the sex one was a bit unlikely although you never knew. That left the house and garden, the mind and body, and the psychic one. The psychic expo was only a week before she was killed and it instantly drew his attention. Maybe the killer was a stallholder? There could be some irony in that; was a fake psychic about to be caught by the real deal?

He did a more thorough search for information on that particular expo and jotted down the name of the organisers. He would contact them tomorrow and get a listing of the stallholders. Hopefully they kept that information. If he could get the list, he and Phil could start checking to see if any of them had a record.

He printed out some info about the expo and shut the computer down. He headed downstairs to the evidence room. Maria, a uniformed officer close to retirement, was on duty at the front desk, which was where the evidence room log was kept. The room itself was through a door behind the desk, in full view of the CCTV cameras.

Maria greeted him warmly. He'd known her since he first started in Fairfield Station. She'd always been a genuine and up front person. When Susan went missing she was one of the few people who'd approached him about it directly. She'd told him outright that she knew he'd had nothing to do with it. He'd been

HINDSIGHT

touched and very grateful for the show of support. When she saw him, her eyebrows shot up in surprise.

'What brings you here at this time of night?'

It was Maria's way to know exactly who should be around at any given time. Ed felt a pang of guilt. He wasn't going to be able to tell her the whole truth and he felt bad about it.

'Two things, CS are here tomorrow about the Janet Hodgson case and I just want to go back over some of the evidence. Is it all here still or did they take it with them?'

'Most of it's still here. They were pretty confident they had their guy and they didn't think there was anything very useful in the items you collected. They took all the crime scene stuff but, from memory, left the rest.'

She shifted her considerable bulk off the stool she was perched on and waddled off into the room behind her. She was a fantastic cook who enjoyed her own cooking. She came back a few minutes later and plonked a cardboard box in front of him.

'You said there were two things? What was the other one?'

'A favour. I was hoping you would let me have Susan's diary. It has the phone numbers and addresses of some old friends jotted in it.'

'You going to run upstairs and copy the page straight away?'

'Yeah, that'd be great.' Ed knew he was pushing it. He didn't want to get the woman in trouble but at the same time he didn't want a record of the diary being signed out to him. Sorenson would go mad if she knew he was working the case. It was a small miracle that she'd let him work with Cass.

'I'll go get her box.' She turned to walk back into the evidence room.

'Don't you need to look it up?'

'There are some cases that I'll never forget the location of,' she said quietly and with such compassion that it brought a lump to Ed's throat.

She disappeared again and came back a few minutes later with the box for Susan's case. She placed it gently on the counter. Ed looked at it. He rested one hand on the lid. How could something as ordinary as a brown cardboard box sum up the wonderful life that had been Susan? It didn't seem fitting that the essence of her was bundled into something so bland and utilitarian. He wasn't sure how he felt about diving into the contents. There were ghosts in there and he was afraid to let them out.

He eased off the lid. A whiff of musty air escaped, telling him that it had been a long time since anyone had spent any time on her case. It wasn't a cold case any more. He gently sorted through the contents, trying hard not to look too carefully at anything. It didn't take him long to find what he was looking for: Susan's leather-bound diary. It was something she always carried on her; touching it felt like touching a part of her. He quickly lifted it out of the box. He couldn't afford to get all sentimental now. He had work to do.

'This is it, thanks, Maria.'

'Make sure you bring it back tonight.'

'Will do, thanks again.'

HINDSIGHT

'Any way I can help,' she said. For others it would have been a throwaway line. Maria really meant it. Ed was grateful for people like Maria. Small kindnesses made all the difference.

He headed upstairs, settled back at his desk and opened the diary. Its gold embossed pages gave off the faint and unmistakable scent of Susan's perfume. He tried to remember the name of it. Tears welled up in his eyes. He still missed her terribly. He flicked through the pages, looking at the scrawled entries in her crazy, loopy cursive. He flicked to the day of her disappearance and started working backwards. Every so often an entry would leap out at him, adding extra salt to the freshly opened wound. *Ed's birthday dinner!* she'd written.

He remembered the night. She'd surprised him with a dinner at his favourite restaurant, Russell's Pizza House in McLaren Vale. Phil and Grace were there too. It was a night of laughter, good food and way too much wine. He dragged himself back from the memory; happy times.

He kept flicking, trying not to let other memories crowd in. He had to go right back to March to find the entry he was looking for. There it was, the 25th; she'd gone to a mind and body expo in Adelaide with her friend Julia. He remembered it now. She came back talking about crystals and astrological charts. He'd poohed-poohed it all and she was annoyed with him for being so close-minded. He tried to imagine her face if he told her he was now working with a psychic. She would think he was taking the piss.

He could feel his pulse racing. He now had two victims who'd been to expos in the months leading up to their disappearance.

Was it just coincidence? He stood up and opened the Janet Hodgson box. There were a few things they'd taken from her flat and some bags of evidence from the scene but that was it. He rummaged some more. Tucked down the side of the box was her diary. It was small and black, the sort that was given away with magazines. He flicked through it, starting at the day she was murdered and working backwards.

There was nothing. Disappointment made him sink back into his seat. Still, it didn't mean she hadn't attended one, it just meant she wasn't good at keeping a diary. They would have to talk to her work colleagues again.

Then there were the other three cases they could check. The one benefit of the CS being involved was that they would have access to the other files. If the expo angle really was the link between the victims it was something tangible they could start working on. If all or most of the vics had attended these things then they could start to look at stallholders, security and anyone else who'd been involved in all of the events attended by the victims. It would narrow down the search and, with luck, give them only a few likely suspects to focus on.

He yawned. He'd been running on adrenaline for the last hour and it had finally worn off. It was time to go home. He couldn't do any more today and he was a bit disappointed. Part of him had hoped for a miracle; that he would find the connection, access the list of people who had worked at the expos and come up with a possible suspect all before bedtime.

Tomorrow CS would be briefed, they would take over the

running of the case and Sorenson would boot him off it once and for all. It was maddening. Just when he felt like he was close to an answer to explain Susan's disappearance he would be excluded. Phil would keep him in the loop, but there was only so much she could do, assuming that CS let her keep working the case.

He sighed as he picked up Susan's diary and Janet's box. He took the stairs and dropped the items back. He thanked Maria for her help and then headed for his car. It was well after 10 PM and he just wanted to sleep. As he drove the dark streets on his way home he was acutely aware of how alone he was. He was the only person crazy enough to be out on such a bitterly cold and miserable night. At least he hoped he was. Please God, let the killer be home tonight.

CHAPTER 23

When Ed got home he snacked his way through anything resembling food that he could find before crashing into bed. He expected sleep to come quickly but the minute he closed his eyes thoughts of Susan crowded in.

Images flashed through his mind and he launched himself out of bed and rushed to the bathroom. He heaved, retching until his eyes watered and his throat was raw. He sat back against the bathroom wall. What they found could be worse than not knowing; still, he would rather know than live his life wondering.

He got up and splashed cold water on his face then looked at himself in the mirror. It wasn't pretty. He turned the light off and crashed into bed. Exhaustion finally won out and he was asleep within seconds.

The next morning he was awake by seven, bleary-eyed, head pounding. He showered, took a handful of pills and headed straight for the station. He wanted to talk to Phil before Sorenson and the rest turned up. Thankfully Phil was already in, looking disgustingly perky.

'Jesus, look what the cat dragged in,' she said, looking Ed up and down, taking in rumpled clothes, mussed up hair and stubble. 'Tough day yesterday?'

'Yeah, really tough. I've got heaps to tell you. I need food and coffee if I'm going to face Sorenson today. Can we head for Enzo's and I'll fill you in?'

They settled into their usual spot and Phil waited, not very patiently, while Ed wolfed down a bacon and egg sandwich. He was chewing the last mouthful when Phil's curiosity finally got the better of her.

'So? What did little Miss Freaky see?'

'It was what she heard.'

He told Phil about the expo angle and the research he'd done the night before.

'You think our guy might be a stallholder at one of these new age expo things?'

'He could be security or one of the organisers. We — sorry, you — can contact the organisers and try to get some lists of all the stallholders and anyone else involved. Also, with Janet you can canvass her colleagues again and see if anyone remembers her attending any expos recently.'

'With a bit of luck we'll get some common hits and I can run the names for any priors,' Phil said.

'Yeah, I got the names and numbers of the organisers for the expos that Susan and Marcy Lucas, the 2009 vic, attended.'

'Great, saves me doing it.'

'If Sorenson will let me, I'll help you do some of the leg work. What time are our friends from CS due?'

'Eleven, I think,' Phil said.

'Sorenson is probably in by now. I'd better tell her what happened with Cass, while you make a few phone calls and try to get the lists.'

'Yeah, fingers crossed that these new age types are into record keeping.'

Sorenson was in her office and saw them return. She beckoned to Ed.

'Better go give her the good news.'

'Yeah and get myself officially removed from the case.'

Sorenson demanded every detail about Cass's visions. Then he told her about his own investigations into the expo angle, carefully leaving out the bit about foraging through Susan's case file.

'It seems we've got a serial. I'm going to include Susan as one of the potential vics, so I'm sorry, but you're off the case,' she said.

'Can I at least help Phil chase the expo records?'

Sorenson frowned. 'I don't suppose there's any harm. When Byrnes and Rawlinson get here you can attend the briefing to assist with handover but after that you're off. I'll keep you informed of any developments just like any other relative of a vic; no privileged access to information, and absolutely no participation in the case. Got it?'

'Got it, and thanks.'

'Don't thank me. If the killer had struck again last night I'd have hung you out to dry for not telling me sooner. Let's hope we don't get any reports of missing persons today.'

He tried to read her expression. He couldn't quite tell if she meant it or not. He thought she probably did.

'See what you and Phil can come up with before CS arrives. It would be nice to have a shortlist of possible suspects.'

'Wouldn't it just?' He walked out of her office and back to the squad room. Phil was hovering over the fax machine.

'What's up?' Ed asked.

'Spoke to the organiser of the 2009 expo. Nice woman, off with the fairies but thankfully her fairies are into keeping records. Nothing electronic of course but she told me she has handwritten records of all the stallholders, the organising committee and contractors they hired for security, waste disposal and everything else.'

'She's faxing it through?'

'Yes, her neighbour has a fax machine. She's taking her special book over there now.'

'Her special book?'

'Yes, apparently it's covered in blue velvet, blue is the colour of communication, you know.'

'Right.'

'Personally I don't give a shit what it's covered in as long as what's inside has the information we're looking for.'

'What about the one Susan went to?'

'The woman I spoke to sounded more in touch with this millennium. She had electronic records but they were stored on disks and she needed to find them.'

'She knew where they were?'

'She thought so. She was going to look and ring me back.'

The fax machine chugged into life. They stood there, holding their breath as the pages started to churn out. Phil snatched the first one off and turned it over. It was covered in neat lines of cursive; name, address, phone number, the type of stall they were running and their payment details. It was a beautiful thing. They stood grinning at each other. The fax machine went silent. Phil grabbed the rest of the sheets and they went back to their desks.

'Give me half and I'll start running some names as well,' Ed said.

'Are you allowed to?' Phil asked, jerking her head in the direction of Sorenson's office.

'Yeah, I have the nod to help you until Byrnes and Rawlinson show up. After that I'm officially the invisible man.'

They sat in front of their computers. For the next half an hour they plugged away in silence, entering name after name and searching for criminal records. Other officers came and went around them. Samuels hovered for a while, being nosy, but they both ignored him and eventually he drifted away. Phil's phone buzzed, making them jump.

'Detective Steiner. Ah, Cheryl, thanks for calling back. How did you go? Excellent! That's great. Can you send them through? You can? Terrific.'

She reeled off her email address and ended the call.

'She found them?'

'Yep, all the records were on one disk, stallholders, contractors and organisers. She's sending it all through now.'

'The gods might finally be smiling on us,' Ed said.

'I really hope so. Here it is. I'll print it out now.'

Ed waited impatiently for the files to print. He grabbed the sheets.

'They're not as thorough as the velvet book woman's but they're enough to start some cross-checks.'

'Yeah, we can narrow our search to the ones that were at both.'

'I'll read off this list and you check the velvet book for matches.'

They were both rigid with tension. They were on the hunt and could sense they were getting close. Slowly and meticulously they started going through the two lists. Every time they hit a common name, Ed made a note. After about twenty minutes they were done. They had seventeen names plus two companies that had provided services for both; one did waste disposal, the other promotional materials.

'We don't have time to look at the companies but I reckon we can run the other names before CS show up,' Phil said.

'Let's do it. I've already run a couple. Split the rest and let's get moving.'

They frantically started to plug the details in. Half an hour later, they were finished.

'I got one with a DUI, one with a sealed juvie record and one with an assault. You?' Phil asked.

'I only got one, but it's a good one. Jason Weissman, thirty-one, restraining orders, assault, sexual assault. He's a real gem and you want to know the best bit? He's practically local. He lives in Mount Compass.' Ed sat back, his eyes burning with a fierce intensity.

'That's got to be our guy. What did he do at the expos?' Phil asked.

Ed rummaged through the papers. 'Velvet book has him down as a reiki massage therapist.'

'Great, just the sort of guy you want giving women massages. Did Susan have a massage?' She asked the question reluctantly.

Ed sat there for a few seconds, staring into space. 'I can't remember her mentioning it but she liked a good massage.'

Phil sighed. 'I'm really sorry, Ed.'

'Yeah, me too but at least we're gonna get the bastard,' Ed said.

'Yep, when the goons get here we can ask them to look into the case files and see if there's anything about the other vics attending expos. With a bit of luck we can get another hit.'

'Yeah, and you can start calling Janet Hodgson's colleagues and see if they remember her going to anything like that. You never know, we might just get the full set if we're really lucky.'

'Fingers crossed, but we should push Sorenson to let us bring this guy in for questioning even without the others,' Phil said.

'Bring Cass in too and see if she can do an unofficial ID on the guy.'

'You're kidding right?' Phil snorted. 'Any ID she gave wouldn't mean shit.'

'Maybe not, but she could at least give us some kind of confirmation that we had the right guy.'

'I suppose so. Let me think about it. I'm still coming to grips with all that psychic shit.'

'Oh great, it's glum and glummer,' Phil muttered, taking in the grim expressions on Detectives Byrnes and Rawlinson's faces as they arrived. 'So, you're glad to be back here then?'

'Couldn't be more delighted,' Byrnes said.

Sorenson noticed them and stepped out of her office. She was quick off the mark, not wanting any slanging matches before the briefing.

'Morning.' She nodded at the CS detectives. 'Let's go into the meeting room. We've got a lot of ground to cover.'

They settled themselves around the table; Byrnes and Rawlinson on one side, Ed and Phil on the other and Sorenson at the head.

'Let's get started. As I told you yesterday, Detective Dyson had a hunch that our killer might have been operating in the region for a while. He did some research and came up with four other names who may have been victims of our killer.'

'You really think you have a serial?' Rawlinson snorted.

'Yes, we do,' Ed said quietly.

'You realise that we have experts and computer programs that review all homicides looking for patterns?' Byrnes said.

'They're not all homicides. Three are missing persons,' Ed said.

'Same applies,' Byrnes scoffed.

'Detective Byrnes, this is not personal. We're all on the same team,' Sorenson said, staring him down.

'What's the connection between the vics?'

Sorenson nodded at Ed to give the details.

'All the vics went missing or were killed in consecutive years starting in 2008. They all went missing in either June or July and they all had eyes that were a particular shade of green.'

'Green eyes? That's it? No other similarities?'

'No.'

There was silence while the two detectives digested the information.

'How is your supposed serial finding his victims or haven't you had time to work that out yet?' Byrnes's voice was syrupy sweet.

Sorenson shot him a look but let Ed answer him.

'As a matter of fact, we have. We think he found all the vics by posing as a stallholder at expos. So far we've worked out that two of the vics attended expos shortly before they died or disappeared.'

'Only two? That's hardly conclusive,' Rawlinson said.

'True but we have a consultant who works with us who confirmed the expo link between the killer and one of the vics,' Sorenson said.

'A consultant?'

Ed looked over at Phil, knowing that what was coming wasn't going to be pleasant.

'She's a psychic. She has an ability to visit a crime scene and see what the vic saw just before they died. She saw and heard the killer at one of the sites she visited,' Sorenson said.

Rawlinson snorted. 'You're kidding, right?'

Byrnes sat there looking from Sorenson to Ed and Phil then back again. 'I hope there's a punch line coming because there fucking well should be,' he shouted. He stood up and leant over the table. 'Do you mean to tell me that you've had a fucking psychic running around the crime scenes?' He thumped his fist on the table.

'Detective, sit down!' Sorenson yelled. 'And moderate your tone or I'll have you on report.'

He sat, folding his arms across his chest and staring venomously at the Fairfield officers.

'The psychic Ed used is reliable and discreet. There is no issue with her. Assuming the whole squad room hasn't heard you yelling, the only people that know of her involvement are in this room. Now if you don't mind, we'll finish this briefing.' Her eyes were like shards of blue ice as she looked around the room. Her comment was greeted by silence so full of tension the air practically rippled with it.

'Right, there are a few more things we need to cover. Phil, did you find anything this morning?'

'Yeah, we got lucky. We reckon we have a possible suspect. He was a stallholder at the expos that two of the vics attended and he has a record a mile long that includes violent and sexual assault. He also lives around here.'

'We think it's worth bringing him in for questioning,' Ed said.

'You do realise that we'll be taking over this case now that it's a Tier 3?' Byrnes asked.

Phil started to reply but Sorenson cut her short.

'I was hoping we could work the case with you, especially since it looks like most of the vics and the killer are from this region. I have a teleconference booked with DCI Fisher in half an hour to advise him of the latest developments. I'm happy to discuss it with him if you'd prefer?'

Byrnes glared at her. His jaw muscles clenched and unclenched a few times as he struggled to get his temper under check. 'If Detectives Dyson, Steiner or any of your other officers are going to work this case then they do it strictly under my lead. They don't scratch their arses unless I've approved it first.'

'Of course CS would be in charge, that's understood.' She flashed something that vaguely resembled a smile but had about as much warmth to it as an average arctic winter. 'Detective Dyson won't be working this case. He has a conflict of interest.'

'What conflict? He's been working it up until now, hasn't he? Don't tell me there's a chance he's compromised the case as well?' Byrnes's voice went up a few notches again.

'One of the victims is Detective Dyson's missing wife.'

'Oh for fuck's sake! What is wrong with you people?' Byrnes bellowed.

'That's enough! This is the last time I warn you!' Sorenson yelled back.

They stared at each other until Byrnes finally looked away.

'Now, if everyone has themselves back under control, we all have work to do. I need to brief the senior leadership group. Then I need to brief the rest of the team here. Ed and Phil, I want you to run through what you've done this morning in detail and outline the rest of the cases you think are linked.'

'Yes, ma'am,' Phil said.

She left the room and the four of them sat there looking at each other.

'Well, I could use a coffee. Shall we grab one before we get into it?' Ed said finally.

Grunts and nods of assent meant they were all seated at a table down the road five minutes later. It still felt like they were two opposing teams facing off but the informal setting and coffee went some way to overcoming hostilities.

'This's pretty good coffee.' Rawlinson sounded genuinely surprised. It probably hadn't occurred to him that anywhere outside a five-kilometre radius of the city could make a decent brew.

'So what made you think there might be a serial operating?' Byrnes cut to the chase.

'It was the eyes. Janet Hodgson and the other three women had exactly the same colour eyes as my wife.'

'That's a big leap to make,' Rawlinson said.

'Yeah, I knew it at the time but I guess I've been searching for answers about Susan for so long that I pretty much jumped at the idea.'

'So how did you find the other vics?'

HINDSIGHT

The question was asked casually enough but Ed knew he was entering dangerous territory and had been preparing his answer. 'Since Susan went missing I've been taking an interest in missing persons and homicides in the area.'

Byrnes gave him a penetrating look but Rawlinson jumped in before he could voice any of the difficult questions that Ed was bracing himself for.

'How did you hook up with the psychic?' Rawlinson asked.

'Sorenson recommended her. She knows her family. She's legit,' Phil answered.

Ed had to hide a smile. It was amazing; her dislike for Byrnes and Rawlinson had her defending Cass. Who would have thought it? 'I'm confident she's the real deal as well. I saw her in action yesterday and there was nothing fake about her,' Ed said.

'How did she come up with the expo connection?'

'When she has a vision she actually experiences what the vic saw, heard and felt just before they died. She got a glimpse of the guy who killed Marcy Lucas in 2009 and heard her say he was the guy from the expo.'

'Hmm, and your wife?' Byrnes asked.

'I remembered she'd been to an expo in the months before she died,' he lied.

'So you really think that the stallholder is your guy?'

'We think he looks pretty good for it; worth asking more questions and trying to get a search warrant for his house and car anyway.'

'All right, Steiner, you and Rawlinson can go and pick him up. I'll organise for the records to be sent down for the other cases if you give me the details. We'll see if there's any record of them attending expos,' Byrnes said.

Nods of agreement all round.

'Oh, and Dyson? Bring your psychic in. I want to meet her and she might as well have a look at your suspect, nothing official, of course. After that you're off the case.'

They headed back to the station. Sorenson was already briefing the rest of the officers. They listened with rapt attention as she gave an outline of the situation, stressing that a serial killer was only a possible line of enquiry.

'Questions?' she asked.

'Is it true you've been using a psychic?' Samuels asked.

Sorenson glared at him. 'Who told you that?'

'Some of us overheard your discussion in the meeting room this morning,' he said with a smirk.

Sorenson looked like she wanted to eat him alive but she managed to answer with a modicum of civility. 'Yes, a psychic has provided us with some valuable assistance.'

'Are they still working on the case?' Samuels asked.

'Jesus, the guy has more balls than brains,' Phil whispered. 'Any minute now Sorenson is going to rip his head off and shit down his throat.'

'We have no plans for her to participate any further at this time. Her involvement in this case is strictly confidential. It's not to leave this room.'

She answered a few more questions and then called the briefing to a close.

'It's not every day we get a case this big around here,' Phil said.

'Let's get this clear. The chances of this turning out to be a serial are pretty fucking slim but I'm prepared to humour you just in case you've bumbled your way to finding a genuine psycho,' Byrnes said.

'We'll see, until then we have a shitload to do,' Phil said.

Ed grabbed his keys. He had a feeling it might take some convincing to get Cass to come in for an ID. The sooner he got over there and talked to her the better.

It was going to be a big day. With a bit of luck they might have the person responsible for Susan's disappearance in custody by the end of it. A wave of white-hot rage swept over him as he thought about what he'd like to do to him.

Half an hour later he was standing on Cass's porch again. Anita answered the door at his first knock. She didn't look surprised to see him. Ed wondered if that was part of her talent. Did she know in advance who was going to come calling?

'Is Cass home?' As soon as the words were out of his mouth he realised how absurd the question was. Of course she was home.

'Come in, yes, she's here and she's awake. I heard her in the shower about twenty minutes ago so she should be down soon. Come into the kitchen. Do you want a cup of tea?'

'Coffee would be great if you have some?'

'I can manage that.'

Anita Lehman was dressed in a black turtleneck jumper and jeans; quite different from the flamboyant, gypsy-looking outfits she'd sported on his other visits. Her hair was pulled back from her face. She looked elegant. She looked tired too. Ed felt a pang of guilt. He was pretty sure he was partly responsible for that. She must have been worried about Cass the day before.

He sat in the same chair. He was starting to feel like a fixture in their kitchen. Even the cat hardly batted an eyelid when he walked in. The sleek black head looked up from its food bowl for the briefest moment before going back to enthusiastic scoffing.

'That cat is eating every time I'm here.'

'Yes, he's a passionate devotee of his food bowl. He didn't get to be the size he is just by chance.'

'Hmm, it's a wonder the locals don't think you're witches — three women with a black cat.'

'Trust me, some of them do.' She passed him a coffee and slid a plate of homemade biscuits in front of him.

'They're my mum's homemade choc-chip biscuits. Beware, they're very moreish.'

'I'm going to get fat if I keep visiting you like this.'

Cass walked into the kitchen a few minutes later just as he was tucking into his third biscuit.

'Morning, Mum. Hey, Ed.'

'Gee, I must really be spending too much time here if you were actually expecting to see me at your table.' He smiled at her.

'Nah, I saw your car from my window.' She gave him a faint

HINDSIGHT

smile back. She still looked tired; there were dark shadows under her eyes and her skin was pale and waxen.

'Sit down, Cass. I'll pour you a coffee. Do you want some breakfast?'

Ed didn't bat an eyelid at the idea of breakfast at midday. He was starting to get used to the weird hours Cass kept.

'No, no breakfast thanks, Mum. I'm not hungry. I might have something later.'

Anita passed her a mug of coffee. She turned to Ed. 'Do you need to speak to Cass in private?'

'No that's fine, Mrs Lehman. Please, stay.'

She sat down and they all sipped in silence.

'I have some news for you,' Ed said finally.

Two pairs of eyes looked at him expectantly.

'I went back to the station last night and checked Susan's diary. It's still in her evidence box. She went to an expo as well. It looks like the killer was a stallholder. We have a suspect that we're going to bring in today for questioning.'

'Oh, good, I mean that's terrible, but it's good you have a suspect,' Cass said.

'Yeah.' He looked down at his hands wrapped around the blue and white china mug. Now that it had come to the point where he had to ask her to come and do the ID he was at a loss for words. Seeing how exhausted she looked reminded him of the high personal price she'd paid to help him already. Asking her to do more didn't seem right.

'You didn't come here just to tell me that.'

'No, I didn't.'

'You want me to come and look at the man you bring in.'

'Yes. Will you do it?'

Anita Lehman had been silently watching the exchange. She sighed deeply.

'Mum?' Cass asked.

'It's all right, Cass. Don't mind me. I just worry for you like any mother would.'

'Except you're not like every other mother. Is there something I need to know?'

'No, nothing different from what I've already told you. You need to do what you feel is best.'

'I have to help him.'

'Yes, I know.'

Ed wondered what Anita had told Cass. It was one thing dealing with an anxious parent but an anxious parent with the ability to predict the future was something different altogether. It was no wonder there hadn't been many men in Cass's life. It added a whole new dimension to being intimidated by your partner's mother.

Cass sighed. 'Let me have something to eat and then I'm all yours. Mum, I will have some breakfast. Something tells me I'm going to need it.'

Twenty minutes later they were in his car on the way back to Fairfield. His phone buzzed, signalling an incoming text message. He tossed it to her. 'Can you have a quick look?'

'It's a message from Phil. It says, "We've got him, on our way back now."'

Ed nodded. He didn't trust himself to speak.

'Are you OK?' Cass asked.

He nodded again, staring at the road ahead.

The trip passed in silence. Ed pulled into the car park and was out of the car before Cass had a chance to unbuckle her seatbelt. He was hell-bent on getting inside; she felt the exact opposite. She reluctantly opened the door and got out. He strode off and she had to almost run to keep up with him. He led her through the squad room and straight to Sorenson's office. Knocking on the door, he barely waited for a reply before he barged in with Cass puffing along behind.

'Sit down.'

Cass slid obediently into a chair. Ed remained standing.

'Miss Lehman has agreed to do an unofficial ID,' he said.

Sorenson threw Cass a brief smile and nod before focusing on Ed.

'I've just got off the phone. Your third vic, the missing PR rep? The McLaren Vale station had her diary in their evidence file. She attended a lifestyle expo three months before she disappeared.'

'So that's three out of six now.'

'Yes, I have Samuels trying to get the list of stallholders to check for your suspect. Phil is phoning all of Janet Hodgson's colleagues again as we speak to see if anyone can remember her attending an expo or something similar.'

Ed paced back and forth in front of Sorenson's desk. There was something frightening about the intensity radiating from him.

'You need to stay here while they bring the suspect in. I don't want you to move a muscle until he's in one of the interview rooms. Understood?'

'I have to see him.'

Sorenson sighed. 'You shouldn't even be in the same building. You can view him briefly once he's in the room. I'll come with you.'

'I don't need you to come.'

'It's not open for debate. Cass, thank you for coming, you can wait here while I take Detective Dyson around. When we come back I'll arrange for one of the detectives to take you to the room so you can see the suspect.'

'Will he be able to see me?' Cass felt nauseous at the thought.

'No, you'll be looking at him through one-way glass.'

Sorenson's phone buzzed. She picked it up and had a brief, monosyllabic conversation.

'He's here. Let's go, Ed.'

They left, shutting the door behind them. Cass sat there, feeling strangely detached, like she was dreaming all of this and would suddenly wake up. The door opened. She turned around expecting it to be Ed and Natalia.

'Sorry, I didn't realise anyone was in here,' the officer said, smiling at her. 'Are you the psychic?'

'Um, yes, I guess so,' Cass said, uncomfortable with the label.

'I'm Senior Constable Samuels. What's your name again? DI Sorenson mentioned it this morning but I'm terrible with names.'

'Cass, Cass Lehman.'

'That's right, pleased to meet you, Miss Lehman, I'll just leave this file. See you around.'

He plonked a file on Sorenson's desk and ducked back out again. Cass was still thinking about her new title when Sorenson came back in with another officer.

'Cass, this is Detective Byrnes. He'll take you around to the interview room now.'

'Thanks for coming, Miss Lehman. This way please.'

She followed him out of the office and down a corridor to a room at the end. There was a large glass window and behind it, Cass could see a man being interviewed by Detective Steiner and another police officer in a suit. She studied the man sitting opposite the two officers. He was in his thirties with brown hair. He was ordinary looking, average height. He fitted the description she'd given Ed. It could be him.

'Can I hear him talk?'

'Why do you need to hear him talk?' Detective Byrnes asked.

'Because I will never forget the killer's voice,' she said simply.

Byrnes hesitated for a few seconds, scrutinising her expression. Then he reached over and flicked a switch on the wall. A small speaker crackled into life and they could hear what was being said.

'Can you remember where you were last Monday night?' Rawlinson asked.

'Monday?'

'Yes.'

'I was at home.'

'Can anyone confirm that?'

'No, I live by myself.'

The man had a deep, husky voice. It was different from the higher pitched, almost feminine voice she'd heard in her visions. It wasn't the same man. Cass turned to Detective Byrnes.

'It's not him.'

'You're sure?'

'He sounds nothing like the man in my visions.'

'But he matches the description you gave.'

'He looks similar but it's not him. I'm sorry.'

'This man was at expos that two, maybe three of the victims attended. Are you absolutely sure?'

'I am.'

Byrnes led her back to Sorenson's office. Ed was there, waiting. He looked so brittle he could snap. He looked at her first, then at Byrnes. Byrnes shook his head and then left the room, shutting the door behind him.

'I'm sorry, Ed.'

He said nothing, staring out the window at the grey winter's day. It looked like the colour had been stripped out of everything.

'You could be wrong.' He ground the words out through clenched teeth.

'I don't think so.'

'Does being a psychic mean that you're never wrong?' He turned his gaze on her and she was startled by the animosity she saw there. He was really angry.

'That's a shame, Cass, we were all pretty hopeful,' Sorenson said.

HINDSIGHT

She looked at them both, not sure what to say. 'I'd like to go home now.'

'Let's go,' Ed said. He strode out of the office and once again she was left to run along behind him. She couldn't help wondering how someone who'd been so sensitive and caring the day before could turn into such a schmuck today.

The drive home was just as tense as the drive in. They sat in icy silence. She could feel the hostility radiating from him. She watched the passing scenery, feeling miserable and more than a bit annoyed. He was the one who'd wanted her help and this was how he thanked her? It wasn't her fault that they had the wrong person.

He pulled into her driveway and sat there with the car running.

'I'm not wrong,' Cass said quietly.

He turned on her. 'Everything points to this guy. While you were with Detective Byrnes we got confirmation that the same guy was at the expo the third vic went to as well. It's got to be him.'

'It's not him. You need to look again.'

'So we're supposed to ignore a suspect who looks prime for this just on your say-so?' he yelled.

'Do what you think you need to, but the killer's still out there,' she snapped.

'You're wrong.'

She got out of the car and slammed the door. He reversed out of the driveway and sped off in a cloud of exhaust fumes. Cass stood there staring after him.

CHAPTER 24

He drove his van into the car park. He was early but it was important that he got a good spot. This fair wasn't as well organised as the bigger expos and they hadn't pre-allocated sites. Ideally he would get a spot where he could see the people approaching him. That way he could do some spruiking. It was hard work being chatty with complete strangers. The only thing that kept him going was the thought that the next person who walked over could be the one. It was like a treasure hunt.

The stall he chose was in an excellent spot. He couldn't believe that no one else had snapped it up. The fair had been set up in a U-shape with tables and chairs and a stage in a central green area. His stall gave him a perfect view of people approaching from all directions. As a bonus he was close to a coffee stall. He would be able to talk to people who were standing in the queue waiting for their coffee.

He had an hour and a half until the fair opened. It probably wouldn't get busy until about lunchtime. Luckily it was a clear day. For the first time in almost a week the rain had subsided and the sky was a pale wintery blue. He wandered over to the coffee stall and turned on his most charming smile.

'Good morning!'

The woman running it had her back to him sorting through boxes of cups and unloading them. She turned around, tucking a strand of hair behind her ear.

'I'm running the iridology stall next door.'

'Iridology, hey? That doesn't sound very medieval to me,' she said, smiling.

She was probably in her thirties. She had a nose ring and a tattoo on her neck. Her hair was dyed that unnatural shade of jet black that made anyone over twenty look much older than they were. Not the sort of woman he liked.

'Oh, you'd be surprised. It's a very ancient art, its origins date back almost eight hundred years.'

'Really? I didn't know.'

'I don't suppose your coffee machine is up and running yet? I'm frozen. I could really use a hot drink.' He smiled again.

'I think I could manage one cup. I'll even do it gratis if you'll do a quick reading for me before all the punters get here.' She gave him a broad smile, showing a set of teeth that would have benefitted from a trip to the orthodontist.

'You've got yourself a deal. Come and sit down and I'll have a quick look and jot down any areas you need to focus on.' He walked back to his stall and she followed.

'Sit over there. I need to turn a light on so I can see your irises better.'

She took a seat and he sat down opposite her. He switched on the light and looked at her eyes. He was so startled he almost exclaimed out loud. She registered his surprised expression.

'What? Is it something serious?'

'No, you have really unusual eyes. Did you know that only about fifteen per cent of the population have green eyes?'

'No, but people always say my eyes are my best feature.' A slight blush coloured her cheeks.

'They'd be right. I see lots of eyes but I don't often see people with such beautiful green ones.'

'Thanks.' The blush deepened. 'So what health issues do I have?'

'I can see some issues with your circulation and there's a mark in your left iris. Have you ever had issues with your kidneys?'

'That's amazing! I had lots of trouble with my kidneys as a kid. I also suffer from varicose veins. I can't believe how spot-on you are! Is there anything else?'

'Not much, you look pretty healthy. You need to make sure you limit your intake of fatty and acidic foods, but other than that you have a clean bill of health. Do you want me to jot it down on a chart for you?'

'No, I can remember it.'

'If you get a chance come back later and I'll do a full reading and chart for you.'

'Thanks. You'd better come over and get your coffee.'

'Sorry, I've forgotten your name?'

'Lucy.'

'I'm Brian.'

He followed her over to her stall. His heart was pounding and he was so excited he could barely contain the energy flooding through him. She was perfect. Those eyes were the closest to Ginny's that he had ever seen. He wanted to shove her into the back of his van and drive away. Of course he couldn't. He was going to have to slog it through the day. It would be a complete waste of time and energy. He didn't know how he would manage it. Still, at least he could console himself that he'd found a match. What luck! Now he and Ginny would be able to celebrate their anniversary after all.

He realised that Lucy was waiting, looking at him expectantly.

'Sorry, did you say something?'

'Gee, Brian, you looked like you were a million miles away. I asked what sort of coffee you wanted.'

'Sorry, I'm still half asleep. It's a bit early for me. I'll have a latte please.'

'Sure.'

'Are you from around here, Lucy?'

'Yeah, Willunga, a local born and bred.'

'Are you into the medieval stuff?'

'No, not really. I just sell coffee, although I'd really like to see

HINDSIGHT

the jousting. Don't think I'll get a chance though. It's in the next field and I doubt I'll get away.'

'What do you do when you're not selling coffee?'

'Are you trying to crack on to me, Brian?' She said it jokingly but there was a slight edge to her voice. He decided he'd better back off. He'd obviously pushed too much.

'No, I'm happily married. I was just curious. Sorry, it's a nasty habit of mine to ask lots of questions.'

'That's OK.'

He heard the relief in her voice. Saying you were married always put people at ease, as if being scary was limited to single people.

'I run a small art gallery and coffee shop on the main street in Willunga. It's called Divinity. It's in an old church.'

'Good business?'

'Great — my sister's holding the fort today. All the tourists will be out for a drive now the rain's broken. Here's your coffee.'

He smiled to himself as he walked back to his stall. *We're going to get to know each other much, much better, Lucy.* He almost danced on the spot with delight.

The rest of the day dragged by. He saw a procession of clients, but struggled to maintain his focus. His eyes kept being drawn to Lucy. She was doing a booming trade and luckily she was so busy she was oblivious to his scrutiny.

He found only two other clients with green eyes, real green that is, not hazel or green flecked. He carefully recorded their details. There was nothing like planning ahead. He might not find anyone better at the next few expos.

Finally things started to wind down. It was getting cold and only a few diehards were left. A lot of the stallholders had already gone. The dreary band playing the last session on the centre stage finally finished. It sounded like a dirge. How appropriate. He chuckled to himself.

He got his van and pulled it up behind his stall. It was important to get his things packed up before Lucy finished. The line at her stand was still going. He had no intention of coming back the next day and he wanted to be ready to follow her as soon as she left.

He took a deep breath, trying to ease the knot of tension in his stomach. He didn't have time to plan carefully like he normally did. There'd be no opportunity to monitor her habits and work out the best way. It was risky but he was feeling lucky. She'd been sent to him. He was meant to have her.

Finally she put up a closed sign and started the tedious process of cleaning the machine and jugs, bagging up rubbish and sorting things out ready for the next day. After what felt like forever she pulled down the shutter on her van, locked it and came out of the back door. It was starting to get dark, the sun had slipped behind the hills and there was a cold mistiness to the air. It would be a frosty night.

He walked quickly around to the driver's side of his van and jumped in. He watched Lucy walk towards the car park about five hundred metres away. He let her get a good head start and then he drove slowly towards her. She was striding along, anxious to get out of the cold. He pulled up next to her. He looked in his rear-view mirror. There were no cars behind him, no other people walking in front or behind. The few remaining stallholders were busy packing up. No one was paying any attention. He smiled and wound down his window.

'Can I give you a lift to your car?'

She stopped and looked at him. 'It's not very far.'

'Oh come on, don't be silly. It's freezing out there. You'll be an icicle by the time you get there.'

She stood by his car, undecided. He didn't push her, not while her instincts were telling her she shouldn't. It was always a mistake to seem too eager. She looked towards the car park.

'Suit yourself, I just didn't want you to catch cold.' He started to wind up the window. Pretending you didn't care always worked well.

'No, wait — you're right, thanks.'

She jogged around to the passenger side of the van and climbed in. He started to feel the humming and throbbing of his own pulse as adrenaline pumped through him. He looked in the rear-view mirror again; no one was close to them. That was perfect. Fate was smiling on him. He continued his slow drive across the boggy grass.

'You had a busy day today.'

'Flat out. I'm so tired I can barely keep my eyes open.'

'Really? I might be able to help you with that.' He chuckled, enjoying his private joke.

Lucy frowned, not understanding. 'I need sleep. Just as well I don't have any plans. What about you? Are you and your wife doing anything tonight?'

'Yeah, big plans.' He sniggered.

The van hit the car park and he sped up slightly.

'That's my car over there.'

He drove over to the car and stopped.

'Just before you get out, Lucy, would you mind passing me the small blue box in the glove box? It's got my diabetes meds in it. I forgot to take my insulin earlier and I'd better not risk driving home without it.'

'Sure thing.' She opened the glove box and handed it to him. 'Thanks for the lift.' She tried to open the door. She jiggled the handle a few times then turned to him in frustration. 'I can't seem to get the door open. Can you give me a hand, please?'

'Sorry, Lucy, I'm afraid I can't.'

'What?' She looked at him in incomprehension. 'I need you to open the door.' She shook the handle harder.

He smiled at her, holding up the syringe. 'Just relax, Lucy.' He plunged the needle into her thigh. She screamed and lashed out at him, then turned back to the door, frantically scrabbling at it.

He put his foot on the accelerator, driving away from Lucy's hatchback.

'Brian! Stop, please! Let me out!'

He ignored her. They reached the end of the car park and he turned onto the main road, gaining speed. Lucy's movements slowed down. She stopped pounding on the door and splayed her hands on the glass in silent supplication. Her head nodded and thumped against the window. He stopped on the side of the road and reached over to pull her into an upright position, fastened her seatbelt and folded her hands in her lap.

'There we go. That's much better. We can't have you drawing attention to us, can we? Don't worry, we'll be home soon. I'm so glad you didn't have any plans for tonight. My wife and I have a real surprise in store for you.'

Lucy's breath came in short, desperate puffs. She blinked frantically. Her eyes were stretched wide and her pupils were so dilated that the irises were almost invisible. Inside her head she was screaming.

CHAPTER 25

I woke up on Sunday morning feeling disoriented. Something wasn't quite right. There was hardly any light filtering in around the curtains, which told me it was still early. I looked over at the clock. It was just before seven, much earlier than I normally struggled out of bed.

Every so often when Gran decides to have a sleep in, Shadow will pester me until I get up and feed him. His stomach alarm usually goes off at around 6 AM. His waking-up-the-help routine involves standing on my chest and purring loudly into my face until I open my eyes. I stagger downstairs to feed him and then head back to bed. He joins me ten minutes or so later for his post-breakfast nap.

But this morning I couldn't blame Shadow for my awake state. He was missing in action, which was strange in itself. I laid there for a while trying to work out what had woken me. Then I heard it again, voices on the veranda followed by a knock on the door. I wondered who the hell would be visiting us at such an ungodly hour. I heard the front door opening followed by voices. The first was Gran's, then there was what sounded like a barrage of other voices, all talking fast and loud.

I jumped out of bed and went over to the window. As I lifted the curtain I heard the front door slam. Intrigued, I peered down. At the front of the house were six or seven cars. In the front yard the drivers were milling around. One of them looked up and saw me looking out of the window. There was a flurry of excitement and before I knew what was happening flashes started going off and they were snapping my photo. I dropped the curtain like it was on fire and stepped back from the window. I sat down on the bed and tried to think. Why on earth would a gaggle of media be camped out on our front lawn?

While I was trying to kick my brain into gear there was a knock on the door and Gran came in.

'I thought the noise would probably have woken you up.'

'What's going on, Gran?'

Gran sighed and sat down next to me. She took my hand in hers and stroked it. 'They want you, dear.'

'Me? What have I done?'

Gran pulled a folded paper out from under her arm and handed it to me. I looked at the front page. FLEURIEU SERIAL KILLER? the headline screamed. It was followed by the strapline,

HINDSIGHT

PSYCHIC PROVIDES VITAL CLUE, and there, for all the world to see, was my picture.

I scanned the article. It described police suspicions about a serial killer abducting women in the region, then came the bit about me. There was a potted history of my life, the fact that I lived in Jewel Bay with my mother and grandmother and, for the grand finale, a paragraph about assisting police with my psychic abilities. I looked at Gran.

'Who would have done this?' I asked.

'There must be a leak at the police station.'

'I can't believe someone would talk to the press! It's completely irresponsible. Not only is it a complete violation of my privacy, it's plain stupid. The killer will know the police are investigating now. They might never find him.'

'It says here that police brought someone in for questioning yesterday.'

'The guy that Ed took me to see yesterday isn't the killer. They've got the wrong person.'

When Ed had dropped me home I'd walked into the house fuming about his pigheadedness. I stomped into the kitchen and banged around making myself a cup of coffee and cutting a huge piece of the chocolate cake that Gran had left on the table. Mum came in a few minutes later to find me drowning my sorrows in a sea of chocolate ganache. She'd laid a hand on my shoulder.

'Do you want to talk about it?'

'I can't, Mum. I'm so mad at him that it makes me want to scream.'

'Gran and I are going for a walk before dinner. Do you want to come?'

My first instinct was to say no. I wanted to retreat to my room and stew. I was feeling sorry for myself. I'd expected to be treated like some kind of hero; the person who'd provided the vital clue, who could identify the killer and help them tie the case up in a nice neat bow. The killer should have been caught and Ed should have been eternally grateful to me for solving the mystery of his wife's disappearance. Instead everything had gone pear-shaped the minute I saw the man in custody.

It was Mum's worried frown that made me change my mind. I decided it would do me good to get out and not think about killers and missing women for a while. I parted company with the chocolate cake and spent a much healthier afternoon striding along the paths that snaked along the coastline. Every twist and turn was familiar — I've been walking them for as long as I can remember.

The freezing wind whipped off the sea, clawing at our faces and making our noses and cheeks glow red. We walked fast to keep warm and soon I was puffing and sweating under all my layers. Gran and Mum were both very fit and we set a cracking pace, pausing only when we got to the top of a particularly steep climb. The waves were lashing the rocks below and white foam soared into the sky every time a big one hit.

We stood at the top, trying to catch our breath. The vigorous exercise had lightened my mood. I felt better than I had in days.

'Do you want to talk about what happened now?' Mum asked.

'You know, I actually don't, but it's not because I'm angry any more. It's the opposite. I feel so good that I don't want to spoil it by thinking about all of that stuff again. What I really want is to spend the rest of the day just doing normal things, as if none of it had happened.'

'An excellent idea,' Gran said, putting her arm around me and giving me a squeeze. 'What do you fancy for dinner? How about something special?'

'You know I love everything you cook, Gran. I don't care what it is.' I smiled. It was true. The only time I could ever remember Gran cooking something I didn't like was when she decided that we all needed to detox about five years ago. What followed was a week-long parade of raw vegetables and vegetable juices that had Mum and me sneaking off to our bedrooms to devour secret stashes of chocolate.

'How about roast chicken and vegies followed by baked rice custard with stewed rhubarb?'

I could feel myself salivating. Gran's roast chicken was a culinary masterpiece and rice custard was one of my childhood favourites.

Mum laughed. 'We'll have to do this walk again tomorrow just to make up for all of that!'

'I expect we will. C'mon then, let's get back. If we're going to eat at a reasonable hour I'd better get started.'

After that, every time my treacherous mind wandered to thoughts of Ed or the case I forced myself to think of something else.

By nine o'clock I was full up to the eyeballs and starting to fall asleep. We'd retreated to the lounge room and Mum was watching some forgettable movie on TV. I dragged myself upstairs and crawled under the covers, falling into a sound sleep almost immediately. Killers and ghosts stayed away and I was just me, well fed and in my own bed.

Now that feeling of wellbeing was in tatters. My private world had been invaded. What was I going to do? I was hostage in my own home.

And the killer knew who I was.

A wave of panic swept over me. All the air seemed to have been sucked out of the room. I struggled to draw breath, my chest heaving. I could hear a weird noise; Gran was talking but I couldn't understand what she was saying. I realised the noise was me trying to breathe. The room started to recede and go black. Next thing I knew I was lying on the bed with Gran and Mum standing over me having a debate about whether or not to call an ambulance. I looked at them through half-closed eyes. I couldn't muster the effort to open them properly.

'She's breathing normally now,' said Gran, who was holding my hand.

'I don't know. She's never done that before,' Mum said. She was hovering and every few seconds she tugged on her ear, a sure sign that she was anxious.

'It's OK, Anita. I've managed to calm her down. Her pulse is normal. She just had a panic attack. Nothing unusual about that when you wake up to find a bunch of paparazzi camped on your doorstep.'

I tried to speak. My voice came out as a rusty whisper. I cleared my throat and tried again. 'I'm OK.'

'I think you need to be checked over, Cass, you fainted,' Mum said.

'I just panicked, like Gran said,' I whispered.

'I don't know,' Mum said.

'Could I have a cup of tea please, Mum?' I sounded a bit more normal.

'Anita, why don't you make a pot?'

Mum flapped out of the room and Gran pulled a chair over next to my bed. I propped a couple of pillows behind me. She stroked my hand for a while, saying nothing. I knew what she was up to. She was channelling all her energy into easing my stress. I could feel it seeping away, a warm fuzzy blanket of contentment replacing it. I gently took my hand away. As good as it felt, I knew how much it took out of Gran to do this and with each year that passed it took her longer and longer to recover. I was young and fit and, as crappy as I might be feeling, I was well able to recover without her help.

'You don't need to do that, Gran, I'm feeling better.'

'Are you sure?'

'Yes.' I looked towards the window. I could still hear voices from the front yard.

'You don't have to speak to them. They'll get sick of waiting and go away eventually,' she said.

'I hate feeling like I'm being dissected by everyone who's sitting down to breakfast with their morning paper.'

Gran nodded. There wasn't really anything she could say to make it any better. We sat there saying nothing. Shadow poked his head around the corner of the door and dashed across the room and onto the bed. His tail was up like a bottlebrush and he made a bee-line for the comfort of my lap.

'I think he feels a bit put out by the invasion as well.' Gran chuckled.

I stroked the large black head that was nudging my hand and demanding attention. Mum came back at that point, juggling a tray laden with tea and associated paraphernalia. She smiled as she took in the scene before her.

'You look much better,' she said.

She pushed a few books to one side and plonked the tray on my desk. She was busy pouring when the phone on my night table jangled into life, making us all jump. I reached for it but Gran gently pushed my hand aside.

'It could be the press. I'll get it.'

She answered and listened.

'Hold on.' She put her hand over the phone. 'It's Ed. Do you want to speak to him?'

I thought back to how pissed off I'd been the day before; how bloody-minded he'd been. The man was an emotional Neanderthal. He was the last person I wanted to talk to. 'Not really, but I will.' I grabbed the phone from her. 'Hello?'

'Cass, I'm sorry.'

The apology took me by surprise.

'Sorry for acting like a moron yesterday, or sorry for the fact that I'm splashed all over the morning news?' I snapped.

He sucked in a sharp breath at my surliness. 'Sorry you're in the papers. We don't know how it happened. Sorenson is out for blood. She's announced an internal inquiry to find out who's responsible.'

'None of that helps my situation. I can't even get out of the front door at the moment.'

'Media?'

'What do you think?' I knew I was sounding petulant and childish but I just couldn't help myself.

'Do you want me to send someone to move them on?'

Send someone? He couldn't even be bothered coming himself. That pissed me off even more. 'Don't bother. You and your lot have done enough damage already. I have to go now, goodbye.' I threw the phone down. Mum passed me a cup of tea and we sat there lost in our own thoughts. To me everything felt the same but subtly different. Our small, protected world had been knocked off its axis, spinning out of control in a universe full of unknown threats.

CHAPTER 26

It was nearly dark by the time he got back, which suited him perfectly. The funeral home was in one of the commercial parts of Clifton. There weren't any other houses so there was little chance of anyone seeing him pull up, but you never could tell who would be out and about.

He pulled into the driveway and hit the button for the roller door. The secure garage he'd added to the side of the building was one of the best things he'd done. It meant he could drive a car inside and unload without anyone seeing what he was doing. He turned to Lucy.

'Here we are then, home at last. I hope you like it. Ginny and I have been very happy here.'

A tear trickled out of the corner of Lucy's eye and started to run down the side of her nose.

'Now, don't be silly, Lucy. Tears won't help. You really are very lucky, you know. You're one of the special ones. It's not just anyone who gets to meet Ginny and help us celebrate our anniversary.'

He smiled. He was feeling better than he had in days — full of energy and enthusiasm. Ginny would be delighted with Lucy. She was perfect. He stepped out of the van and did a little dance of pure happiness then went around to the passenger side to unload Lucy. He lifted her out, puffing with the exertion.

'You really are a dead weight aren't you, Lucy?' He giggled.

He carried her inside and took her straight down to the basement. He didn't want to introduce her to Ginny until he had her prepped and ready. He hefted her onto the steel table then fussed around, straightening out her limbs and adjusting her clothes so she was decent. Once he was satisfied, he carefully fastened her wrists and ankles with thick leather straps. Last of all he gagged her and fastened a final strap across her forehead.

He looked into her eyes. They were darting left and right, frantically searching the room. A familiar smell assaulted his nostrils. He glanced away from her face. A dark patch was spreading over her jeans and rivulets of urine were running into the shallow channel that bordered one side of the table. They always peed themselves.

'Just as well this table is built to handle bodily fluids, isn't it?'

He stepped away from her again and came back with a bucket.

He unplugged a hole at the end of the table and let the thin stream of bright yellow fluid trickle into it.

'Peeing is fine but if you can try not to poo I'd appreciate it. The smell makes me nauseous and I am sure you don't want to lie there in a pool of your own faeces. You can stop looking too. There's no way out of here other than the stairs we came down. At the top there's a heavy wooden door with a lock on the outside. You aren't going to be leaving anytime soon.'

He took an IV bag out of a fridge, hooked it onto a stand and wheeled it over. Then he took a needle and tubing out of a set of stainless steel drawers under the table. With infinite care he felt the inside of Lucy's arm for a vein and inserted the needle. He attached the drip and then taped the needle in place. He stepped up to her head and looked into her eyes again.

'I hope that didn't hurt too much. The drip is very important. It's a special mix of fluids and glucose to keep you healthy.'

Tears started to flow out of Lucy's eyes again. A strangled sound came from her mouth as she struggled to breathe.

'Shhhh. It's all right. I think you'd better get some sleep. We don't want your eyes all bloodshot now do we? I was going to introduce you to Ginny tonight but I think it can wait until tomorrow. I could use a good night's sleep myself before we get started.'

He walked over to the fridge again and got out a small vial and a syringe. He drew up some of the drug and then injected it into the IV line.

'This will let you sleep for a good ten hours. Night-night, sleep tight.' He smiled as her eyes fluttered shut.

When he woke up on Sunday morning he was surprised at how late he'd slept — it was nearly noon. He headed downstairs to check on Lucy. The drugs would have worn off ages ago and her drip bag would need changing.

'Morning — no, afternoon, Lucy. Sorry, I overslept. I meant to come and see you much earlier than this. How are you today?'

She tried to scream, the noise stifled by the gag he'd secured across her mouth.

'Now, don't be silly. No one can hear you so there is no point getting all worked up. I'm going to change your drip bag.'

He walked across to the fridge and took out a fresh bag, Lucy's eyes following him as far as the head restraint would allow. She was in a bad way. He'd given her the sedative at about 7 PM. It had worn off in the early hours of the morning, well before first light. She'd been lying there struggling to get free for hours and was bathed in sweat and exhausted. Her wrists were raw and bleeding where she'd struggled against the leather restraints.

He changed the bag and leant over her, staring into her eyes. 'Ginny and I will be down to see you later. I can see you're a bit worked up so I'm going to give you something to relax you.' He took a syringe and vial out of the drawers under the table, drew up the dose and injected it into the drip line. Lucy struggled, trying to resist. He watched her face as her eyes went from wide with fear to unfocused and half closed.

'Good girl, I'll see you again soon.'

HINDSIGHT

He walked back upstairs, feeling energised and ready for a busy day. He opened the front door and grabbed the newspaper sitting on the porch. His stomach rumbled loudly and he smiled to himself. Hunting days always left him feeling famished. While he was hunting he couldn't face the idea of food. He hadn't eaten anything all day yesterday.

He opened the freezer and shuffled through the stack of frozen meals looking for something that took his fancy. Chicken tikka? Sounded good. He plopped it into the microwave and sat down to wait. He unrolled the paper and shook it open.

The headlines screamed out of the page at him. His eyes devoured the story. He sat back, oblivious to the whirring of the microwave and its chirruping to announce his meal was ready. Was it him they were talking about? It had to be. It couldn't be anyone else. But how could they know? Those stupid plodding police would never have worked it out, he'd been too careful. It must have been that woman, the psychic.

He looked back at the paper that he'd dropped in his lap. Cass Lehman. He'd always been wary of psychics — there were plenty of them at the expos. He'd thought they were just ordinary people who were good at reading cues from gullible people but he'd stayed away from them just in case.

So what had this woman seen? What if she saw more? She might see what he looked like, where he worked. The pungent smell of curry was heavy in the air. He shoved his chair back and rushed to the sink, vomiting bile into it. He waited for the wave to pass, then sat down shakily.

He couldn't let one stupid woman ruin everything. He looked at her picture. She didn't look anything special; attractive, if you liked that sort of thing.

He staggered the half-a-dozen steps to the kitchen dresser in the corner and yanked the phone book out of one of the cupboards. Thumping it onto the table he flicked through, searching for her name. There were no listings for Lehman in Jewel Bay. He sat there thinking. What was he going to do?

Something niggled in the back of his mind. He looked back at the paper. There it was! A mention of her living with her mother Anita Lehman and grandmother Gwen Carmichael. He looked through the phone book again and found the listing straight away.

He grabbed the phone off the wall and dialled the number. A woman answered.

'Hello?'

'Hello, can I speak to Cass please?'

'If you're media, she's not taking any calls.'

'Media? No, I'm not media. I'm from the Crime Service in Adelaide. My name is Detective Richardson. Who am I speaking to please?'

'Her mother, Anita Lehman. I'm not sure that she'll want to talk to you either. What do you want?'

Her tone was faintly hostile. That was interesting. Perhaps Cass's relationship with the police wasn't that rosy after all. 'I need to ask her a couple of questions. We're really very grateful for her assistance.' There was a long pause. He started to wonder if she was still there.

'Hello?'

'Yes, I'm here,' she answered. 'I'll see if she wants to talk to you. I'm not making any promises. She wasn't too happy after she spoke to Detective Dyson this morning.'

'Thank you, I appreciate it.' So she'd spoken to the police already. Maybe about the newspaper article. He waited as the silence stretched on, starting to feel nervous. A lot depended on how the next few minutes played out. The hand holding the phone was slippery with sweat.

'Hello?'

'Hello, Cass?' He dropped the tone of his voice a few notches; deep and masculine always seemed to reassure.

'Mum said you're with the Crime Service.'

Straight to the point. 'Yes, I'm Detective Richardson.'

'Were you at the station yesterday? I don't remember you.'

'Yes, but we weren't introduced.'

'Were you the detective in the interview room with Detective Steiner?'

'Yes, that was me.' Why not?

'I thought your voice sounded familiar. You have the wrong man, you know.'

He paused, filing away this piece of information, and smiled to himself. 'Yes, I know.'

'You do?'

'That's why I'm calling.'

'What do you need from me?'

'It's a big imposition, especially on a Sunday, but I was wondering if you might be able to come in and look at some photos of possible suspects?'

'Now?'

'No, this evening. We have a few things to do this afternoon but I can swing by and get you at about six.' He wanted to wait until it was dark, just in case she knew what he looked like. She didn't answer him straight away. 'I'm sorry, you probably have plans …'

'No, no plans. Are you sure it can't wait until tomorrow?'

'We're working around the clock on this one. Your help would be really valuable.'

More silence. He didn't interrupt her. He felt sure she would agree, but something about her tone told him not to push too hard.

'I suppose I could spare an hour. Did you want me to drive in?'

'No, I'll swing by and pick you up.'

'I'll see you at six.'

'Would you like me to come to the door or are you happy if I just honk?' He knew how she would answer.

'Honking is fine.'

He ended the call and sat back in his chair. His neck and shoulders were full of tension. He didn't normally like to wing it like that, but it had gone perfectly. Now he just had to hope that no one else from Fairfield Police contacted her today. He didn't think it was very likely. It was Sunday after all and thanks to her mum he knew she'd already spoken to Detective Dyson.

HINDSIGHT

He went over to the microwave. He took out the curry and dumped it in the bin. He grabbed a banana from the fruit bowl and headed upstairs to the bedroom. He wanted to spend some time with Ginny. She wanted to meet Lucy and he knew she would want to change her clothes and fix her hair and make-up before he took her downstairs. She was very particular about the way she looked. He needed time to get himself ready too. He wanted to wear a wig and make-up when he picked up Cass. He still wasn't convinced he believed in psychics but he couldn't take any chances. She'd said she knew that the police had the wrong person in custody. If she was legit that might mean she knew what he looked like. No harm in being careful.

It was just after 1 PM. With a bit of luck he would pick her up and be back by seven. He'd take the Commodore; it looked more like a police car than the van.

He wouldn't kill her straight away. It might be nice to have an audience other than Ginny for a change, plus he didn't want to run the furnaces twice when he could just as easily do both her and Lucy at the same time. Might as well roast two birds in the one oven. He laughed, delighted with his own wit.

CHAPTER 27

I put the phone back in its cradle and stood there thinking. I should have felt vindicated; pleased that they were acknowledging they had the wrong person, but I still felt pissed off. Maybe because Ed hadn't called me to tell me himself.

What did I expect? One minute I was telling him to get lost and the next minute I was upset that he wasn't calling me. Maybe he was right. Maybe I was a nut-job or bunny-boiler or whatever it was he'd called me.

I gave myself a mental slap. Detective Richardson would be on my doorstep in a few hours. I needed to grab a shower and get changed.

I tried to remember Detective Richardson. When I'd looked in the interview room I was so focused on the man they were interviewing I hardly took any notice of the officers in the room. I couldn't put a face to him. There was something tugging at the back of my mind about our conversation but it was like quicksilver: every time I got close to grabbing the thought it just slid away.

I reluctantly let it go and went into the lounge room to tell Mum and Gran what I was up to. When I opened the door the scene before me was like an elixir. There were the two people who were my whole world, sitting doing the things they always did. Mum was watching one of her favourite shows, a box of chocolates on the side table next to her. Shadow was firmly ensconced on her lap, his extra-large proportions oozing off the edges in pools of inky black fur. Gran was sitting in one of the armchairs reading a book. The familiarity soothed away my angst.

'I have to go out for a while a bit later,' I said. They both looked up.

'Out?' Mum asked.

'Yes, Detective Richardson is going to pick me up and take me back to Fairfield Station to look at some photos of possible suspects.'

'So they've changed their mind about the man in custody then?' Gran asked.

'Yep, seems that way.'

'And it can't wait until tomorrow? You still look so tired.' A worried frown furrowed Mum's brow.

'Apparently they're working around the clock, so no, it can't wait. He's picking me up at about six. It shouldn't take long but just in case it does, don't wait up for me.'

HINDSIGHT

'We'll probably be home after you. We've got bridge tonight,' Mum said.

I smiled, bridge night was just an excuse to get together with a group of old friends to drink wine and exchange gossip.

'Make sure you dress warm, it'll be bitter out there.' Gran was always the one who appeared to worry less, although experience had taught me she was just better at keeping it to herself.

'Don't worry, I'll rug up.'

I threw on jeans and a black polo neck with a heavy green woollen coat and grabbed a black angora scarf and fur-lined leather gloves for good measure. It was overkill, but it made me feel better. The car and the station would be warm but the thought of even a minute in the brutal night air was enough to have me dressing for Arctic conditions.

I loped back downstairs for a quick cup of tea and a snack before I left. If TV cop shows were to be believed then the tea and coffee on offer at the police station would rate somewhere between shoe polish and battery acid. I was sitting at the table about halfway through a sensationally good cuppa and a toasted tomato and cheese sandwich when I heard a horn honking out the front. Why was it that the cup you don't get to finish is always a really good one? Sighing, I chucked the rest down the sink and headed for the front door, yelling goodbyes as I went.

The front door closing made a resounding thud that carried across the thin air. I hurried over to the waiting car and jumped in. The interior light didn't work so I couldn't really see Detective Richardson. He planted his foot and we lurched off while I was still struggling to get my seatbelt on.

'Cold enough for you?'

'Yes, it's freezing out there,' I said. Feeling nervous, I babbled on. 'So when did you decide you had the wrong man in custody?'

He smiled. 'I had my doubts right from the beginning. The man we had just wasn't smart enough to have pulled it off. The guy we're looking for is clever; the police haven't caught him in six years.'

'But it wasn't obvious. You only found two of them. The rest were just missing persons. Do you think the two you found were mistakes?' I asked.

'Mistakes? No, not mistakes. This killer doesn't make mistakes.'

'You sound like you almost admire him.' I forced a laugh.

'I do — this man isn't your typical killer, he's an artist.'

'Uh huh.' I decided to drop the conversation. It hadn't quite gone the way I'd expected. I stared out the window at the black landscape, dark fields and charcoal sky. It was a moonless, starless night, the sky a blank canvas. My mind wandered to thoughts of the work I still had to do. It took me a few minutes to realise that we'd missed the turn to Fairfield and were travelling along the Adelaide road. I sat up and looked across at Detective Richardson.

'You missed the turn.'

'Yes.'

'Didn't you say we were going to Fairfield Station?'

'I did, but I really need to take you somewhere else first.'

The fine hairs on the back of my neck started to prickle.

'Where?'

'To my place.'

'Why would we go to your place?'

'You ask too many questions.'

My heart started to pound. 'Can I see your ID?'

He glanced across at me. It looked like he was smiling.

'Sure, there's a blue box in the glove box. Could you pass it to me? My ID's in there.'

I opened the glove box and spotted the small blue container. It didn't look like something you'd keep ID in. It rattled as I handed it to him. My nervousness grew to fever pitch. I watched him open the blue box with one hand and fumble around inside. He pulled something out.

At that moment we flashed under a brighter street light at an intersection and I caught a glimpse of what he was holding. It was a syringe. Realisation struck me and I sucked in a breath to scream.

He lunged, trying to empty the needle into my leg. I lashed out at his arm, connecting so violently my hand went numb. The syringe flew out of his hand onto the floor. Both of us dived for it.

The car did a wild zig-zag across the road as we struggled, grunting and puffing. A horn blared as a lone oncoming car skidded off the road to avoid our mad projectory. I ground my fingers against the rough carpet on the floor, breaking nails and banging my head on the dashboard. My seatbelt arrested my efforts with violent jerks. My lungs were brutally crushed in the effort to bend over and I could hardly breathe.

He forced the car onto the verge and stamped on the brakes. My head pounded against the dashboard so hard that my eyesight blurred and I could barely regain focus. I took a breath and lunged down again. I felt a rush of pure animal pleasure as my fingers found the syringe. I pricked my fingers but managed to grab it. I sat up, pushing in the plunger to expel whatever was inside.

Panting, my heart pounding and tears running down my face I threw the syringe away and grabbed the door handle. It wouldn't budge. I shook it then looked for the door lock. There wasn't one. Whipping around, I looked at the man next to me, who had gone very still. His face was in shadows still but I knew who he was now. I knew that voice. He'd tried to change it but part of my brain had recognised it on the phone, I'd just been too stupid to realise it.

'What do you want?' I cried.

He shook his head slowly then he lashed out. I felt a blazing pain in my left temple and then there was nothing.

I woke up sick and dizzy. I vomited down the front of myself. My head was throbbing with a relentless pain that started at my

HINDSIGHT

temple and stabbed at my eyeballs. I lifted my head and tried to work out where I was.

I was sitting on a chair. I tried to move my hands and legs and couldn't. My arms were tied behind my back and my ankles were tied together and anchored to the chair. The room I was in was very dark, I could only make out shadows. I strained my ears, trying to hear something but all I could hear was the rasping of my own breath and the rushing of blood in my ears. I struggled against the bonds on my wrists but the effort was too much and everything went black.

When I came to again I wasn't alone. I blinked and realised that he was standing in front of me.

'Hello, Cassandra, glad you could join us.'

'You bastard, let me go!' I screamed.

'That's enough!' He slapped me hard. My head felt like it was going to explode. 'In my house you will show me and my wife some respect!'

His wife? I was so focused on him I hadn't realised there was anyone else in the room. I looked at him; the man from my visions who I'd felt kill three different people. He was about my age, his hair was short and brown and his features were regular. He was Mr Average.

I looked into his eyes. That's where the difference was. There was something wrong about them; too much white showing, not enough blinking. It was hard to pinpoint, but it was enough to make me sick with fear.

'This is my wife, Virginia.'

He stepped to one side. I jerked back so hard my head smacked against the back of the chair and I groaned, a low guttural sound that was part disgust and part animal reaction.

'Say hello!' he yelled.

I tried to swallow. My mouth was bone dry.

'Hello,' I whispered.

'That's better. Ginny darling, this is Cassandra, the one I was telling you about.'

He walked over to the thing that was propped up in the chair. I forced my eyes back to it — the corpse of a woman. The skin was stretched and dry, pulled tight over the bones. The lips were drawn back over the teeth in a bizarre imitation of a smile. Her long blonde hair looked so brittle and dry it would snap if you touched it. Where the eyes should have been there were empty, black holes.

'Isn't she lovely? I fell in love with her the first time I saw her, you know. I knew we were meant to be together.'

'Lovely,' I croaked.

'The only problem is, she can't see. Every year we have a special celebration for our anniversary and I get her a new set of eyes so that we can have a few days where we can look at each other. Don't you think that's romantic?'

'Yes.'

'I'm glad you think so because that will make it easier for you to understand why I can't let you ruin it for us.'

'I understand, really. I promise I won't tell anyone. I don't even know your name or where we are. You could just blindfold me and drive me somewhere.' The words tumbled out of my mouth and tears started to run down my face. 'Please, let me go.'

He smiled. 'My name is Brian. You are in Jenson's Funeral Home and I am afraid that you won't be going anywhere. You can stay and participate in our anniversary celebrations tomorrow. We don't normally have guests and Ginny tells me that she would enjoy your company for a little while.'

'But I don't have green eyes,' I said desperately.

He looked at me in surprise. 'You know?'

'Yes.'

'Do the police know?'

'Yes,' I whispered.

He paused. 'Don't worry about your eyes. You're right, they're not the right colour. You can watch me take the eyes from our other guest.' He pointed behind me.

I struggled to look around but I was tied so tightly to the chair I couldn't turn my head far enough to see what he was talking about.

Brian walked over and shoved my chair around. There, strapped to a stainless steel table, was the motionless body of a woman.

'Oh God, is she dead?' I whispered.

'Dead? Of course not. The eyes have to be fresh. She's sedated, that's all, just like you would've been if you hadn't knocked the needle out of my hand. That wasn't very nice, you know.'

I stared at him. He was worried that I wasn't being nice? Any vestige of hope I had was snuffed out and I dropped my head, feeling weary and defeated.

'That's right, you rest. I want you to be ready for tomorrow. It's going to be a big day.' He forced a gag into my mouth, tying it roughly behind my head. Turning his back on me he went over to the corpse in the chair and carefully picked it up before heading up the stairs. He turned out the light when he got to the top and shut the door hard behind him.

I sat there in the dark feeling small, alone and more afraid than I'd ever felt in my life. I strained my ears, trying to hear the sound of the other girl breathing. Tomorrow I was going to see her have her eyes cut out. Then he would kill both of us. A strangled cry exploded from me and I gave in; huge wracking sobs shaking me as I cried into the darkness.

CHAPTER 28

Ed woke up early Monday morning feeling jangled. The dream he'd been having was still with him. He was searching for Cass. He could hear her calling him and he kept following the sound of her voice but every time he thought he was close the voice slipped away again.

Finally he saw a woman standing at the top of a cliff. The wind was whipping her hair around her shoulders and she had her back to him. He called Cass's name but she didn't turn around so he walked up behind her. In the water a ship had run aground. He grabbed the woman by the shoulder, telling her they had to get help for the people in the water. 'What people?' she asked and then turned around. He pulled back in shock. Instead of Cass's face it was Susan's, but where her eyes should have been there were gaping black holes.

Ed tried to banish the images from his mind. He'd had too much time to think, that was the problem. The weekend had been long and tedious. After he'd dropped Cass off on Saturday he'd gone back to the station and wandered around, trying to find something to do that made him look busy but let him keep an eye on what was going on. He resorted to checking the other stallholders that he and Phil had cross-matched earlier in the day. He looked up their addresses, registered vehicles and any other information he could find. None of them looked half as promising as the guy they had in the interview room. Still, Cass had been so certain he wasn't their guy.

By four o'clock he was finished and was starting to feel like a spare prick at a party. Only the guy with the sealed juvie record looked even slightly promising. His address was listed as a funeral home in Clifton. The business had a van and a couple of hearses registered to it but there was nothing unusual about that. He had no convictions as an adult and without knowing what he'd done as a minor there was no reason to suspect him.

Having run out of reasons to hang around he'd headed home and spent Saturday night and Sunday resisting the urge to call Phil every five minutes. The only other person he'd spoken to was Cass and that had been over in less than thirty seconds. It was time to call her again and try to rebuild burnt bridges.

It was Anita. 'Hello?'

'Hello Mrs Lehman, it's Ed Dyson.'

There was a slight pause.

'Yes, Ed, what do you want?' Her voice was pleasant enough but he could hear an underlying edge.

'I just wanted to speak to Cass. I feel bad about everything.'

'Cass will come around, but she was disappointed that it was that other detective that called instead of you.'

'Other detective?'

'Yes, to ask her to come and look at pictures of possible suspects after you realised the man you had wasn't the right one.'

Ed was more than a bit surprised. He was also annoyed that he was finding out third hand that the suspect had been released. He knew he was off the case but surely Phil could've told him they'd kicked the suspect loose?

'Was it Detective Steiner?'

'No, it was one of those CS detectives, let me think, he did tell me his name …'

'Detective Byrnes or Detective Rawlinson?'

'No, neither of those, um, let me think a bit … Richards? No … Richardson! That's it! Detective Richardson.'

Who the hell was Richardson?

'You're sure it wasn't Rawlinson?'

'No, it was definitely Richardson. Why?'

'Did she go to the station?'

'Yes, he came and picked her up last night.'

'What did he look like?'

'Look like? You don't know him?' Worry was creeping into her voice.

'No, I wasn't in yesterday. Did you meet him?'

'He didn't come inside, he tooted and Cass ran out to the car.'

'Can you go and get Cass for me please?' The knot in his belly had turned into a fist. He was trying not to worry Anita but he was gripping the phone so hard that his knuckles popped.

'I think she's still asleep but I'll go and see.' She put the phone down with a clunk and he waited, pacing. After a lifetime she picked up the receiver again.

'Ed, she's not there! Her bed hasn't been slept in.' She was breathing fast and he could hear the tears in her voice.

The bottom dropped out of his world. He stood there trying to comprehend what was happening. He forced himself to talk to the woman crying on the other end of the phone.

'Anita? I need you to keep it together. I'm going straight into the station now. She's probably still there. I'll ring you as soon as I get there. It's only five minutes from my place.'

He grabbed his mobile phone and keys and ran for the door. Swearing in frustration, he threw himself into his car and drove to the station at a manic pace, screeching to a stop on the double yellow lines outside the front door. He ran into the squad room. As luck would have it the only person in was Samuels.

'Is Phil in?'

'Not yet.'

'Sorenson?'

'Same deal.'

'The CS guys?'

'Ditto.'

'Fuck!'

'Something I can help with?' Curiosity emanated from his every fibre.

'Was there a Detective Richardson from CS here yesterday?'

'Detective Richardson? Not that I know of. I only saw the two of them, Byrnes and Rawlinson.'

'Did they kick loose the suspect?'

'I don't think I'm supposed to tell you anything about the case.' Samuels smiled as he said it, enjoying the feeling of power, however small.

'Don't be a prick, Samuels, I need to know.' The fierceness of Ed's response wiped the smile off Samuels's face.

'They let him go yesterday.'

'Did Cass come back last night?'

'The psychic woman?'

'Yes!'

'Not that I know of. Check the visitor log.'

'I will.' Why hadn't he thought of that? He had to get himself together. He was no use to anyone if he was running around in a blind panic.

Ed jogged down the stairs to the front foyer. He swiped into the secured area and grabbed the visitor log. Heart pounding he scanned the entries; nothing. He turned and ran to the car, dialling the Lehman house as he ran. Anita answered on the first ring.

'Hello?'

'Anita, it's me. She's not at the station.'

'Where is she then? Oh God, what if —' Her voice shredded his heart.

'Shhh, I'm going to find her. I'm not going to let anything happen to her. I'm on my way to your place now. Think back to yesterday, even the smallest detail could be important.'

The drive to Cass's house felt eternal. He battled with his inner demons the entire way; thinking about what might be happening to Cass if the killer had her, then beating back the thoughts and trying to stay positive. He had to stay positive. He couldn't let her or her family down.

It shocked him to realise that in the few short days he'd known her he'd started to feel close to her, responsible for her. He liked her and her family. He wanted time to get to know her better. The thought that she might be snatched away by the same person who had taken Susan from him flooded him with a red tide of rage so powerful that he could barely focus on the road.

He screeched into the driveway and leapt out of the car. Before he'd covered the few short steps to the front door, Gwen threw it open and rushed towards him. Her face was pale and tear-streaked. For the first time since Ed had met her she actually looked her age. She threw her arms around him and cried on his shoulder. Her grief stopped him in his tracks and he stood there, helplessly patting her back until she calmed down enough to look up at him.

'I'm sorry, I just can't believe it. Please, Ed, you have to find her. She's our whole world.'

'I know, I'm sorry.'

'Come inside, we'll tell you what we can.'

He followed her inside and into the kitchen. Anita was sitting at the table, gazing sightlessly into a cup of tea. She didn't look that different but her immobility told the story. Every time he'd visited she'd been either buzzing around the kitchen or off doing something else. Not once had he seen her sitting so still. It was like someone had switched off a bright light.

'Mrs Lehman, I'm so sorry,' he said quietly.

'It's Anita,' she said without emotion. 'Mrs Lehman makes me feel ancient.'

Ed sat at the table and took her hand. 'I'm going to find her.'

Anita dropped her head and stroked his hand without speaking. After a couple of seconds her grip tightened, she placed her other hand over the top and went rigid with concentration. Ed sat there, hardly daring to breathe. If she was having a vision he hoped to hell it was a good one. Finally she looked up. Her eyes were slightly glazed but she focused on his face quickly enough. He let out a long breath that he didn't realise he'd been holding.

'I saw flames.'

'A fire?'

'No, it was more like a combustion heater. No, that's not right either.' She closed her eyes and frowned. 'It's a furnace. The place where Cass is has a furnace. You're going to go there and find her.'

'Did you see anything else?'

She thought hard, closing her eyes again.

'There were containers on a shelf, lots of them.'

'What sort of containers?'

'They were odd, some were metal. They were all pretty fancy.'

'Were they urns? Was it a funeral home?' Ed felt a flicker of hope. The guy with the juvie record. It had to be him.

'Could be. I don't get complete pictures, just glimpses. I don't see how that helps you though. There must be hundreds of funeral homes out there.'

'Yes but only one where the guy who owns it also works at expos.'

'What?'

'I'll explain later. I know where Cass is. The sooner I get there the better.' He jumped up and was halfway to the door before Anita's voice stopped him.

'Wait!'

He turned and looked at her.

'It's dangerous. I saw you in pain. You need to be vigilant. Cass is depending on you.'

He nodded, not wanting to think about the risk to himself. All that mattered was finding Cass before it was too late. He ran out of the house and threw himself back into his car. He remembered the name of the funeral home. He dialled Phil's number as he started to drive.

Phil answered on the second ring. 'Wassup?'

'He's got Cass, Phil. It's the guy with the juvie record. I can't explain it now. I'm on my way to Jenson's Funeral Home in Clifton.'

'Shit! Fuck, Ed, even if you're right you can't go there by yourself.'

'I'm not waiting for backup. If I wait it might be too late. Call Sorenson.'

'She'd tell you to wait. Shit, this guy's fucked up. You can't go in alone.'

'Just get there as soon as you can.' He hung up.

Ten minutes later the scanner in his car chirruped into life. He expected it to be Fairfield but it was Noarlunga putting out a call. A young woman from Willunga hadn't shown up for work. She was last seen at a medieval fair on the Saturday. Ed tried to work out what it might mean. Was it possible that the killer had taken another vic as well? Surely not, just taking Cass would have kept him busy. The girl would probably turn up. Still, he didn't like it. He should call Phil and tell her. He grabbed his phone and dialled. It beeped in his ear; no signal, he was in a black spot. It would have to wait.

He turned his attention back to the road ahead, counting every kilometre that passed. *Hold on, Cass*, he pleaded silently, *I need you to be strong and survive.*

CHAPTER 29

I spent the night alternating between despair and bitter anger. My wrists and ankles were raw and bleeding from struggling. The one small victory I'd had was to force the gag out of my mouth with my tongue and teeth and by worrying it on my shoulder. There was something to be said for slippery, clean hair.

Every so often I called out softly to the girl lying on the table. I wanted her to know she wasn't alone; small comfort that must have been, given that I couldn't do anything to help her. I cried so much that I was hoarse and every blink of my eyelids felt like sandpaper. I lost track of time. I was exhausted, my head was pounding and the stabbing pain behind my eyes was excruciating.

Despite everything, I eventually fell asleep. I don't know how long I was out but the next thing I knew a loud noise woke me and I lifted my head, groaning at the pain. Then a different type of pain hit me. My bladder was so full I would wet my pants if I didn't use the toilet soon.

'Good morning, Cassandra. I see you've managed to remove your gag. That was naughty of you.'

His voice brought all the events of the night rushing back.

'Don't make me remind you of your manners again.' He walked around in front of me and smiled. There was no mirth in it.

'Good morning,' I mumbled.

'That's better, manners are important. If you are going to have breakfast with me and Ginny, I expect you to be on your best behaviour.'

'Can I use the toilet?'

'What do we say?'

I recognised the tone. It was the one every parent used with their toddler. It was so surreal I could hardly comprehend it. Here was a man who had killed so many women, worrying about whether or not I said please.

'Please?' I whispered.

'Yes, you may. I'm going to undo your wrists and ankles but before I do I want you to understand something. How I treat you and Lucy is in your hands. If you try to run away, if you try to hurt either me or Ginny, I will kill you both as slowly and painfully as I can. Understand?'

'Yes.'

'Good.'

HINDSIGHT

He bent down to undo the ties around my ankles. He walked around behind me and did the same with my wrists. The rope was stuck to my flesh and as it came away it left raw, oozing wounds. Trying to flex my hands or feet caused sharp stabbing pins and needles. I struggled out of the chair. He pushed me in the direction of the stairs. I glanced over at Lucy. I'd been wondering why the effects of the drugs hadn't worn off, now I could see. He had her hooked up to a drip. She was lying there, staring sightlessly at the ceiling. I hoped she wasn't aware of what was happening to her.

I stumbled the short distance to the stairs. I could see the room better now that I was standing. It was a basement. The steel table with Lucy was in the middle of the room. The wall on the right had a large metal door and some kind of electronic control panel with gauges and buttons.

He made an impatient noise and nudged me to keep walking. I recoiled from the contact and moved slowly forward. Feeling still hadn't returned to my feet and I felt like I was walking on blocks of cold meat. I slowly made my way up the stairs. Eventually I made it and I pushed the door open and stepped into a kitchen.

'Toilet is through that door. Remember, don't try anything silly. There's no way out of here. All the doors are deadlocked and the windows have security bars on them.'

I shuffled over to the door he'd pointed to and for a few minutes all I could focus on was the blessed relief. That done, I looked around the small cubicle; it had one small window, with bars on the outside. That was it. Taking a deep breath I stepped out. He was waiting for me, standing casually by the kitchen table in the centre of the room. On the table was a neat pile of clothes, a hairbrush, a cosmetic bag and a towel.

'Ginny doesn't get much female company so I want you to look your best. Through that door is a bathroom. Go shower and change. By the time you're finished, breakfast will be ready. Don't take too long please. I don't want to keep Ginny waiting. It's our anniversary, and we have a big day planned.' He laughed.

That laugh sent a fresh batch of chills knifing down my back as I remembered the other times that I'd heard it: when he was killing Janet, when he was taunting old Mick. How could such a monster walk around looking so normal? There should have been something about him that gave some hint about the twisted soulless thing beneath his skin.

I walked over to the table, picked up the pile and went into the bathroom without speaking. Like the toilet there was no lock on the door. The room was bare and utilitarian; plain white tiles on the walls and floor, very basic sanitary ware and cheap fittings. There was a small white vanity unit with one cupboard and three drawers. A glimmer of hope flickered as I looked at it. I turned on the shower and spent a few quick minutes looking through it. I was desperately hoping there would be something I could use as a weapon. My hopes faded quickly. There was nothing: no razors, no scissors.

The only thing I spotted was a small bottle of what I thought were sleeping pills. I stashed them under the pile of clothes. Just maybe I would get the chance to slip some into his breakfast.

HINDSIGHT

The chances were slim but it was better than nothing. I quickly showered and dressed in the clothes he'd given me, all except for the underwear — I refused to wear the underwear he'd placed in the pile. Just wearing the clothes was bad enough. They made my skin crawl. Were they a dead woman's clothes? I shuddered at the thought then folded my old clothes and put them in a neat pile next to the door.

I took five capsules out of the bottle I'd found. Working quickly in case he came in, I took a piece of toilet paper, opened each and tipped its contents into the centre of the paper and then carefully folded it and slipped it inside my bra. I sealed the capsules again and put them back in the bottle and replaced it where I'd found it. My heart was thundering in my chest and I was so nervous I could hardly stop my hands from shaking. I opened the door and stepped back into the kitchen. I stopped dead, arrested by the scene before me.

Brian was standing at the stove, cooking what looked like pancakes. Three places were set at the table and seated in one of the chairs was the macabre figure he called his wife. It was even more horrific in the bright, morning light. The face was a death mask, lips drawn back over clenched teeth, skin yellowed with age and the flesh beneath it wasted away so that the outline of the skull was clearly visible. It was the gaping holes where the eyes should have been that riveted my gaze. I didn't want to look but I couldn't look away.

'Say good morning, Cassandra,' he said.
'Good morning,' I whispered.

'Ginny has been looking forward to you joining us for breakfast. I hope you aren't going to disappoint her?' The quiet menace in his voice made me shiver.

'No, no, I won't.'

'Sit down.'

I tore my eyes away from Ginny and sat at the table. I surveyed what was in front of me. He'd placed three glasses of orange juice on the table. My heart started to pound. He turned around and looked at me.

'You chat among yourselves. I'm nearly done here.'

I battled down my feelings of revulsion and tried to think of something to say. He was watching me, waiting to see if I was going to do what he wanted. I tried to swallow.

'So, Ginny, tell me how you and Brian first met.' My voice sounded strange in my ears, hollow and high-pitched.

He smiled and turned back to the stove. He started to talk as he went back to cooking the pancakes, telling me about how Ginny had moved in across the road from him and how it had been love at first sight. While he was distracted I quickly took the folded paper from inside my bra and with shaking fingers I emptied its contents into the glass in front of his chair. I was expecting the powder to dissolve into the juice straight away but it didn't, it just sat there, floating on top, stark white against the bright orange.

He turned around at that moment and I forced my eyes away from the juice, hoping he wouldn't notice. Thankfully he was still busy telling me about his and Ginny's whirlwind romance as he

HINDSIGHT

dished out the pancakes; he didn't look at the juice. I risked a quick glance at it and to my relief the powder had disappeared, leaving some froth on the top, hopefully not enough for him to notice.

'I hope you're hungry. We don't have company very often so I went a bit overboard.' He smiled at me. I realised he was waiting for me to say something.

'I'm hungry,' I said, hoping the lie would satisfy him.

He sat down and to my complete astonishment he bowed his head and started to say grace. My mouth dropped open in total disbelief. He must have felt my stare because he looked up and glared at me until I dropped my head.

'Dear Lord, thank you for the blessings you bestow on us, thank you for bringing us our guest today and thank you for the food we are about to receive, Amen.'

He reached for his glass. I held my breath, willing him to drink it all down; hoping he wouldn't notice the froth sitting on top or realise there was something wrong with it. He took a sip and then screwed up his face in disgust. He held the glass up to his nose and sniffed. A wave of panic hit me. I gripped the edge of the table. Should I try to run for it? He looked at me, frowning.

'I must apologise, Cassandra, the juice isn't right, it must have turned. Can I get you something else to drink? Water, perhaps?'

'A glass of water would be good, thank you.' I actually meant it. My mouth was so dry it felt raw. I was dizzy. He got up, cleared the juice away then fetched three glasses of water, placing them on the table. Then he sat back down and started to eat. I sat there, motionless, partly overcome with relief, partly numb from the stress.

'You're not eating.'

'Sorry,' I mumbled. Raising my arms took supreme effort but I managed it. I grabbed the water and drank half of it down in one draught. Then I turned to the plate of pancakes in front of me. The thought of eating was totally repugnant but what choice did I have? I took a mouthful and forced myself to chew and swallow. He watched me expectantly. Oh God, he's waiting for praise.

'Very nice,' I said. In truth I could have been eating cardboard. All I was concerned with was keeping up the charade, hoping that with enough time a miracle would happen and someone would find me, find us. My mind wandered back to the girl downstairs. I hoped she was still alive.

'So tell me, did your mother know you were a prophetess when she called you Cassandra? Surely it can't be a coincidence?'

'No, it's not a coincidence.' The truth was that when Mum chose the name, she chose it thinking there was little chance of my having precognitive talents like she did. Of course Mum's knowledge of ancient Greek mythology was crap and the ancient Cassandra could see both the past and the future. She was a terribly tragic figure; kidnapped and taken to a foreign country only to be murdered. The name fitted my talent and at the moment I couldn't help thinking the bit about being tragic fitted pretty well too.

'I guess you didn't foresee your fate, did you, Cassandra?' He sniggered.

His laugh made my skin crawl. He repulsed me. I gagged on the piece of pancake in my mouth. His smile turned to a frown.

'Tell me about your gift. How was it that you managed to help the police put it all together?'

'I really don't like to talk about it,' I said. I couldn't bear the thought of revealing even one small detail about my personal life to him.

'You're not very good company are you, Cassandra?' His mirth evaporated. 'I don't see any point in continuing this if you're not going to make an effort.' He pushed his chair back and stood up. He started to snatch plates up off the table, dumping them in the sink. I quickly finished my water. He snatched the glass out of my hand, making me recoil from his touch.

He turned to the thing he called Ginny. 'I'm sorry, darling. I know you don't like it when I lose my temper but I think it's best if we just get on with things. Our guest doesn't appreciate our efforts.'

I sat there trying to work out what to do. If I tried to placate him I could just make things worse. I didn't know what getting 'on with things' meant but I didn't think it was going to be good for me or the girl downstairs.

Instinct got the better of me and I jumped out of my chair. I dashed for the only door I could reach and tried to wrench it open. It was locked. Before I could turn around he was behind me. He grabbed me by the hair and yanked my head back, making me squeal.

'That was very stupid, Cassandra. Now I have no choice. I have to tie you up again.' He grabbed one of my arms and twisted it behind my back. Tears welled in my eyes. Keeping hold of my hair, he walked me back towards the door to the basement.

'I'm sorry. I panicked. I won't do it again. Please don't tie me up,' I pleaded.

'It's too late for sorry. You had one chance and you blew it.'

'Please, Brian, Ginny doesn't want you to hurt me,' I begged.

'Don't pretend you know Virginia!' he roared. 'Only I know what she wants!' He yanked my hair again, so hard that I yelped.

He marched me down the stairs to the basement and forced me back into the chair I'd spent the night in. I tried to get up and away from him but he twisted my arm with such savagery that I thought I heard something snap. The agony of it sucked the breath out of me. I sank into the chair, sobbing with pain and frustration.

'Have you forgotten what I told you? If you make this difficult I will make your death and hers as painful as I can.'

I had barely glanced at the prone figure on the table I was so intent on my own struggle and the pain he was inflicting on me. I looked over at her now. Her skin looked like wax it was so white. *Hang on.*

He left me sitting there and went back upstairs. I tested the rope around my ankles and wrists. It was rock solid. Every movement of my left arm was agony. The pain radiated from my shoulder, down my arm and across my back. My fingers were tingling and starting to go numb. I was half gasping, half whimpering with the effort and tears of frustration were running down my face.

HINDSIGHT

I didn't want to die. I didn't want to watch that poor girl die. This was not how my life was supposed to end; surely Mum would have seen something when she looked at my future?

I heard the door open again and his footfall on the stairs. I refused to turn and look at him. His face was already imprinted on my mind and I was afraid that even if I managed to survive I would never be able to shut my eyes again without seeing it.

He walked past me carrying Ginny in his arms and gently lowered her into the chair next to the desk. He wheeled it over so it was next to the surgical table and just out of my line of sight. Then he walked back to me. Every part of me tensed. He grabbed my chair and wrenched it around so I had full view of the table. Then he walked back over to where Ginny was and took one of her hands in his.

'Are you ready darling? It's so exciting isn't it? I can't wait for you to be able to look at me again.' He smiled tenderly at her and stroked what used to be her cheek.

Abruptly he turned and stepped over to the table with Lucy on it. He looked at her, checked her pulse and checked the drip. Satisfied, he went over to one of the cabinets against the wall and started placing instruments on a metal tray.

'Stop!' I yelled 'Please, don't hurt her.'

He ignored me, methodically placing things on the tray. Tears were flooding down my face again. He was going to kill her and take her eyes right in front of me and there was nothing I could do to stop him.

'Stop it! You can't do this! Ginny is dead. She doesn't need eyes!' I screamed. I yanked against the ropes, ignoring the pain, desperate to try to just do something to stop him. 'Help! Someone help us! Please!'

He opened a drawer and pulled out some bandages. He walked over to me and grabbed me roughly by the jaw. His hand moved in front of my face and I lunged forward and bit down hard. He yelled in pain and tried to yank his hand back. I bit down harder and tasted blood. He swung at me and his fist smacked into my jaw with a crack. With angry grunts, he forced my mouth open and pushed a roll of bandage inside, then with swift motions he wrapped another bandage around my head and over my mouth, tying it hard and tight.

Satisfied, he walked back to the table. He carefully disinfected and bandaged his hand then he added a couple more things to the tray. He snapped on a pair of gloves and picked up a scalpel off the tray. Leaning over the girl he smiled.

'Hello, Lucy. I'm sorry, but this might hurt a bit. I hope you understand though, your eyes are going to good use. Ginny and I are very grateful, aren't we, darling?'

The blow to my head had stunned me and I felt like I was watching everything down a tunnel. The edges of the picture started to go fuzzy and black. A single thought flashed through my mind — *Oh God he's really taking her eyes while she's still alive* — and then mercifully, I passed out.

CHAPTER 30

Ed pulled up in front of the funeral home and sat in the car, looking at the building. He didn't like what he saw; bars on every window. The front door had multiple locks on it and the only other way in was through a roller garage door that was securely fastened. High fencing blocked access down the other side of the building. The only option was to go barging through the front door. He would try knocking but if no one answered, Ed was going to have to try to kick it down. The problem was if he kicked in the door his element of surprise would be blown. If the killer was inside and he had Cass … He checked his phone. The signal was back. He rang Phil. She answered on the first ring.

'What the fuck, Ed? I've been trying to call you. We're nearly there.'

'How long?'

'Ten minutes.'

'Too long. It might be too late. I'm going in.'

'Don't do it, man! Just wait!'

He hung up and turned off his phone again. Sucking in a deep breath he felt under his jacket for his gun, touching it for reassurance. He could end up getting both of them killed but he would never forgive himself if she died while he was waiting. He got out of the car. Closing the door softly, he looked at the front of the building again. There was no sign of any cameras. He took the direct approach and walked straight up to the front door trying to look casual. If the killer was watching he could always hope that he didn't recognise him as a police officer and think he was a customer.

He was about to press the bell when he heard it, the unmistakable sound of a woman screaming. Adrenaline kicked in and he threw himself against the door, kicking it savagely. His first kick rattled the door in its frame but it was solid timber and the locks were strong. He kicked again and again, grunting with the effort. The timber around the locks started to splinter and after a few more kicks the door flew open, banging into the wall. He pulled his gun and rushed inside, looking around for any movement and straining to hear anything that might tell him where she was. Silence greeted him and that frightened him more than the screams.

He headed deeper into the building, pausing at each doorway to throw it open and quickly look inside. He found a viewing room, an office and the room where the bodies were prepared and stored. He thought about checking each of the stainless steel drawers that lined the walls but decided the chances of Cass being alive and in one of those were remote.

He kept going, finding himself in a small kitchen at the back of the building. To the left was a short hallway that led to stairs to an upper level. He stopped to listen again. He thought he heard a faint scraping sound from behind one of the doors off the kitchen. He went his way towards it, trying to calm his breathing and make as little noise as he possibly could. He grabbed the handle and turned it slowly, easing the door open. He found a set of stairs that disappeared into a basement. Cautiously, his heart hammering in his chest, he stepped onto the landing and peered into the room below.

The sight that greeted him made him stop in shock. The first thing he saw was the body of a young woman strapped to a surgical steel table. One of her eyes was missing and blood was running down her face. With a lurch that was part relief, part despair, he realised that it wasn't Cass but another girl.

The next thing he saw was Cass. She was strapped to a chair and her head was slumped forwards. He could see bruising on one side of her face and blood in her hair. Her hands were tied behind her and there was more blood oozing from underneath the rope. He couldn't tell if she was alive or not. Fury swept over him. Where was the son-of-a-bitch who had done this?

He scanned the rest of the room and that was when he saw the final atrocity, the one that took his breath away. There, seated in the back corner of the room, partly in the shadows, was the corpse of a woman. Long blonde hair fell around what used to be a face but was now barely more than a skull with petrified flesh stretched over it. He gagged violently. *Susan? Oh God, it's Susan!*

He ran down the stairs and towards the corpse. He had to see for himself. Was it her? What had he done to her? He was halfway across the basement when a blow to his head sent him reeling. Half turning as he stumbled, he finally saw the man who had killed Susan, the man who had killed Janet Hodgson and pushed Old Mick in front of a truck. Rage took over and he raised his gun, his only thought was that this thing didn't deserve to live.

The killer struck him again, landing a blow on his arm with what looked like a length of steel pipe. He heard the bone crack and his gun went flying out of his hand. Yelling in pain and anger, Ed made a grab for him.

'You piece of shit, you killed my wife and now you have her sitting there like some freak show exhibit? I'm going to kill you!' Ed swung at him again but the punch missed its target and glanced off the man's shoulder.

The bastard was too quick. He dodged out of reach and rained more blows on Ed's head and shoulders. Dazed, Ed sank to his knees. The killer lashed at him with his other hand and Ed felt a sharp pain as a blade sliced into his neck. Gasping, he grabbed at the wound and felt blood running through his fingers.

The killer bent over him and sneered into his face. 'Wife? She's not your wife. That's Virginia, *my* wife. Your wife was a piece of rubbish. I took her eyes and threw her body into the furnace. She was nothing.'

HINDSIGHT

The last thought Ed had before the killer finally knocked him out was that he'd failed again; failed Susan, failed Cass and the woman on the table, and failed himself. The eyeless face of the corpse swam in front of his eyes and then receded into darkness.

He didn't know how long he was out of it but the next thing he knew he was lying on the floor struggling to open his eyes and focus. His vision was blurry. His head was splitting and he couldn't move. He felt so weak. He tried to lift his arm but it felt like someone had pumped lead into his veins. He concentrated on trying to clear his vision. If he could see where the killer was maybe he could bide his time and recover some strength.

He blinked a few times then looked around the room again. Images swam and then slowly came into focus. The killer was standing over at the table, bending over the woman who was lying on it, only it wasn't the same woman. With a jolt he realised it was now Cass lying on the table. Was he dreaming this? No, the pain was real. The bastard really did have Cass on the table. What was he doing to her? He tried to move again but he seemed to have lost all control over his limbs.

With despair, he watched as the killer worked on Cass. He'd removed the ropes and gag and he was tethering her to the table with leather straps. When he was finished he turned away and walked over to a cabinet against the wall. As the killer turned away, Ed thought he saw Cass move slightly. Was she still alive? Please God. If they could hang on, Phil would turn up with help.

Then it happened. Cass went stiff and arched her back. Tipping her head back she let out a scream that turned his bowels to water. The killer whipped around. His eyes were wide with shock. She screamed again, a long guttural sound like nothing Ed had ever heard.

'Stop that!' the killer yelled. 'Stop it right now!'

Cass ignored him — or more likely didn't hear him — because the screams just kept coming, each one as painful as the last. The killer stood there, stunned to immobility for a few more seconds before striding over to her and grabbing her shoulders. The instant he touched her, he froze. His entire body went rigid and Ed, who had a clear view of his face, watched as his expression turned from anger to a mask of pure terror. His eyes bulged and strange gargling sounds came out of his mouth, which was stretched wide in a silent imitation of Cass.

She was still screaming but with each scream her voice got weaker and weaker. Listening to her and not being able to help was like nothing Ed had ever experienced before. It destroyed what was left of his self-control and tears started to run down his face. He watched the macabre display before him, wondering if it would ever end. Finally Cass went silent and the killer let go of her. He sank to his knees and curled into a ball, rocking backwards and forwards and making strange gasping noises. Ed realised he was crying before oblivion swept over him again.

CHAPTER 31

When I woke up it was from what felt like an endless dream. In the first part of the dream I'd been running through thick fog. I was terrified of something and desperate to find my way to safety, but every time I thought I was about to escape, the mist stretched out its fingers and wrapped itself around me again and so I had to keep running. That dream was replaced by another where I kept waking up and doing all the things I do in the morning only to find that I was only dreaming being awake.

When I finally opened my eyes for real it wasn't to get up and go through my morning routine. I blinked a few times, confused and dazzled by the stark whiteness that assaulted my eyes. I couldn't work out where I was. Why wasn't I at home? I turned my head and realised I was hooked up to tubes and a drip. The drip made me panicky for some reason and I tried to reach over and pull it out of my arm.

'Cass, Cass, darling, shhh, it's all right. It's Mum. You're fine. You're in hospital.'

I tried to push the oxygen mask away from my face but I couldn't seem to raise my arm to do it. I was so tired. Mum realised what I wanted and gently eased the mask down so I could talk.

'What happened? Why am I here?'

'Don't worry about that. You were injured, you're going to be fine though. You just need to rest.'

I knew there was something I needed to remember but it kept slipping out of my grasp. The effort was too much. I fell asleep again, only this time the dreams were of faces with no eyes.

I woke up sweating with my heart pounding. I looked around the room. Gran was sitting by my bed. She was holding my hand and the lines on her face told the story: she'd been sitting there channelling all her energy into me. The oxygen mask was gone but the drip was still there.

'What's wrong with me, Gran?' I asked.

She patted my hand gently and answered my question with one of her own.

'What's the last thing you remember?'

My brain felt fuzzy and reluctant. 'I remember going for a walk with you and Mum and then we had a really good dinner.'

'Yes, what happened after that?'

'I don't remember.'

'Try, sweetheart.'

HINDSIGHT

'Can't you tell me?'

'The doctor's asked us not to. He thinks it's better if you remember by yourself.'

For some reason that upset me, and I started to cry. Gran sat there and cried with me. I knew something terrible had happened and I was scared of what it would be. I fell asleep again after a few minutes and the next time I woke I was by myself. I felt stronger and some of the fog had gone. I looked around. The room was quiet. It looked out over a courtyard with a few plants and some benches. It was daytime. Pale sunlight streamed in through the window. I lay there, wondering how long I'd been in hospital and what hospital I was in. I thought back to the conversation I'd had with Gran. I remembered dinner. What happened the next day?

An image of a newspaper flashed through my mind. The words 'serial killer' leapt off the page. I sat up. Memories started to flood into my mind. I remembered a phone call from Ed then another phone call later in the day. Oh God! Then there was the car, struggling with him, the basement, Ginny and the girl. Oh my God, that poor girl! What had happened to her? Finally there was the moment I woke up on the table. I started to sob.

He'd put me on the table where he'd killed all the other women; there were three of them. Their death experiences hadn't hit me one at a time, they'd all come at once, a chorus of suffering. The pain and anguish had been unbearable. I remembered screaming in agony and fear.

My breathing was coming in short gasps and panic started to overwhelm me. I couldn't breathe. I reached over and pushed the call button hooked over my bed. A nurse poked her head in a minute later. By then my breathing was so tortured I was starting to see black spots in front of my eyes. The nurse rushed in and pushed an alarm button. She put a mask over my face. A doctor appeared and quickly summed up the situation. I was given an injection and within seconds I slipped into a deep, sedated sleep.

When I woke up again there was no blissful fog, no respite before awareness kicked in. This time I remembered everything; every horrible detail played out in my memory from the time I got into his car to the time I passed out watching him leaning over the girl, and then there were the visions. With fresh horror, the realisation swept over me that one of them was Ed's wife. I had experienced Susan's death.

All three women had terrible deaths. The monster had taken their eyes while they were alive and aware of what was going on, but paralysed from whatever drug he'd given them. The pain was excruciating and the horror of not being able to move was only made worse once they lost their sight. I felt their desperate fear at not knowing what he was going to do to them next. He killed them with a lethal injection soon after he'd taken their eyes but those few minutes of fear, pain and uncertainty had been the worst agony I'd ever experienced.

I was so absorbed in my thoughts that I didn't realise Mum was sitting next to my bed. She had her nose in a magazine and didn't realise I was awake until I started to cry again. She jumped up and wrapped her arms around me.

'It's OK, Cass, let it out.'

'It was terrible, Mum. I felt him take their eyes. I felt their fear.'

She sat there holding me and I told her everything in one long rush, the words tumbling out. I lost track of how long I talked but finally I was spent. The words and the tears stopped and I just sat there, resting my head on her shoulder like a small child. I fell asleep like that and didn't wake up again until light was flooding through my window.

I felt a bit better; still exhausted, still emotionally wrung out and immeasurably sad about what had happened but this time I had questions and I wanted them answered. I was alone again and so I rang the buzzer, impatient. A nurse came in.

'You look much better. Are you ready to have your drip out and have some real food?' she asked brightly.

'I'm not really hungry. What I want is to speak to Detective Dyson. I want to know what happened to the girl and the killer. I need the number of the Fairfield Police Station.'

The smile dropped from her face. 'Detective Dyson?' She licked her lips nervously. 'I'll see if I can find someone to talk to you.'

Her reaction frightened me. Why couldn't I speak to him? How had I got away from the killer? Had Ed been involved? Was there something wrong with him? Was he dead? The thought made me feel sick.

I had to find out. I had to get to a phone. There wasn't one in my room. I pushed my legs over the side of the bed and realised the drip was in the way. Impatiently I yanked it out of my arm. Blood started to ooze out of the wound. I snatched a tissue from the box next to my bed and held it hard over the spot. I stood up and immediately sank back onto the bed again. My legs wouldn't support me.

I was sitting there trying to work out how to get to a phone when a man who was obviously a doctor walked into the room with the nurse in tow. He exuded an air of quiet calm.

'Hello, Miss Lehman, I'm Doctor Sanderson. What are you doing out of bed? Nurse, please check Miss Lehman's arm. Now, how about you tell me what it is you want to know and I'll do my best to answer your questions?'

'I want to speak to Detective Ed Dyson of the Fairfield Police Station.'

'Detective Dyson can't speak to you. He's currently in our High Dependency Unit. He's in a serious condition but we expect him to make a full recovery with time.'

The sick feeling in my stomach eased slightly. He wasn't dead. He was in bad shape though. 'What happened to him?'

'He was brought in with you. He had been attacked and sustained some very serious injuries.'

'With me? How? What injuries?'

'I'm afraid I can't tell you any more as you're not a member of his family but if he continues to recover well you should be able to see him in a day or two.'

His tone told me that there was no point arguing. The nurse patched me up and tucked me back into bed. The doctor checked me over and prescribed some mild sleeping tablets if I needed them.

'You should be able to go home in a day or two, Miss Lehman.' He smiled at me, patted my hand and glided out of the room.

I sat there stewing. I needed to know what had happened to Ed. He must have come to find me. He must have saved me. I suddenly realised I'd forgotten to ask about the girl. I thought about ringing the bell again but decided I'd be better off waiting for Mum or Gran to come back. They could probably tell me what was going on. Two hours dragged by, punctuated only by the arrival of some insipid soup with jelly and ice cream on the side.

I picked at the jelly, trying not to let the demons crowd into my head. Finally Gran stuck her head around the door.

'Gran, what happened to Ed and the other girl? I need to know.'

She filled in some of the blanks. She told me Ed came charging in and had been attacked by the killer. He'd lost a lot of blood. He had a fractured skull, broken ribs and a gash to the neck.

As for Lucy, she was alive but that was about as good as the news got. I had to drag the rest of it out of Gran but she caved in eventually. The killer had taken her eyes but for some reason he didn't kill her straight away. The chaos with me and Ed probably upset his routine. I couldn't help wondering if she would have been better off dead. According to what Gran could find out, she was deeply traumatised and was being treated in the psychiatric ward of the hospital. She would recover physically but whether or not she could cope mentally was anyone's guess.

It wasn't until I was about to be discharged that I finally summoned up the courage to ask about the killer. I'd resisted the urge up until that point, but I needed to know if I was stepping back into a world that included that madman. Mum and Gran were both with me and we were waiting for the doctor to come around to sign my discharge when I asked. I saw a look pass between them and it was Mum who decided to answer me.

'We were wondering when you'd ask about him. He's alive but in custody.'

'Police custody?'

'No, he's in a facility for the criminally insane. It's secure. There's no chance he'll get out.'

'Has he been charged with all the murders and everything else?'

'Yes. Natalia seems to think he won't be found guilty, though. He'll be found incompetent to stand trial.'

'He was competent enough to kidnap me and kill all those women,' I said, anger sending blood flooding into my cheeks. 'Why did he do it?'

'They're not sure. As a teenager he was arrested a few times for being a peeping Tom and then for indecent exposure. They think the first victim, Virginia, was a neighbour he developed an infatuation for. They haven't been able to ask him any questions. When the police found him, he was incoherent. They said he was rocking backwards and forwards, muttering and crying. He's been the same ever since.'

'Why?'

'We're not sure, Cass. We thought maybe you might know?' Mum asked.

'I don't remember. The last thing I remember is the visions.' The thought sent an involuntary shudder over me. I was trying very hard to forget those visions. Every night they visited me in my dreams. I wondered if I would ever feel safe and happy again.

I didn't find out any more until a cool spring day weeks later. Ed and I were sitting in a patch of sun out the back of our house. We were like a couple of old people, both of us tucked into comfortable chairs with rugs over our knees. Ed was sipping a cup of one of Gran's better-tasting herbal brews. He was a temporary fixture at our place. He hadn't been released from hospital until almost a week after I went home and even then the doctors would only let him go if there was someone around to look after him.

While he was in the hospital, we'd visited him every day. Mum and Gran thought he was a hero: he'd gone charging off to rescue me and almost died in the process. When Gran found out about his predicament there hadn't been any question about who was going to look after him. He was coming home and staying with us and there would be no arguments about it.

Phil and her partner wanted to take him in but their one-bedroom cottage wasn't big enough and neither of them could afford the time off work to look after him. It was us or a live-in nurse. Ed had put up feeble resistance but in the end he was no match for three determined women.

He'd been with us a week before he and I finally talked about what had happened that day. We'd been spending the afternoons in each other's company, reading, watching TV or sitting outside if the weather was good. We chatted about all sorts of things: our school days, books, friends, movies. We'd developed a comfortable, easy friendship.

I knew I had feelings for him that were a lot more than just friendly but I didn't have the energy to investigate them. The whole experience had left me emotionally fragile. I was still suffering the most horrendous nightmares and even the short trips out of the house to see him when he was still in hospital had left me in a state of nervous tension.

He'd talked about Susan a few times but he never asked me the one question he must have wanted answered more than anything. I knew he would ask when he was ready. When he finally did ask it took me by surprise. I was listening to him talk about a trip he and Susan had taken to Thailand; he had an amazing way of describing things. I was sitting back with my eyes closed, picturing the places he was describing when out it popped.

'Did you see how Susan died?'

I sat there for a few seconds, not saying anything, trying to work out how to answer. I had rehearsed what to say so many times but the reality of it made those words seem wrong.

'Cass?'

HINDSIGHT

'I heard you. I'm just trying to work out how to answer.'

'Just tell me the truth,' he said. He reached over and took my hand. I opened my eyes and looked into his blue ones. There was a world of anguish in them and I knew that if I told him everything it was only going to make things worse.

'Susan died from a lethal injection the killer gave her. It was quick.' That much was true anyway.

'Was she frightened? Was she in pain?' The words came out of his mouth in a hoarse whisper.

'Oh, Ed, I'm so sorry. Yes, she was scared and yes, she was in pain.'

'Her eyes?'

'Yes.'

He bowed his head and his shoulders started to shake silently. I reached out and wrapped my arms around him. We sat there like that for a long time while he cried. Mum stuck her head out of the door to check on us, saw what was happening and quietly went back inside.

Eventually he stopped crying and pulled away from me. We both sat there, staring out at the garden. Shadow was curled up in a pool of sunshine. A Murray magpie, one of a pair that had been residents in our garden for years, cheekily hopped past his nose, busy searching for food for its nest full of babies.

'That bird has balls,' Ed muttered.

'Not really, he knows how lazy Shadow is. That cat expects five-star service all the way. He hasn't caught anything since he was about eighteen months old.' I smiled as I said it but I was feeling pretty tense. There were questions I wanted to ask him as well. I wasn't sure if I should ask him now or not.

'Go on then,' he said.

'What?'

'Ask me.'

'You've been in this house for too long. You're starting to develop a talent of your own,' I said. It was uncanny how often he could read my mind. 'I want to know what happened.'

And so he told me. He told me about his struggle with the killer. He told me how he'd seen the corpse called Ginny and he'd lost the plot, thinking it was Susan. He told me how he'd lain there on the floor, watching as the killer bent over me, unable to move, willing Phil to arrive. Finally he told me how he'd watched me wake up and start to scream.

'You screamed over and over again. It was terrible, Cass. Were you having a vision?'

'I was. I had three at the same time. It's never happened like that before.'

'Well, the screaming freaked him out. He grabbed you to try to make you stop but then he just stood there.'

'Why?'

'I don't really know. The look on his face was like nothing I've ever seen.'

We both sat there in silence, pondering this.

'Eventually you stopped screaming and then he just dropped to the floor, curled up in a ball and started to cry.'

'He was crying?'

'Yep. Cass, do you think maybe you somehow transferred the pain and fear that you were feeling to him when he touched you?'

I turned in my chair and stared at him. 'You think that's what happened?'

'I've thought about it so many times since that day and it's the only explanation that makes any sense to me.'

'But no one has ever felt anything when I've been having a vision before,' I said. I didn't want to believe what he was telling me. It turned my talent from something that was isolating and hard to live with into something downright scary.

'How often has someone touched you when you've been having a vision?'

'I don't know. People tend to keep their distance.' I searched my memory. I wouldn't remember anyone touching me. During a vision I was totally oblivious to my surroundings; it made my talent dangerous, but surely someone would have said something before now if they'd touched me and felt something?

'I didn't,' he said.

'What? What do you mean?'

'I grabbed you when you were experiencing Old Mick's death. I thought you were going to fall onto the road.'

'And did you feel anything?'

'Yeah, I guess I did. I felt a massive jolt of pain. It only lasted for a split second. I was too busy worrying about stopping you from falling into the path of a truck to really think about it. At the time I didn't think it was anything to do with you.'

I sat there, staring into space. I didn't want it to be true. Tears filled my eyes.

'Cass?' Ed was looking at me, a worried frown on his face.

'I'm a freak. I'm going to be one of those old spinsters who dies alone and gets eaten by her own cats.'

He reached out and grabbed my hand. He stroked it gently until I stopped crying then he turned it over and pressed a soft kiss onto my palm. Waves of shock and pleasure swept over me.

'Not if I have anything to do with it,' he said.

ACKNOWLEDGEMENTS

The person I need to thank first and foremost for encouraging me and giving me the belief that I could do anything if I put my mind to it is my Mum. Unfortunately she can't be here to see my first novel on the shelves, but I know wherever she is, she's watching and smiling. Thanks Mum, love always. You were my first inspiration.

I'd also like to thank my Dad for supporting me through my years of study. You also taught me the value of a good education, determination and perseverance, qualities that are endlessly valuable in the writing industry.

My next shout-out goes to my husband Peter who has enthusiastically cheered me along this journey all the way and put up with endless evenings of trying to talk to me and getting nothing but monosyllabic answers when I'm writing. Thanks Pete, you are my rock. I'm also grateful to my children Emma and Liam whose love and hugs mean more than they will know (until they have kids of their own).

Thanks also to my friend from the South Australian Police who patiently answered my questions and also gave me the idea for one of the scenes in this book — you know who you are and which scene I'm talking about!

The wonderful staff from the Professional Writing School at Adelaide's College of the Arts also deserve a mention. Thanks for teaching me some valuable skills and giving me lots of good advice that I am only now beginning to appreciate. Special thanks to Jane Turner-Goldsmith and Kirsty Brooks for their mentoring.

Now to the people whose talent and dedication have made it all come to life — the wonderful team at Pantera. Thank you Ali and John Green for taking a chance with me. Your hard work, enthusiasm and patience know no bounds. Thanks also to the wonderful editing, support and marketing team that works at and with Pantera to make it all happen; Kylie Mason, Desanka Vukelich, Graeme Jones, Karen Young, Luke Causby from Blue Cork, Andrew Dunbar and Georgie Dee. I hope this is the first of many books I work on with all of you.

Melanie Casey

If you like *Hindsight*
then look out for
the next book in the Cass Lehman series
(coming in 2014)

CRAVEN

'So what do you think? It's charming isn't it?'

The bright, chirpy voice of the real estate agent made me jump. I turned to look at the woman. She was quite attractive, or at least I imagined she was. It was hard to tell what she really looked like under an inch of artfully applied makeup. Her hair was a pale, winter blonde and her eyes were a pretty shade of blue. She was clutching the list of names she'd compiled during the open inspection in beautifully manicured hands, heavily laden with rings. I felt rumpled and scruffy. I tucked my hands with their chewed nails into my pockets.

'Yes, the house is lovely, but a woman died in this bathroom?' I said.

The agent blinked in surprise; her well-practiced expression of happy confidence wavered. 'Ah, yes, yes, there was an incident with the previous owners.'

'An incident?' I steadily returned her gaze, refusing to let it go at that.

'The woman who lived here had an accident in the bath,' she said.

'You mean she was murdered by her husband.'

The agent's mouth fell open briefly before she managed to gather her wits. 'No, I'm sorry, Miss …' she consulted her folder, 'Lehman … I don't know who told you that but there was no murder. The woman pulled her hairdryer into the bath and was electrocuted. It was just a terrible accident …'

For more information, please visit:
www.PanteraPress.com

MELANIE CASEY

Melanie Casey was born and lives in South Australia with her two young children and her husband (who didn't know he was marrying a writer when he walked down the aisle).

After studying English Literature and Classical Studies, Melanie shifted in to Law, and now works in government.

A chance meeting with a highschool English teacher in the supermarket made Melanie realise that she should be doing what she'd always loved, writing! Another period of study, this time at the Professional Writing School of Adelaide's College of the Arts ensued, helping Melanie to acquire the skills she needed to put her plan into action.

Hindsight is her debut novel, and is the first in a series of crime novels featuring Cass Lehman and Detective Ed Dyson.